i

SOURCES, DISCLAIMERS, ACKNOWLEDGMENTS

Before the fiction begins I feel it necessary to emphasize a few facts. First and foremost, please note that the central character of this novel is, indeed, fictional. In the novel, the character called Jack Dobbs is described as the first Native American to play in a major league, but, in reality, that was not the case. Baseball historians consider Louis Sockalexis, who played for the Cleveland Spiders in the late eighteen-nineties, to have that honor.

It is well known that Louis had as rough a time breaking into baseball as did Jackie Robinson, and Jewish ballplayers, Irish-American ballplayers and others have suffered similar trials. Racism, indeed, is one of the themes of this novel, and, because of that, it contains many words that are now considered offensive and many that were offensive even in 1900. My intention was to remain true to the historical period and the attitudes of too many people in those supposedly halcyon days.

Less importantly, I must also point out, before someone else does it for me, that the song Rufus and Liza sing at the May Day Dance, "The Belle of the Barber's Ball," was written by George M. Cohan in 1909, and so could not possibly have been sung in 1900. The second song they sing is "Hello My Baby," which, happily, was written by Joe Howard and Ida Emerson in 1899. "Daisy Bell," heard frequently in these chapters, was written by Harry Dacre in 1892.

I have also taken a few other small liberties. There wasn't actually a high school in Contra Costa County until 1901, for example. Also note that the baseball box scores and statistics presented in this novel are a compromise between historically accurate formats and formats familiar to baseball fans today.

It is also difficult for me to know how to adequately credit the sources I used to write this book. If it was a work of pure history, I'd simply fill the pages with footnotes citing chapter and verse. But this is fiction and such an approach seems inappropriate.

Let me begin by saying that many books, websites, and what have you were used to construct the fiction that follows. The most important of these were *Days Gone By*, Volumes 1 & 2, by Nilda Rego; *The History of Concord*, by Edna May Andrews, et al; *Port Costa*, by Dick Murdock; and several old issues of the *Contra Costa Gazette* which dwell on microfilm in the public library.

I cannot say enough about Ms. Rego, who reviewed the work for accuracy, and from whose researches I derived many of my tales "of ordinary people, sometimes doing extraordinary things, but mostly just trying to survive."

Nor can I give enough credit to the people who wrote and produced the *Contra Costa Gazette* in the spring of 1900. I have taken many of their "Local Brevities," clipped them, reshaped them, and pasted them into my little collage. I beg the indulgence of those good folk.

Last but hardly least, my thanks to Kristen King, whose editorial skills guided me, to James Hanna who encouraged me, to Dave Singleton whose comments on my "almost final draft" were indispensable, and to Elana O'Loskey for punctuating and proofing the final draft. Thanks also to Al Garrotto and Sue Clark for critiquing my early drafts; to Jim Breivis, catcher and orthopedic surgeon, for helping with various medical details; to author G.S. Rowe for help with turn of the century baseball statistical formats; and to model builders Tom and Bill Rubarth for help with details concerning the ferry *Solano* which, in its fictional form, I have rechristened the *Benicia*.

Finally, thanks to Mr. J. Thomas Hetrick of Pocol Press for his enthusiasm and understanding, and a huge thanks to my good friend Rick Shubb, bluegrass musician and inventor of the world-famous Shubb Capo, for his encouragement, support and for coming up with the title, *The Fade-away*, which I consider to be absolutely perfect.

The Fade-away

George Jansen

Pocol Press
Clifton, VA

POCOL PRESS

Published in the United States of America
by Pocol Press.

6023 Pocol Drive
Clifton, VA 20124
http://www.pocolpress.com

Publisher's Cataloguing-in-Publication

Jansen, George 1944-

    The fade-away / George Jansen. – 1st ed. – Clifton, VA :
Pocol Press, 2007.

        p. ; cm.

        ISBN-13: 978-1-929763-31-3
        ISBN-10: 1-929763-31-X
        Includes bibliographical references.

        1. Pitchers (Baseball)–California–Fiction.
    2. Baseball–Corrupt practices–United States–Fiction.
    3. Baseball stories. I. Title.

    PS3610.A574 F33 2007
    813.6–dc22   0705

Cover art of author by Bryan Costales.

"Somewhere in this favored land the sun is shining bright..."
–Ernest L. Thayer

1
DOCTOR SAM FULLER
President, Port Newton Athletic Club

It was Friday, April 13, 1900, the first year of the new century or the last of the old, depending on your point of view. It was Eastertide, too, and Good Friday. But at the old Railroad Exchange Saloon in Port Newton, California, we always remembered it as the night Jack Dobbs floated into town. And I mean that *literatim*: the son of a bitch floated right on into town.

Young Calvin Elwell was tending bar that night, hard-cooking the eggs and salting down the meat for the free lunch. Rosa Paredes, old and addled, pumped the pedals of the player piano in back, "Daisy, Daisy, give me your answer do." Me and Foghorn Murphy, the owner of the joint, sat at his favorite poker table playing five card stud and hashing over the town team's chances in the upcoming baseball season.

"We don't *have* a chance, Doc," Foghorn said, and Foghorn was the manager no less. "I'd ask God to send us some pitching, but He's dead, I understand. Saw it in the papers down at the Beehive Cafe just this morning."

I tossed a dime into the pot and told him I'd seen the article myself.

"He's not dead, exactly. Put out to pasture is more like it. Outlived His usefulness, you might say."

"Dead," Foghorn muttered. "Happened somewhere in Germany, back in the last century."

Outside, a west-bound freight thundered down the Port Newton waterfront. The floor shook. Our beer mugs trembled, and Foghorn dealt the cards.

Mine was a jack, which paired me face-up, a monster of a hand when only two fellows are playing. I bet the limit figuring Foghorn would fold his tents and slip off into the night. But instead, he bent over until his cheek rested on the green felt of the poker table, lifted up a tiny corner of his hole card, and eyeballed it.

"I don't recall seeing it in the article," he went on, cheek flat on the table, "but it occurred to me that if God really is dead, then the devil must be too."

I hadn't considered that possibility, and it rocked me, I'll say. For if He really was dead–irrelevant, useless or whatever–then it made a certain amount of sense that the devil was too. And if both of them were goners, then what of good and evil? Had good and evil also ceased to exist? Or was it just that the apprehension of virtue now depended solely on the eye of the beholder?

"Raise two bits," Foghorn said.

"What?"

"You heard me. I raise two bits."

Now that rocked me even more than the devil business. I had that pair of jacks, all right, but Foghorn had a king showing and, by raising those twenty-five cents, he was trying to convince me he had another in the hole besides.

Foghorn Murphy, by the way, was the fellow who invented the Martini Cocktail, or so he always claimed. But Andy Mellus over in Martinez stole the recipe from him: two thirds Old Tom gin and one third French vermouth. Otherwise, the Martini would be called the Newton and to this day, too. Or so Foghorn Murphy always claimed.

"I call your two bits," I said, tossing a half dollar into the pot. "And I raise you two bits more."

Foghorn called the raise, then dealt my last card and Fortune smiled. It was a jack, which gave me three, face up, and I figured the son of a bitch's goose was cooked. But instead of cursing his luck, Foghorn stopped dealing altogether and started up on baseball and divine intervention again.

"Maybe a few Hail Mary's would serve to procure us some pitching," he said. "I mean if the man upstairs really is dead, maybe we'd have better luck if we asked the woman... *Ave Maria.*"

He dealt himself his last card–the goddamnable king of hearts it turned out to be–and if he had that third one in the hole as he'd been trying to convince me, it was my goose that was cooked. I bet a nickel.

"Raise a buck," Foghorn said.

"Raise a buck? The limit's two bits. You can't change the rules in the middle of the game."

"And why the hell not?"

I had no ready answer for that, but as it is my habit to call a known bluffer whenever practical, I took a silver dollar from the stack of coins in front of me.

"He who hesitates is lost," Foghorn said.

But hesitate I did. The laws of probability are one thing, but a dollar is a dollar after all. And lost I soon became, condemned to wonder for the rest of my days if Foghorn Murphy really did have that king in the hole. For at that precise moment Captain T.A. Alvarado of the State Fish Patrol burst through the back door of the Exchange.

"Doc! Come quick! We need you!"

He was wrapped in a navy blue pea jacket and had a woolen watch cap pulled down over his ears. He'd been out on San Francisco Bay patrolling for oyster pirates that night, apparently with some result.

"Doc! Come quick!"

My first, terrible thought was that there had been a shootout or set-to of some sort, and I grabbed my medical bag. The captain disappeared out the door whence he had come, and Foghorn and I hustled after him, through that same door and down the long, narrow walkway on the dock side of the Front.

It was dark and starless that night–primeval, I'm tempted to say. Across the Carquinez Strait lay the town of Benicia, shrouded in fog. To the east stood Granger's Wharf where the hermaphrodite brig *Martha W. Tufts* lay at rest, visible only for the lights hung in her rigging. To the west loomed the ghostly form of Newton Wharf & Warehouse, closed and shuttered since Old Man Newton dipped into the till of Newton Savings & Loan, bankrupted half the town, then drowned himself in the cold, deep strait.

"There!"

Captain Alvarado pointed down at the deck of the little sloop *Esmeralda*, tied up at the dock below and bobbing like a cork in the unsettled waters.

Long John Sheets, our town constable, guardian and protector–not to mention the best hitter on our ball team–

stood in the bow dressed like the captain but bareheaded and boyish, hair tangled by sea and fog.

"Johnny," I called. "I feared you were shot up or some such."

He laughed at me with grand bravado. One hell of a fellow, Long John. He'd begun life as the seventh son of a hay farmer over in Pacheco. A barefoot farm boy he'd been, with underwear made of sugar sacks, but he'd pulled himself up by the bootstraps and made himself a life in Port Newton.

"Me? Shot?" Long John laughed. "Hell, no, Doc. We just pulled another floater out of the Strait is all."

There at his feet in a puddle of salt-fresh water, lay an unconscious man. Brown skinned, he appeared to be, aged about thirty-five years and dressed in a soaking wet, black tuxedo.

"Is the son of a bitch alive?" Foghorn asked, as we peered down from the dock.

"He's still breathing," Long John said.

"He's a big one, isn't he?" Foghorn said. "An Injun, unless I miss my guess."

As I climbed down to the deck of the *Esmeralda*, Long John began the tale of what had happened. The railroad ferry, laboring between Benicia and Port Newton, had just churned past them in the dark night. They'd heard some splashing, investigated, and come across the fellow in the tuxedo who, by then, was going down for the third time.

"Long John threw him a line," Captain Alvarado said, "and reeled him in, just like pulling in a big fish."

Long John made a big grin and shook his head. "The minute we landed him, the son of a bitch passed out. Hasn't been a peep out of him since."

I steadied myself on the deck and found the brown fellow's pulse.

"Heart like a goddamn mule," I pronounced.

Long John pointed to the bloody towel he'd wrapped about the Indian's noggin.

"Looks like somebody plunked him with a club. Tried to rob him, maybe."

I gestured towards the dock, the ladder that climbed it, and the Railroad Exchange beyond. "Let's get him inside. It's cold out here, and I'm not as limber as I used to be."

4

We looped a line under the big Indian's arms. Long John coiled it and tossed it up to Captain Alvarado.

"How many men you got up there, Cap?" Long John called out.

"Just Foghorn and me," the captain replied.

"Well, that'll have to do. You game, Foghorn?"

"I'm always game, Long John."

"You fellows pull from above, and we'll push from below. You limber enough for that, Doc?"

"I imagine I have no choice."

When all was at the ready, a count of three was made, and we commenced to heave ho. That Indian was well over six feet tall and must have tipped the scales at two hundred twenty-five pounds. When we got him up and over the railing, we lost our grips, and he fell with a thud onto the planking.

"Damn red devil," Foghorn said, puffing a bit.

"Get his legs!" Long John commanded.

Me and Foghorn grabbed hold of the Indian's south end while Long John and the captain took the north. The four of us manhandled him down the dock then through the back door of Foghorn's saloon.

"Heave!"

We gave a grunt, all at once, and tossed Long John's big fish up onto the hand-carved mahogany bar that Foghorn had salvaged off the wreck of the *Delta Princess* back in 'ninety-five.

"Damn. My back," Foghorn said.

"Don't ask me about backs," I told him. "No doctor alive understands backs. Have a shot of whiskey. That's my advice for backs."

By now, some of the boys began to filter into the Exchange. Just a few at first: a couple of railroad men from the yard; a deck hand off the ferry; two stevedores from the sugar wharf in Crockett. Rough and tumble boys, they were, and they gathered around the Indian like he wasn't even there, ordering up Port Newton Steam Beer and partaking of bread, cheese, hard-cooked eggs, and that greenish roast beef that Calvin Elwell, the bartender, had salted down.

"Is he a Hoopa?" Cal asked, surveying the Indian laid out in front of him. Cal played second base on our team, by the way, and not badly, either.

"Apache is my guess," Foghorn said.

Rosa Paredes, the addled old lady who'd been pumping the player piano, wandered over, took one of the eggs Cal had boiled and began to peel it. Rosa, who told fortunes and read palms, stopped, bent over, sniffed the Indian, then the egg, then the Indian again.

"*Un bebé del agua*," she said. "Made by fairies."

"Fairies?" Foghorn laughed. "Fairies don't wear tuxedos."

She showed Cal the peeled egg. "*¿Usted tiene sal?*"

"Sure, Doña Rosa," Cal said, pulling a saltcellar out from under the bar. "We got plenty."

Long John pushed everyone away from the big Indian. "Give him room to breathe!" Then I got down to work. I lifted one of the Indian's eyelids to have a look–red and bloodshot, it was. I undid the towel Long John had wrapped around the wound in the head.

"Bleeding's stopped," I said. "But you're right, Long John, looks like somebody plunked him a good one."

Foghorn shook his head. "He smells of whiskey. An Apache all liquored up. What the hell's the world coming to?"

I broke open a vial of smelling salts and shoved it under the Indian's nose. In my experience, such an act almost without fail caused a patient to burst forth into consciousness, but this time, it did not. Instead, he began to snore.

By now, Long John was going through the big fellow's pockets with the practiced thoroughness of a Holmes. Then, like a magician with two score rabbits in his hat, he began pulling out objects that seemed far too numerous for those pockets to contain.

"Brass watch," Long John said. "Half-drowned but still ticking. One handkerchief. One lucky rabbit's foot. A pair of dice."

He gave them a tumble across the bar and they came up seven.

"Loaded, most likely."

Long John ran his hands up and down the inside of the big Indian's legs.

"Ho, what's this?"

He pulled up the right pant leg, and there, strapped to the inside of the ankle, was a feisty little revolver. Long John slipped it out of the holster and unloaded it.

"A thirty-two," he declared. "And I'll be damned if it isn't a knife-gun." He unfolded the stiletto blade that was hinged underneath the barrel, snapped it into position, and held the infernal device up high for all to see. The boys began to yammer all at once.

"A fellow could do some real damage with that little son of a bitch."

"Gamblers and thieves are all that carries a thingamajig like that."

"*Gitanos*," Doña Rosa said. "Gypsies."

"And from how he wears his gear," Long John added, pointing at the holster on the Indian's ankle, "I'd wager he's left-handed."

He pulled a black, leather wallet from the Indian's jacket pocket, removed the three water-soaked one-dollar bills it contained, and handed one to me.

"Your fee, Doc." He pocketed the other two for himself. "Carrying charges." Then he continued on through the wallet.

"A one-way ticket, Sacramento to Oakland. A cigarette card depicting a chorus girl, a pawn ticket from Honest John's Honest Loans on Main Street in Watsonville, and, lastly, a California League baseball schedule from the year eighteen hundred and ninety-nine."

I passed the smelling salts under the big Indian's nose once more but again with no effect.

"Drunk, is what he mainly is," I told the boys. "He'll sleep it off by noon, I'd reckon."

"Noon?" Foghorn said. "You ain't gonna leave some savage passed out on my bar until noon. What if he pukes?"

"Do what you always do when somebody pukes," I told him. "Clean it up."

"Can't you cart him off to County Hospital, Doc? Isn't County Hospital the place where he belongs?"

7

"Well," I said, not feeling in need of a long, midnight drive, "best not to move him. He might be concussed, you know. Let him sleep it off right here. That's the wisest course, in my professional opinion."

Foghorn turned to Long John. "Can't you dust out a cell for him? Why, the man's obviously a malefactor of some sort. An Injun, I mean, drunk and with a pistol like that?"

Long John shook his head. "He hasn't broken any laws I know of."

Riley Towne, publisher, editor and jack of all trades at the *Port Newton News*–the same fellow who'd reported that God was dead–pushed through the crowd of working men that now surrounded the bar.

"Stop being such a damn priss, Foghorn," he said. "I thought you had some business acumen about you. An Indian splayed out on a bar is as good a draw as seals playing horns by Port Newton standards."

"Seals playing horns?" Foghorn pondered. "I never heard of such a thing."

"It's true," Riley told him. "Seals *can* play horns, if they're educated to it."

"Sounds like crap to me."

"All you need is a little puffery." He lit a tailor-made cigarette and coughed. "A goodly dose of the old ballyhoo, if you catch my drift, and that Indian will be as good a draw as seals playing horns. That's all I'm trying to tell you."

Riley Towne understood that Foghorn Murphy was the most corrupt man in town, and once he'd baited the hook it didn't take but a moment for Foghorn to swallow it.

"Ballyhoo, you say?"

The bargain was quickly made. Column inches in the *News* were traded for free steam beer and roast beef sandwiches at the Exchange. You scratch my back, I'll scratch yours. Nothing wrong with it. It's just how things were done in those days, and times were hard in old Port Newton.

2

THE PORT NEWTON NEWS
Monday, April 16

TOWNE TOPICS

BASEBALL SEASON OPENS
PORT NEWTON ROUTED 16–2
THE PROCESSION OF THE BENICIANS

The opening game of the 1900 baseball season did much to dispel the fears of our citizens who have inveighed against the playing of baseball on Sunday, and especially on Easter Sunday. Those good folk can take comfort, now, for your editor can assure them that nothing resembling baseball occurred at the old ballpark on Newton's Bluff yesterday afternoon.

It was slaughter, plain and simple.

The visiting club from Benicia ripped drives that screamed like shells from a field howitzer while the Newtons' fielders dove for cover. Once upon the sacks, the Benicia club ran wild, stealing nine bases while the Newtons' catchers flung ball after ball into the vast netherworld of center field.

The day began when the Benicians made a tasteless arrival in our fair city, riding across on the ferry then forming up behind the depot. Unruly fans, the Benicia Marching Band, and the ballplayers themselves then marched up Railroad Avenue. As the band struck up a Souza march, a Brobdingnagian banner emblazoned with the legend "Benicia, Champions 1899" was unfurled.

A half dozen other championship banners were then exposed, including that particularly ancient and hated one from the 1888 season when a falsified score sheet showed the Benicians defeating our lads 19–17. The score, in actual fact, was 16–12 in favor of Port Newton.

After this uncouth display, the assembled throng began a progress down Railroad and then up Ferry Street to

Newton's Bluff while the trumpets blared and the glockenspiels spieled.

Sad to say, the Benicians present to witness the carnage that followed outnumbered us Newtonians by ten to one. But the years have been lean of late, and withal, it was the best crowd seen hereabouts since Professor David Drake attempted a balloon ascension from Founder's Park in 1894.

So melancholy and debilitating was the game itself that the only incident worth recounting occurred when the captain of the Benicians, Anthony J. Rossi, stepped to the plate without bothering to bring a bat.

"Carrying a cudgel of any sort was wholly unnecessary," Big Tony later explained. "That so-called pitcher of yours had become so unhinged that he hadn't a snowball's chance in Hell of throwing a strike, and I simply saw no necessity in toting any heavy lumber around."

The "so-called pitcher" in question was Port Newton's ace hurler Charles "Icebox" Meyers. Had "The Box" been able to recapture, for even a moment, that same cool he exhibited in halcyon days of yore, the result would have been three straight strikes to Big Tony.

But the chilly one has, for some years, been warming to a tropical degree, and his knees wobbled under him like swaying palms. The Benician rooters bayed and howled, the count went to three balls, two strikes, and Charlie aimed a lollypop down the middle which ended up finding, not the catcher's glove, but the plate in front of it.

"Ball four!" the umpire cried, and as Rossi crept towards first base, imitating the slithering motions of a snake, the Benicians broke into howls of laughter.

Dr. Sam Fuller, president of the Port Newton Athletic Club, said that Rossi's act was the most unsportsmanlike affront he had seen in many a year.

"We play these games for recreation, amusement, and fellowship," Dr. Sam went on. "Taunting and ridicule may have their place in the professional leagues, but we are civilized men and should be above such things."

For their efforts, the Benicians were rewarded with a purse of twelve dollars. Betting on the game was also light, and Mr. Gerald "Foghorn" Murphy, treasurer of the Athletic Club and manager of the team, opined that this was because the Newtons' chances had been deemed poor from the outset.

"I would have bet on the Benicians myself," Foghorn said. "But I couldn't find anyone to take the other side of the proposition."

LOCAL BREVITIES

Mrs. Belle Pavolini of Martinez and Mrs. D.A. Mulligan of Black Diamond were killed, instantly, Sunday evening when the Number Seven train, eastbound from Oakland, struck the wagon in which they were riding. Ruthie Pavolini, aged six years and also riding in the wagon, was taken to County Hospital, where Doctor Sam Fuller discovered that a portion of her skull had been crushed. An operation was performed but, at present, little Ruthie's chances are not thought to be good.

The Indian that Constable Sheets pulled from the Strait early Friday morning still sleeps as if dead, but snoring, on the bar at Foghorn Murphy's Railroad Exchange Saloon. Dr. Sam, while surprised at the deep and lengthy nature of the Indian's repose, said that such a thing is not impossible in cases like this.

"The man showed clear evidence of suffering an injury to the head," he said. "And that, combined with the mental trauma caused by his brush with death could, in my estimation, cause a sleep of such lengthy duration."

Whatever the case, visitors all agree that the gigantic Indian, laid out on Murphy's bar, is a sight worth beholding.

On Saturday the barkentine *Sagittarius* arrived at the sugar refinery in Crockett with 20,000 sacks of raw sugar aboard. A large force of stevedores was put to work immediately but many more were left upon the dock. The grain ship *Francis W. Wilcox* will tie up at Granger's Martinez Wharf today, and it is thought a steady run of work lies ahead in that city.

Buy land in Port Newton now. It will never be cheaper.

Constable Sheets and Hector Fernandez, the engineer on one of the switch engines that shunts railroad cars onto the ferry, went back to their hometown of Pacheco on Good Friday, taking Hector's wife and countless children along with them. Hec reports that some of the Mexican traditions of old California still hold sway in Pacheco. To wit: On Good Friday, the young men of the town hang an effigy of Judas then go around "collecting" anything they can find–buggies, wagons, plows, even sheep and cows. These items are placed around the effigy and after Mass on Saturday, the effigy is burned. Judas' last will and testament is then read, bequeathing the items back to their rightful owners.

"After that," said Fernandez, "we set off some fireworks, have a feast, and raise a few toasts."

Is that why you boys played so sluggish at the game on Sunday, Hec?

The explosion that occurred in the Dyna-King Powder Works at Hercules last Saturday is now thought to have been entirely accidental. Mr. Robert P. Haskell of Rodeo was injured in the blast and a number of Chinamen were killed.

Our own David Drake, professor at the University of California, led an expedition of stargazers up Mt. Diablo yesterday afternoon to observe the full moon that night. He calls the fire of July 4, 1891 that destroyed the observatory and telescope that stood upon the summit, a tragedy for the cause of science.

The lawsuit of Mrs. Ella P. Caldwell against the Newton Savings Association went on trial in Superior Court last week. Mrs. Williams brought a good supply of legal talent with her, but even those fellows can't get blood from a turnip, Ella.

Your editor believes Drexel's New Formula Cough Elixir to be the best of its kind in the world. It is well known that he suffers from discomforted breathing and a hacking cough, but Drexel's Elixir never fails to relieve his pain. McMillan's Pharmacy and Fountain, located at Main and Railroad, maintains an ample supply at reasonable prices.

MEETINGS AND EVENTS
Twentieth Century Club–Monday
The monthly meeting of the Twentieth Century Club will be held at seven o'clock tonight in the home of Mrs. Josie Pimental up Buck's Ranch Road. Mrs. Pimental

informs us that the ubiquitous Professor Drake will be on hand to lead a discussion of Renaissance Italy.

Congregational Church–Tuesday

Mrs. Edith Fuller tells us that, on Tuesday evening, the Willing Workers of the Congregational Church will give a help concert to raise funds for the purchase of hymnals. Piano duets and solos, a cornet solo, and a demonstration of magic will grace the program. Admission will be ten cents. Tasty confections and articles of the ladies' own making will also be sold.

3
SOPHIE FULLER
Senior, Port Newton Union High School

Dear Diary,

She never would have done it if she hadn't been inebriated, but you know Lily Newton, Diary dear. Some wine at dinner, more at supper, then brandy for sleep, and there's that little bottle of Nervina she carries in her purse. Daddy says her nerves are exhausted, and that we should let her have her Nervina and her pick-me-ups after all she's been through. But she's making a spectacle of herself.

It all started on Easter Sunday. Daddy doesn't even go to church anymore and none of us would have to if it wasn't for the Mother.

"Rise and shine Sophie. In two minutes I want to see two feet on the floor."

You'd think it was the Army or something.

"You're your father's daughter, that's for certain."

I told her I most certainly was, and that I'd much rather possess Daddy's sensitivity than have a clockwork heart like hers.

"If I don't see two feet on the floor in two minutes you'll have a clockwork behind. That's what you'll have."

The singing at church was all nice enough. Garnetta did "Onward Christian Soldiers," and I've never heard a finer version. But then Isabella Thayer, the one who was so appalling in *The Mikado* last year, sang something so dreadful it distresses me still–"Many Brave Hearts Lie Asleep in the Deep."

After church Garnetta and I went to the ballgame and witnessed the humiliation of the entire city. I told Daddy he should quit the Athletic Club as it was giving us all a bad name, but he just said, "Jesus Christ," whatever that meant.

So you can understand, Diary dear, exactly why I just couldn't bear going to school on Monday no matter how progressive and wonderful Newton High is supposed to be. And since I'm going to be an actress and poet, or possibly a Bohemian, what should it matter if I matriculate geometry?

That big Indian was laid out on the bar at Mr. Murphy's saloon just begging to be ogled, and, while I was pinning up my hat, I decided I'd invite Lily Newton to go along with me. For propriety's sake, partly, and because I never consider seclusion a healthy thing for a girl, especially Lily. I strolled down the hill towards town, and there she was, working in that awful garden of hers–one foot on the blade of a shovel just like a Negro.

"Not today, Sophie," she told me. "I've work to do."

I told her she *always* has work to do, but she didn't budge an inch, saying that it was spring and she had to plant potatoes. My word!

Lily is a pretty enough girl considering she is almost twenty-six years old. But soon her skin will turn to leather the way she lets the sun tan her like an old cowhide. Some of the kids at school say she digs in her yard because the "Old Man" buried Savings Association money there before he did himself in. But if he had she'd have dug it all up ages ago and departed this mournful town.

"How will anything ever happen to you," I asked her, "unless you get out of your yard and into the world?"

"Some of us have to scrape for a living."

"Oh, come now. This Indian is the biggest thing to happen in Port Newton since... well, since... you know." I meant the Savings Association business, needless to say, but would never dream of mentioning such a thing in Lily's presence.

I grabbed the shovel away from her and commanded she go clean herself up.

"Put on that nice blue gingham you wore to Mattie Hurley's baby shower and that cute little straw hat. We could stop at McMillan's Fountain, if you want."

Shame on me for encouraging Lily's condition, but she always does like to stop at McMillan's for a pick-me-up. The less accomplished kids at school call them "Lunks" from "lunkheads" for that is what they make you. Alcohol, opium, sugar, and soda water, Daddy says.

It was all very Port Newton and all very dull as we walked down the hill, twirling our parasols. The stuffy little cottages, climbed the sides of our tiny valley, all drab and ugly. When we passed the school yard a dirt clod exploded at my feet.

"Hey, Sophie! Don't be so stuck up!"

It was you know who–my precious little brother.

"You'll pay for that, Wilhelm," I called.

He hates it when I call him Wilhelm so he threw another clod, and when it struck right in front of us and veritably exploded, Lily's courage began to flag.

"Oh, Sophie, I don't know. I don't care about any Indian."

"Don't be silly. Constable Sheets might be there, and if you'd come to your senses, maybe you wouldn't have to dig potatoes."

"I don't dig potatoes," Lily said.

"It's nothing to be ashamed of," I told her, although it most certainly is.

And why shouldn't her father have tried to corner the grain market? People think it's just fine if they get rich themselves, but when somebody else does they get all snippy about it. And the scandal about him committing suicide? Well, under such circumstances suicide strikes me as being very Japanese and honorable. Lily says his scent still lingers about the house like a ghost.

The usual fat men were nestled in their chairs in front of the mercantile. The Beehive Cafe hadn't even opened yet. The jitney from the depot was stopped in front of the hotel. No passengers, as usual. The doors of the Savings Association were encrusted in spider webs, padlocked by order of the sheriff.

When we stopped at McMillan's for Lily's pick-me-up, I tried to demur but she would have none of it.

"It'll grow hair on your chest," she said.

I told her that was disgusting.

I did order a "Lunk," finally. But Lily had three and almost fell on her face when we went across the pedestrian bridge over the railroad tracks.

Don't ever tell Mother this, Diary dear, but the waterfront is tremendously exciting to me–billiard parlors, dancehalls, and saloons. There is *life* there, on the wrong side of the tracks–puffing steam engines, the churning ferry, scurrying bicycles, pigtailed Chinamen, the sporting men and painted ladies.

"Yoohoo, Mr. Elwell?" I called, peering over the batwing doors of the Railroad Exchange. "Oh Calvin. Yoohoo."

Poor Calvin, tending bar for a living. He broke into a big grin the instant he saw me and walked over, as we stood by the doors. I decided to torture him a little, just to stay in practice.

"I went to the game, yesterday, Calvin. Just how many errors did you make?"

"Don't remind me," he said.

The big Indian lay atop Mr. Murphy's bar asleep and unshaven, a savage child of the savage woods.

Lily tried to back out. "I don't think we should."

"Oh, don't be silly," I told her. "This *is* the twentieth century, isn't it?"

"Well, just barely," she said.

Calvin offered an arm to each of us. He is a sweetheart, but a girl just can't settle for a boy who'd rather play baseball than apply himself.

I took his right arm and Lily, still cock-eyed from her pick-me-ups took his left. Like the Red Sea, all those distasteful laborers that crowd the place parted, and we bellied up to the bar. A blanket covered the sleeping savage, but his shapely arms and shoulders protruded naked above it. Unable to suppress the temptation, I took an edge of the blanket between the tips of my fingers and lifted.

"My God! Sophie!" Lily exclaimed.

I told her he had drawers on and looked at Calvin. "He does have drawers on, doesn't he?"

"Don't ask me," Calvin said.

That was when that awful old woman, Rosa Paredes, came over to us. The kids at school say she is a witch and throw rocks at her house on Halloween. I cannot condone such shenanigans, needless to say, but she gets what she deserves.

She put her hand on the Indian's chest and accosted poor Lily. "*Un bebé del agua*," she said. "A kiss will wake him."

All this scared the wits out of Lily, so I was forced to step to the rescue.

"You should kiss him if anyone," I told the old witch. "That, I suppose, would frighten him out of his slumber."

She wagged a finger at me. "Such kisses must come from maidens. Perhaps you."

The men all laughed at that, but you know me, Diary dear. I don't take kindly to being laughed at, and I *never* turn down a dare. I straightened my garments and called for a napkin.

"A clean napkin, Calvin," I added, "and a shot of whiskey, besides."

Supplied with both, I wet the napkin with the whiskey and so proceeded to purify the Indian's lips. The laborers gathered closer. I hovered above the sleeping savage, so close I was able to smell his breath. It was so foul that when I kissed him I deflected my lips slightly away from his, as one would do on in a play on the stage.

I took a step back. A muscle in the Indian's face twitched. He gasped. The men began to cheer, but instead of bursting forth with life, the savage lapsed again into snoring. I hung my head as if in brutal disappointment and feigned tears.

"That's all right, Miss Sophie."

"Don't feel bad, girl."

"Buck up there, kiddo."

The men patted my back, offered condolences, and one even gave me the most disgusting handkerchief I have ever seen. Then the old witch turned on Lily once more.

"Now you Miss Newton. Kiss *el bebé*."

"I should say not," Lily replied. "I want no part of Indians or kisses either."

"What harm can come from a little kiss?"

"Plenty," Lily said.

The men began to urge her on, but still I don't think Lily would have relented if it hadn't been for all those Lunks. She looked at me, took off one of her gloves and reached her bare hand towards Calvin. Calvin placed a napkin in it, and she called for a fresh shot of whiskey.

"And not that cheap stuff you usually pass around."

"Good stuff," Calvin said. "And on the house."

But instead of using the whiskey to purify the Indian, as had I, she drank it straight down herself. Then she gasped once and bent over the savage, landing a kiss that lingered long and full on his lips.

4

THE PORT NEWTON NEWS
Thursday, April 19

TOWNE TOPICS

THE INDIAN WAKES
HIS PAST AND FUTURE

The "big fish" that has been laid out on Foghorn Murphy's bar since early Friday woke quite suddenly Monday afternoon. According to some, his arousal was caused by a kiss upon the lips, freely given by a certain maiden of the town. For propriety's sake, her name shall forever remain our secret, although it might not take a Newton to figure it out.

We have interviewed the Indian since his resurrection and can thus state, for certain, that he is not an Apache, a Hoopa, or even a Hindoo, as has been speculated by some of the more unenlightened of our fair city. He is, instead–or was, as he prefers to put it–a member of that same Washoe tribe that once roamed the Carson Valley of Nevada.

"My people were a miserable bunch," the Indian told us when we spoke with him in his temporary lodgings at the Port Newton Athletic Club.

"Don't picture Injuns on horses chasing after buffaloes when you ponder the Washoe. Scavengers. That's what we were. And not so noble in any regard. But my mama left me on the steps of the Carson Indian School when I was but a babe, and there they beat the savage out of me, thank God."

His name is John Poe Dobbs, or "Jack" to his friends. He is a baseball player by profession. He says he pitched for the Gilt Edge team of Sacramento last season and has inked a contract with the San Francisco Wasps for the coming one.

"The California League," Dobbs said, "is on a par with the best of the Eastern leagues and, while I have the ability to pitch in New York, Boston, or anywhere, the coast appeals to me for its climate."

When asked about the speculation regarding his unusual arrival in Port Newton, Dobbs told us that his misadventure in the Strait was the purest of accidents.

"I'd just stepped out on the deck of the ferry to enjoy some fresh air when my feet seemed to go out from under me. The deck was slick, and I must have fallen, hit my head and gone overboard. The next thing I remember is waking up on the bar in Mr. Murphy's saloon when some angel kissed my lips."

Dobbs says he is very grateful to Constable Sheets for fishing him out of the Strait, thus saving his life, and that he will shake Long John's hand the moment he meets him.

When asked why he was found to be carrying a pistol on his person, Mr. Dobbs replied, "Do men have to give reasons for defending themselves these days?"

He further declared that he is determined to stay in Port Newton and rest up for a few days before moving on.

"This town of yours holds a special charm for me, and when Mr. Murphy offered the hospitality of the Athletic Club, I could hardly turn him down."

LOCAL BREVITIES

The men of Bulls Head Lumber, emboldened by the humiliating defeat suffered by our brave baseballers at the hands of the Benicians last Sunday, have challenged us to a game. It will be held at two o'clock this coming Sunday at the ballpark on Newton's Bluff. A purse of twenty dollars, American, will be the prize. Betting for the contest is running heavier than usual with the Newtons being the underdog, but only at odds of five to three.

In other news, George Cavanaugh, a millwright at the sugar refinery in Crockett, was suddenly struck blind in one eye while walking to work on Tuesday morning. Doctor Sam Fuller is at a loss to explain this dreadful occurrence.

Lawyer Elwell reports that estimates were accepted for macadamizing Buck's Ranch Road and the approaches to the town at the meeting of the Board of Trustees on

Thursday. He further says that James Copeland, the contractor of the School Street sewer, made a claim that he extended it up Main four hundred feet further than the contract called for and is therefore entitled to more money.

Lawyer Elwell told us that the chances of Copeland's claim being accepted were infinitesimal. "Contracts are contracts," he said.

The Southern Pacific Railroad has notified us that a new timetable will go into effect next week, and that the 7:45 train from Oakland to Martinez will no longer stop in Port Newton. This is a lamentable occurrence.

Stand by your town and it will stand by you.

Because of the low price of hay, many farmers of the county are plowing under their volunteer crops. It is thought, however, that the beet crop this year will be one of the largest ever.

Buck Farrell is going into the grocery business with his brother-in-law, H.M. Ivory, on Main Street. We have no doubt you'll make a success of it, Buck.

Constable Sheets is seeking an owner for a pug dog and her pups. In the meanwhile he has granted them asylum in the hoosegow. Apply at his office, if interested.

A new gas plant has been installed at the Alhambra Lodge in Martinez. The proprietor, Bailey Estees, says that it is a great improvement over the coal oil previously used for illumination.

Mr. J.P. Daley, candidate for the state assembly, was seen shaking hands in Foghorn Murphy's Railroad Saloon last night.

On the evening of April 21, a farewell ball will be held at Walnut House in Walnut Creek for Mr. A.S. Melchior and the Turner brothers, William and Alton, who plan to sail for the Klondike goldfields on the thirtieth. Miss Nellie Strohl of Concord will favor the affair with several chanties of the sea.

The San Francisco papers contain many complaints from the business community of that city regarding the recent quarantine of Chinatown due to the appearance of the bubonic plague in that pestilential quarter. These businessmen would do well to worry more about the health of their city than their pocketbooks. What is needed is more stringent steps, not watered down self-serving proposals.

Mrs. Edith Fuller tells us that the help concert given by the Willing Workers of the Congregational Church on Tuesday was a great success. The feats of legerdemain performed by Judge E.A. Schmidt were greatly enjoyed, especially his transformation of water into wine. Miss Garnetta McCoy favored the audience with an impromptu exhibition of delsarte, in which she postured human emotions ranging from rage to submission.

Your editor recently tried out one of Patch McKenzie's bicycles and can say without fear of contradiction that his "wheels" are among the best in the world. McKenzie's machines are attractively priced and worth every cent that is asked for them. Test one at McKenzie's shop on Escobar Street in Martinez.

MEETINGS AND EVENTS
Anti-Imperialist Society–Tonight

John Heywards, president of the Port Newton Anti-Imperialist Society, reminds us that Miss Lily Newton will host the society's monthly meeting this evening at the old Newton Mansion up Buck's Ranch Road. Captain Grayson Spintler of the Twentieth Kansas Regiment, who lost an arm fighting the Filipino insurgents at Caloocan, will be the guest speaker.

"I would not mind if I had been wounded in defense of my country," Captain Spintler says, "but this war is being fought in quest of an overseas empire."

Fire Department–Friday

There has been much debate in the last few years about improving the efficiency of our volunteer fire department. The Volunteer Fire Committee, composed of Finnis Hurley, G.B. Rocca and Dudley Valentine, has called a meeting to be held at the International Hotel, Main Street, at eight o'clock Friday night.

A thorough reorganization of the department will be discussed, including the establishment of a new, professional organization which is to be well-equipped and supported by a property tax. There is much opposition to this idea among the brave men of our volunteer fire departments, but the heat of summer will soon be upon us and again we court disaster. Gentlemen's clubs are no longer adequate to the task. Right-minded citizens are urged to attend.

5
DOCTOR SAM FULLER
President, Port Newton Athletic Club

Leave Manifest Destiny and the White Man's
Burden to fellows like William Randolph Hearst, Teddy
Roosevelt, and Henry Cabot Lodge. That's what I thought.
Let the goddamn Filipinos have the goddamn Philippines
and bring the boys home. That was my idea on the subject,
and I was, therefore, an Anti-Imperialist and a member of
the Port Newton Anti-Imperialist Society.

The Society was scheduled to meet at Lily Newton's
one evening, three days after her kiss had awakened the big
Indian. I'd originally planned to attend, but I'd spent the
whole day driving towards Crockett, looking in on patients
with catarrhs, boils, diarrhea, vomiting and female problems.
After a day like that, a man feels like putting his feet up on
the ottoman and having a whiskey soda, which was exactly
what I was doing, at least until my wife set me straight.

"Go get yourself ready, Doctor Sam," Edith said.

"Ready for what?" I asked, petting Percival, our old
yellow mouse-questing cat.

"This is quite a step for Lily," Edith went on. "Being
hostess and all, and it's our duty as friends and neighbors to
support her. Especially after all she's been through."

That, of course, was that. I dumped Percival onto the
floor. "Go make yourself useful," and tossed down my
whiskey.

I'll never know why Old Man Newton thought he
could corner the grain market. Monopolize the grain supply
so completely, that is, as to be able to set the price. But rich
men were doing things like that in those days and Old Man
Newton was rich all right. The son of a bitch owned the
Savings Association, the Wharf & Warehouse, the water
company, two steamship companies, and most of the land
from Port Newton to Berkeley.

But the first Lily, or any of us, realized her father
was diverting Savings Association funds to his own use, was
the morning he told his employees he was going for a walk.

That last, long walk when he drowned himself in the Strait, it turned out to be.

That fateful morning people lined up in front of the Savings Association as usual. But when it didn't open at ten, they grew suspicious. Long John, Constable Sheets that is, had done his best.

"Come on, now, folks. You all just go home, and we'll get this straightened out." And this was way before he and Lily began courting.

Instead of going home, those good Newtonians walked up to Lily's place, climbed the front stairs, and rang her doorbell. Lily hid inside for three days, the shades lowered, the house dark and dreary.

But at the time of which I speak now, the night of the Anti-Imperialist Society meeting, that cold, old mansion—which the Old Man had had the sense to put in Lily's name—glowed as warm and yellow as it had in the happier times. By the time Edith and I arrived, our darling daughter, Sophie, had already sunk her claws into the best-looking young fellow in the place. He was all brass buttons and soldier-boy blue, and Sophie had taken up a position next to him in the reception hall just beyond the front door.

"Daddy? Have you met our brave captain yet?"

I smiled. "I don't believe I've had the pleasure."

"The pleasure is mine," Captain Spintler said.

The poor bastard had lost an arm in battle, and the right sleeve of his uniform jacket was empty and pinned to his shoulder. He, therefore, extended his left hand to me while Sophie played coquette to the hilt.

"Oh Daddy," she moaned. "I've been trying to convince the captain to walk me home after the meeting, but he is such an obstinate fellow."

The captain fell for it hook, line, and sinker.

"Why, I'd be honored to walk you home, Miss Fuller. I wouldn't let it be otherwise, in fact."

The horrors of war, amputation, green jungle, and Aguinaldo's guerrillas had not proved sufficient to conquer him. Yet, here he was, a slave to the romantic machinations of Port Newton's pioneering Gibson Girl.

Edith looked at me with eyes that said, "Do something about your daughter."

It was then, while I was wondering what on earth I could do about Sophie even if I wanted to, that I realized Lily wasn't in the receiving line with the officials of the Anti-Imperialist Society. Lily was my patient, I should add, and the malaise that had seized her in recent years–neurasthenia, the exhaustion of the nervous system–was my prime concern in her regard.

I asked Sophie where she was.

"Oh, you know Lily," Sophie said. "I think she's got a mad on at Riley Towne for writing about the kissing business. And Constable Sheets was looking for you."

"Long John?" I said. "What does Long John want of me?"

"How ever should I know? The boy was looking for you, too."

"Willie?" I said. For some reason Sophie never called her brother by his actual name, but only "Wilhelm" or, as now, "the boy."

Edith said, "You seem very popular tonight, dear."

Sophie gave me a peck on the cheek. "Daddy's always popular, aren't you, Daddy?"

A moment later, I left Edith with Garnetta McCoy, a neighbor girl and good friend of Sophie's. I went looking for Lily and Long John, foolishly thinking I might even find them together. Making my way through the sitting room, behind the reception hall, towards the back veranda, I was pleased to see not just Democrats, but also a good number of Port Newton's Republicans.

Even Riley Towne was there, loitering by the silver coffee service Lily had borrowed from Edith. I started to chew him out for putting that about Lily kissing the Indian in the newspaper, but he just waved me off.

"Hell, it was all over town before I got hold of it. Quit your complaining and come have a look at this."

He dragged me out onto the veranda and pointed towards his new bicycle. It was leaning up against the covered portico, where carriages had deposited wheat kings and railroad barons back in the days when the Old Man ruled Port Newton.

"It's from McKenzie, over in Martinez," Riley said, patting the seat like it was a baby's behind. "I got a bargain you wouldn't believe."

"You sell yourself too cheap," I told him.

He laughed. "And you take yourself too seriously."

Taking a grip on the handlebars he put his legs astride the thing as if he were about to fly off down the hill.

"Want to give it a try?" he asked. "These things are going to liberate humanity. No more shank's mare."

I turned him down, however, and that was when I saw Lily, seated on the porch swing with Father Frank Noone, right fielder on our ball team and pastor of the Catholic Church. He'd been trying to requisition Lily's soul for years, not to mention mine. A lady in distress she seemed to be, and I became intent on rescuing her.

"Good evening," I said. "You're looking lovely tonight, Lily."

And she was, too. Lily had always been a good-looking woman and when she took some trouble with herself–which wasn't often–she was the best-looking young spinster along the Strait.

"Thank you, Doc," she said, but without spirit.

Father Noone offered me the plate of lady fingers he was holding. "They're quite good, actually. Not too sugary."

"Yes, not too sugary," I said, biting into one. "Your meeting seems a genuine success," I told Lily.

"They don't care about the war," she said. "They've just come to leer at me."

"Well, one or two maybe."

"Here, please." Father Noone offered me a napkin, and I realized I was getting crumbs from the damn lady finger all over me.

Lily asked if I'd signed the petition yet, the one the Society intended to send to President McKinley. I told her I would certainly do so, and asked if she knew where Long John was.

"Why do you think I'd know where Long John is?"

"Sophie said he was looking for me, is all."

"I don't keep a watch on him, you know."

I took none of this as a good sign for Lily. She was in one of her moods just as my daughter had warned. Since she was impossible to deal with in such a condition, I shoved off and went looking for Long John.

Out back, near the carriage house, there were rose bushes which Lily had tended with affection. But not so the carriage house, which was in deep disrepair and empty now. But there, among the roses, I found Long John. He was in his best suit and tie and being lectured by Judge Eugene J. Schmidt on the free and unlimited coinage of silver.

"More money in circulation could only bring a return of prosperity," the judge told him.

"Makes sense," Long John said.

Long John never was one to fret much over politics. An uncluttered fellow one might call him. But what was on my mind was the fact that Judge Schmidt had been the umpire at our season opening game. The one against Benicia where Tony Rossi stepped to the plate without a bat and made a fool of poor Charlie Meyers.

"Now don't start up on that again, Doctor Sam," the judge told me.

"But what he did was *illegal*," I said. "A man can't go to the goddamn plate without a goddamn bat."

The judge shook his head. "You'll have to show me that one, Doc. In the book, I mean. Chapter and verse. If a man doesn't want to carry a bat to the plate, I'd say that's his right as an American. And how can a bat that doesn't exist be illegal?" He shook his head. "Your position doesn't make any sense, Doctor Sam."

My blood began to boil, but Long John, knowing the signs by virtue of experience, stepped between us.

"I need to talk with you a minute, Doc," he said. "In private."

He begged of the judge that we be excused and, this granted, he walked me down the rows of rose bushes, towards the back end of the yard.

"You know Ida Mencken, up by Buck's Ranch?" he asked.

I told him I knew her all too well. The poor woman's husband had abandoned her a year before, and her babies had always been sickly.

"Mrs. Buck came to see me this morning," Long John said.

"Yes?"

"She'd not seen Mrs. Mencken in days and so went calling, but there wasn't anybody there. There was this note pinned to a pillow."

He gave it to me. The English was broken. The handwriting was poor.

"Tomorrow," Long John said, "I think I'd best get a couple of Chinamen. Drag the well. The reservoir, too, if needs be."

"Do you want me to go with you?"

Long John shook his head. "I'll come by and let you know if I find anything. I wanted to warn you, is all."

I told him I appreciated that, as weary of such woe as I was, and just then we heard a rustling of leaves in the overgrowth behind us. We turned, and there he was, the big Indian, dressed in an expensive new suit from Frazier's in Martinez.

"Hello there, boys," he said.

He tipped the skimmer that topped his head, as if in a sign of respect.

"Is this where the meeting is? I kinda got lost up there, somewhere." He pointed back up the hill, into the wild eucalyptus. "Took the wrong fork down at the school, ended up trying to cut back through those damn trees. Not much of a pathfinder, I guess."

A big grin broke upon his face. "Why, that's you, isn't it? Constable Sheets? Am I right or am I right?"

"You're right," Long John said, grinning himself now, as was I, for the Indian's smile was infectious.

"Jack Dobbs is me." He shook Long John's hand. "And I guess I owe you a life, or some such, for pulling me out of the Father of Waters and all that crap."

Long John shrugged his boyish shrug. "All in a day's work. How's the head? That was quite a blow, you took."

Dobbs objected. "It wasn't a blow. I fell is all. I told it to the papers. I just fell." He made a laugh. "I'm a clumsy bastard at heart." Then he turned to me. "You're the big cheese at the Athletic Club, aren't you?"

"Well, I'm the president if that's what you mean."

"I guess I owe you a thanks for all that, too. For tending me that night and for the room and board and the loan."

"Loan? What loan?"

"Hey, if it wasn't for you and Foghorn, why, I'd be sleeping in the streets. At least until the team could wire me a bag of money. The Dudes, I mean. The Oakland Dudes. They're just desperate to sign me for next season."

We'd been strolling all this time, and by now, we'd come all the way back, down the garden path to the long, commodious veranda that circled half the house. There, Riley Towne was showing off his new wheel to Judge Schmidt. Father Noone was telling my wife how wonderful the jar of preserves she'd given him last Christmas had been. Lily was still in the porch swing, but alone now, as if shunned.

"Why, that's the girl that kissed me, ain't it?" Dobbs said.

I told him that was the rumor.

"I guess I owe her some thanks, too." He shook his head. "It was an awful place I was in before she kissed me, hot as Hell. Dreaming, I must have been."

He bade us goodbye and started up the veranda steps and, when she caught sight of him, Lily seemed to purposely turn away.

"That fellow doesn't smell right," Long John told me, his voice low and conspiratorial. "He said in the papers that he was going to play for San Francisco, this season, but a few minutes ago, out by the roses, he told us it was Oakland."

I thought for a moment. "Yes, I suppose he did say that."

"You'd think a man would know what team he was going to play for, don't you?"

"Maybe the papers got it wrong. You know Riley Towne. Or maybe Dobbs just misspoke."

Long John shook his head. "In the papers he said he'd already signed. Now he says he hasn't. He doesn't smell right, that's my opinion."

We got no further in this discussion for that was when Willie, my son, found me. "Hey, Pop! Have a look at this!"

All at once he thrust a tattered copy of *The Boy's Book of Big League Baseball* into my hands.

"He ain't just Jack Dobbs," Willie said, pointing at one of the pages. "He's *Chief* Dobbs. First Injun ever in the Big League. Look here. Won twenty-seven games in 'eighty-nine and twenty-nine in 'ninety-two. The moment I saw him, I knew."

"Slow down, Willie," I said, trying to read the fine print of the book by the gaslight exuding through the great windows of the old house.

"He played with the Bostons when they were champs," Willie said. "With Kid Nichols, Tommy McCarthy, and the rest."

"I still don't trust the son of a bitch," Long John said.

On the veranda, Dobbs sat down on the swing next to Lily.

"Before the white man came," I heard him say, "my people ate crickets. Crickets, miss, for godsakes!"

I couldn't make out the rest of it–something about New York City, rib-eye steak, and Mulligan's Chop House.

Willie pointed at the dim page of the baseball book. "See what it says: 'feared for his fade-away.' That was before he went and ruined his arm."

"A fade-away," I said, pondering the wonder of it–a pitch, thrown by a southpaw, that broke down and away from a right handed batter.

Lily gave Dobbs a cup of coffee, and he balanced it, as best he could, on his knee. I'd heard of the fade-away pitch before, but I had never seen a man who could throw one with consistency, so awful was the strain it put on the arm.

He told Lily, "Oh yeah I been everywhere. Boston, Philadelphia, Chicago. Went on Spalding's world tour in 'eighty-eight. Australia, England, Italy. They figured an Injun would be an attraction over there and damn right they were. Arabia, Egypt. The pyramids ain't worth a plug nickel in my opinion, miss. But Paris, well, that's something."

I realized that if a left-hander, like Dobbs, was capable of throwing the fade-away and *also* possessed a curveball–which broke in the opposite direction–he could be a well-nigh *invincible*. All at once I understood why Foghorn–as crafty a leech as Old Man Newton–had lent an Indian money.

6

Extract From
The Boy's Book of Big League Baseball


```
CHIEF DOBBS              BL     TL     6'2"      195 lbs

Jack Poe Dobbs
Born: Genoa, Nev., date unknown

CHIEF DOBBS

YEAR TEAM       GM  WON  LOST  WIN%   ERA    BH   BB    SO
1885 CHICAGO    12    4     8  .333  4.01   115   51    46
1886            41   11    25  .306  3.30   329  134   129
1887            44   16    26  .381  3.99   409   98   120
1888 BOSTON     36   17    17  .500  3.90   309  105    85
1889            47   27    17  .614  3.24   356   87   176
1890            20   12     6  .667  3.81   147   40    86
1891            39   20    15  .542  3.56   302  108   121
1892            51   29    13  .690  3.14   340  137   189
1893 NEW YORK   27    8    20  .286  6.45   364   84    30
     ST. LOUIS  11    4     4  .500  4.28    87   20    14
1894            20    3    10  .231  6.23   198   46    18
1895 PITT       14    2    11  .154  7.07   126   35    16
1896 WASH        4    1     2  .333  6.75    45   15     6
             ---------------------------------------------
     totals    366  154   174  .470  4.02  3127  960  1036

1890-held out, salary dispute
1894-injured, bad elbow
1896-suspended for life from the National League
```

7
Calvin Elwell
Bartender and Second Baseman

Doc blames himself for all that happened back then. But that's Doc for you. He still blames himself for every carbuncle and boil in Port Newton, always has, always will. But it wasn't his fault. Wasn't Foghorn's. Wasn't mine. Wasn't anybody's. Things just go wrong sometimes, most of the time, in fact.

The Chief used to read the dime novels–devoured them daily–Westerns: *The American Indian Weekly*, *Deadeye Dick*, *Rough Riders Weekly*, all those. But what I'm getting at was that he got me to reading them, too, and I read Westerns still to this day. Except it's Zane Grey and Owen Wister, now. When there's a good one playing at the pictures I drive up to Martinez to take it in as the trains don't stop in Port Newton anymore. I take Doctor Sam with me when he's feeling up to it, and we spend a few hours wrapped in a fairy tale.

Things are clean and clear in the Westerns–white hats, black hats, schoolmarms, gunfighters, cattle rustlers. Maybe even a backstabbing Injun or two. But in real life, things are not so simple. In life, there's just people, and people do the best they can with what they've got. Sam, Foghorn, the drunks, and the tarts that used to belly up to the bar in the Railroad Exchange. All of us just roll the dice and, unless they're loaded like those ones the Chief had, we pass or don't pass right in line with the odds.

So it wasn't anybody's fault, what happened later. Sam rails against God every now and again, especially when he's got a drink or two in him, but that's a losing game.

Other times Doc blames Foghorn, and he's some right in that, but you'll never get me to say anything bad about Foghorn Murphy. Foghorn took me in when I needed it. He gave me a job, a place to live, even a family of sorts, if you count drunks and stevedores and boomers.

My father disowned me, you see, locked me out of my own house. But I don't bear any grudges against him, not any more at any rate. I failed out of the university in my first year, and in doing so failed him, too. Father wanted me to follow in his footsteps. I suppose such a thing would have proved to him that he was as good a father as he figured his own father had been. But me, I never wanted any part of being Lawyer Elwell the Third.

I just wasn't the studious sort. I pledged a fraternity, drank beer, chased the girls, and played baseball. Guess I just never wanted to grow up. When I was a boy, I'd put my Sunday school clothes on over my baseball togs, stay camouflaged until I got out of the house, then divest myself of the former and head for the ball field. Baseball was my religion, you might say.

We didn't just watch baseball, in those days, we *played* it. The towns all had teams. The Odd Fellows, the Native Sons, and Knights Templar, they all had teams too. The volunteer firemen, the high school–even the goddamn Dante Society. Just about every organization that could gather together nine men, and sometimes women, had themselves a team. Cynics would say we didn't have much else to do, and they'd be close to right: no radio, no picture shows. Gramophones still seemed a miracle. So the only entertainments we had were the ones we made for ourselves, and, well, you can't beat baseball for entertainment.

Trouble with the Port Newton Athletic Club team was that it was too damn old. Me and Billy Lawton were about the only young fellows left on it. Billy was a wild man and, hell, I was "good field, no hit." What happened was that the flower of Port Newton's youth had departed town when the Savings Association went down and Newton Wharf & Warehouse closed. No sense staying in a place on the downward slide. Why not migrate to the brighter lights of Martinez or Benicia? That was the popular opinion.

When I failed out of the university and Lawyer Elwell locked me out of the house, I almost emigrated, too. Don't know where I might have gone, but that was when good old Foghorn took me in. He gave me a job as a bartender at the Railroad Exchange, a place to stay upstairs, and a true education. I learned all I know, which ain't much, right there behind Foghorn Murphy's prized mahogany bar.

My earliest memories of him, from when I was a boy with my baseball togs hid under my Sunday best, are of him as station agent at the Southern Pacific depot. There he was in the limelight, calling out the arrivals and departures without even a megaphone, just that big, foghorn voice of his.

"6:45 from Oakland, now arriving track one. Bound for Sacramento, Reno, Salt Lake, Denver, and all points east."

It was always exciting, taking the train, and for a boy a train station is heaven. Foghorn singing out. Whistles screaming. Steam belching. Hotter than hell, those locomotives used to be. Motorcars are boring in comparison.

Foghorn Murphy was Irish, as if I needed to tell you, and the son of dirt-poor immigrants. But he never forgot his origins, no matter how high he rose in this world, which wasn't particularly high from the point of view most of the folks who lived up the hill.

When the trains pulled in at the depot, the passengers would mostly debark to stretch their legs while the cars were shifted onto the ferry. Immigrants had tags pinned to them, in those days, and Foghorn would go around looking for people with tags, find every one, shake their hands and give them the benefit of what he'd learned in this life.

"Keep your hand on your wallet."

Spoke four or five different languages, Foghorn did. A little of each, at least. He'd say it to the Italians in Italian, "Keep your hand your wallet." He'd say it to the Mexicans in Spanish; the Irish in Irish; and the Portuguese in Portogee even.

He used to help out old Rosa Paredes, too, the crazy lady. Let her eat the free lunch. Bought her drinks. Let her tell fortunes at one of the poker tables. Let her sleep in back when the hour got late. He never had much love for Chinamen, though. Don't know why. Never trusted them, I think. That is a failing, I suppose, but we are all made in God's image, and He don't seem perfect to me, either.

Foghorn never trusted Old Man Newton or the Savings Association. Put his money in the bank in Martinez even though it wasn't so handy. Got a loan from them and bought the Railroad Exchange. He had a little house off Main Street and even dug his own well so he wouldn't have to patronize the Old Man's water company. Never had any children himself. Never even had a wife.

"Never had time for it," he'd say.

But hear this: when the *Maine* blew up and the Spanish war started, I intended to join up, but Foghorn wouldn't let me. He paid the train fare for every boy in Port Newton who joined, but wouldn't let me join myself.

"You stay home, son," he'd say. "You stay home and don't get your behind blown off."

He doubtless showed himself a hypocrite in that regard, but he was torn, you see. Two of his older brothers fought in the Civil War. The Irish Brigade. One fell at Fredericksburg. Laid all night in the open, wounded, and freezing to death.

"Keep your hand on your wallet." That was Foghorn Murphy's philosophy of life.

And Foghorn really did invent the Martini. Doc always figured it was bull, but I was there when he did it. It was an accident, like most great discoveries. A wrong bottle grabbed, a slip of the hand that held the jigger. After that it took him about a week of mixing gin and vermouth in various combinations to get the formula right and another week of the boys sampling his concoction.

I was as wide-eyed as the rest of the fellows when the Chief showed up, wider even. But I sure didn't like it much when Foghorn stuck him with me in my little room, up above the Railroad Exchange.

"I don't sleep on no damn floor," the Chief said, the first time he saw that cubby hole of mine. "I had enough of sleeping on floors."

He'd had it pretty rough in the National League, being an Indian and all. There were taunts and insults from the fans, the cops, from everybody. People spit on him, threw beer bottles at him. When he first started, players from opposing teams–sometimes even from his own team–would catch up with him after a game and beat the hell out of him. That's why he carried that little knife-gun strapped to his calf. He even shot some son of a bitch once.

"Only winged the bastard," he said, as if he'd wished he'd have killed him, come Hell or high water.

When the Chief's arm went bad, he threw some games for gamblers and got booted out of the league. So in 'ninety-seven, it was up to Sockalexis, the Penobscot Indian out of Notre Dame, to buck the dealer all over again. People only remember him, now. Nobody wants to remember a fellow who sold out his teammates and so the Chief got swept under the rug, just like dust.

"I ain't sleeping on any more floors," he said when he saw my little room.

So it was me ended up sleeping on the hardwood. Wasn't bad. Had blankets and a pillow, but it did start to bruise my hip bones after a while, which didn't help my play at second base any.

First thing the Chief did after Lily Newton woke him with that kiss was go to confession.

"You got a church in this burg? And I mean a Catholic church."

We didn't know what he confessed to at the time. Foghorn tried to pump Father Noone for it. But Father Noone wouldn't spill the beans, at least not then, and that was one reason Foghorn insisted the Chief room with me.

"Learn what you can, son, but keep your hand on your wallet."

I didn't much like being a spy for Foghorn. But people just naturally tell me their troubles, so I figured it wouldn't be hard. Turned out that instead of me pumping him, the Chief pumped me, him on the bed, me on the floor in my blanket.

"What do you know about that woman, kid?"

The Chief always called me "kid." I suppose he knew my real name, at least after a while, but "kid" was good enough, as I always answered to it.

"What do you know about that woman, kid?"

"What woman's that, Chief?"

"The only one that's worth a plug nickel around here. Miss Newton, that is. I can't get the taste of her off my lips. Strawberries. Know what I mean?"

I thought I did at the time. I'd kissed Sophie Fuller more than once, you see, on a hayride all the way up to Buck's Ranch one moonlit, midsummer's night. I don't recall what she'd tasted like. Carbolic acid, probably. I was pretty new at kissing, then, but just when I was getting the hang of it, Sophie cut off my water. What a girl.

The Chief had brought a bottle with him up from the bar. We'd been drinking it all the time, him in bed, me in my blanket on the floor. Once we'd finished with Lily Newton and Constable Sheets–"They engaged or something?"–we started talking about baseball.

"You don't *look* like a hitter, kid, that's your problem. It's half bluff, you know. You got to make the pitcher *think* you can hit the cover off the ball, even if you can't. Got to make him fear you. Appearances, kid, that's what life is all about."

Then he told me how during the off-seasons, when he was in the Eastern leagues, he'd been in a vaudeville act with his "first ex-wife."

"Etta Kane, ever heard of her?"

I told him I hadn't.

He reached for his wallet, which he kept under his pillow at night along with that thirty-two, and pulled out that cigarette card of the chorus girl we'd found on him the night Long John pulled him out of the Strait. It was pretty much ruined by the water, but the Chief dried it out and saved it as best he could.

"She was big around New York City for a few years," he told me. "Hell of a girl, Etta. Polack from Pittsburgh. Real name was Edna Kanecki. We'd hoof a bit and sing a couple of songs. You know, kid, 'Come see the dancing bear.' It's all bluff. Just like hitting. Just like pitching."

And that was the beginning of it, of me and the Chief becoming blood brothers, just like in the dime Westerns. We were both a little drunk when it finally happened. He called for a kitchen knife, slit our palms, and we mingled our blood. But I am getting ahead of myself. This was just the beginning of it all, and the beginning of Foghorn's scheming, too.

8

DOCTOR SAM FULLER
President, Port Newton Athletic Club

I pitched in 'eighty-eight when the Benicians robbed us of the Championship of the Strait. I pitched for years after that, too, and I always figured that my boy children would play on the Port Newton team and my girl children would sit in the little grandstand on Newton's Bluff and cheer and boo and that this world without end would go on and on.

But all that changed when the Savings Association collapsed, and by the time Jack Dobbs floated into town, I was getting pretty weary of the whole damn thing–hard times, defeat, humiliation. I'd still toss a few innings here and there when necessary, but the same thing that ruined Dobbs' arm ruined mine, too. In 'ninety-three, you see, the pitching distance was moved back and after that I no longer had much pace on my fastball. As far as curving the damn thing, well, for me that was always a haphazard undertaking at best.

So it was that I tended to arrive late at baseball practice, in those days, which brings me to the special practice Foghorn scheduled just before the Bulls Head Lumber game. Young Elwell and the Luciani brothers were playing pepper behind third base. Charlie Meyers stood along the foul line breathing hard after running a sprint or two. Long John knocked flies out to Father Noone, who staggered beneath each and every one of them in the weedy outfield.

"Nice catch," Long John yelled, when the good Father actually caught one. "Good try," was his more usual observation.

I set myself up in the pitcher's box, more out of nostalgia than anything, and started tossing balls at the chicken wire backstop that protected whoever dared sit directly behind home plate.

I was just starting to feel loose and almost right when Foghorn came shuffling down the first base line towards home plate. Jack Dobbs was at his side, but what caught my eye was that the big Indian was all decked out in a Port Newton baseball uniform, an old one from that season of the Stolen Championship.

Sharp things those uniforms had been in their day, so dark a green as to be almost black, with a high collar and a big, white "N" over the heart. My only objection to this particular mode of vestment for Dobbs was that a fellow had to be a member of the Athletic Club before he wore the uniform, and Dobbs wasn't. I intercepted the two of them halfway down the line and brought this oversight to Foghorn's attention.

"What the hell, Foghorn? Some things are still sacred, are they not?"

He took my elbow and steered me back towards the mound. "Doc, do you know who this fellow is?"

"Well of course I know who he is. Every son of a bitch in town knows who he is by now. But you can't just let anyone put on a Port Newton uniform, and especially that uniform."

"I thought you knew."

"Knew what? And no crap, Foghorn."

"No crap. Dobbs works for me now, tending bar at the Exchange. He's rooming upstairs with Elwell, and, what's more, he's a member of the Athletic Club."

"A member? The men have to vote on new members, Foghorn, and I don't recall that ever happening. We have rules, after all, and I'm still the damn president, aren't I?"

He shook his head. "No. No. You misunderstand. He's not a *full* member. He's a *probationary* member. It's all in the by-laws."

"What's all in the by-laws?"

"You mean to tell me that you don't know what's in the by-laws? My God, Doc. Don't worry, though, I won't let on to the boys. Hell, it might mean impeachment, if something like that got out."

He whistled, made a wave, and young Cal Elwell, our second baseman, recording secretary, and parliamentarian, interrupted his pepper game and dashed on over.

"Doctor Sam's forgotten the by-laws," Foghorn told him.

42

Cal required no further prompting. He pulled a tattered copy of the by-laws out of the back pocket of his baseball pants. "It's all there, Doc."

"What's all there?"

"A man can be voted probationary membership," Cal said, "by a majority vote of a quorum of the officers of the club."

"But us three are the only officers," I said. "You mean, you two fellows voted him in? You can't do that, can you?"

"Only in an emergency," Cal said, flipping through the by-laws, one way, then back the other. "It's here somewhere."

"Page forty-six, paragraph three," Foghorn told him.

"And what's the so-called emergency?" I asked.

"The Bulls Head game," Foghorn said. "If Charlie pitches we'll lose for sure, and there go all our bets."

"Bets? What bets?"

"We've got to strike while the iron is hot, Doctor Sam. This is the greatest stroke of luck we've ever had. He was going to sign with the San Francisco club, or maybe the Oaklanders. But he likes it here better, God knows why, and none of the boys seem to have any objections. Look at them."

He pointed towards home plate, where Dobbs now stood. Half the team flocked around him like sheep. Billy Lawton, Hec Fernandez, and even Father Noone, who shouldn't have been quite as corrupt as the rest of us, surrounded the big Indian, besieging him with questions.

"What was it like in the Big League, Chief?"

"About like here but more money."

"Did you ever face McGraw and Keeler?"

"Plenty of times."

"Who had the best fastball you ever saw?"

"Amos Rusie. But Keefe had a better change of pace."

The gist of it all was this: Foghorn was bringing in a ringer, a professional who wasn't really a Newtonian but only loosely disguised as one. It was cheating, needless to say, and cheating is always wrong, at least in the ideal. But God was dead, after all, at least according to the *Port*

43

Newton News. Practically speaking morality works more like this: If someone cheats you, why, that's absolutely wrong; but if you cheat someone else, and especially if it is some person or group seen as deserving of it such as umpires, bankers, or politicians, then it is clever and admirable and even better if you don't get caught.

"Well," I told Foghorn, "he'll have to come up before the full membership eventually."

"No bugbear that," Foghorn said. "Why, at the next scheduled meeting, just like it says in the by-laws. Right, Cal?"

"Yes, sir."

Foghorn put an arm around my shoulder.

"Don't worry, Doc. Look at them. The boys love him, and hell, after we beat Bulls Head and put a few dollars in the coffers of the P.N.A.C., and our own pockets too, eh, there won't be a man in the club who'll be against him."

By now, Dobbs was passing out chaws of Black Strap tobacco like a pretty girl selling kisses. Everybody took one, whether they chewed or not. All were laughing and joking except for Long John. He stood by the backstop, swinging a new bat, as if testing it out, with Charlie Meyers who, up until now at least, had been our pitcher.

Dobbs called over to Charlie. "You don't chew?"

Charlie shook his head. "No."

"Not even when you pitch?"

"I teach English and literature, sir, at Port Newton Union High, and I like to set a good example for my students."

Dobbs grinned and strolled towards him. "Glad to find a teacher who's so high minded. All of them I knew were more hitters than pitchers, if you catch my drift."

He reached into his back pocket, pulled out that lucky rabbit's foot of his and a coiled whip of black licorice.

"Got anything against candy, do you?" He bit off a chaw of the tobacco then sunk his teeth into the licorice.

"When you're pitching," he told Charlie. "You chew the licorice along with the tobacco. When you got a load of it, you spit the whole mess into your glove and work it into the ball. Turns the ball black... See? After that, batters can't hardly see it at all."

"Is that fair?" Charlie said.

"Damn right it's fair. This is baseball, not checkers."

Practice went almost as usual after that. I hit infield. Foghorn coached the fielders on cutoffs and relays. Dobbs, who'd excused himself from infield practice because he "already knew all that crap," watched from the bench, chewing tobacco, spitting, and shouting encouragements.

"Look sharp there, boys! Be a man out there! Beat him up, ball!" he'd sing out, whenever one of our infielders booted a grounder.

After infield, I threw a little batting practice. A half dozen swings per man were all we allowed ourselves that day in the interest of time. But the boys did seem more inspired than usual, all wanting to impress the Big Leaguer, I supposed.

Dobbs, by then, had positioned himself at second base, where he clowned, did pratfalls and deigned to scooped up a ball whenever one came so near him he didn't have to move.

"Beat him up, ball!" he called, when one took a bad hop, and the boys all found it quite amusing.

Long John took his swings against me, and turned my feeble fastballs into line drives up the alleys. A hell of a hitter, Long John was, and I'd always wondered if, if perhaps things had broken a little different in his life, he might have been a Big Leaguer, himself. But the Fates had not decreed such a thing and so the barefoot farm boy had become a town constable, risking life and limb for people who never truly appreciated him.

"Nice pitching, Doc," Long John said to me, charitably, when his turn at the plate was done.

When Dobbs' turn came to bat, Charlie Meyers trotted on over to me.

"Let me throw a few," Charlie said. "I'll show that son of a bitch."

Charlie should have known better. Professional baseballers were a rough bunch in those days. No college boys like Mathewson; no peach fuzz babies like Waite Hoyt; no fat, pampered millionaires like Ruth. But what could I say? I tossed Charlie the ball and walked away.

All eyes focused upon Dobbs as he dug in at the plate. He was more concentrated than he had been in the field. Everyone loves to hit I suppose. He pounded his bat upon the plate, and I can see the rest of it still.

Charlie went into a big windup, as if he were readying to dispatch his most powerful fastball–such as it was–but, instead, he tossed Dobbs a cream puff, slow as sugar. The Indian made a mighty swing but missed by a foot, and the boys all put up a nervous laugh.

"Ain't done this in a while," Dobbs said.

His black eyes became squints. He pounded the plate once more. Charlie's next pitch came in hard, and Dobbs only managed to foul it off. When he ripped the third pitch down the first base line, the boys all grunted and nodded their heads. But he only tipped the fourth pitch, missed the fifth entirely, and on his sixth and final attempt, swung with all his might but could only manage a lazy fly towards the middle ground in center field.

"Hell," he said, tossing the bat away with disdain. "Pitchers ain't supposed to be hitters."

And that was when Charlie made his first big mistake.

"You've proven yourself a pitcher, then," he called out.

Dobbs, to my surprise, seemed to take no notice of this but there was more to come. After batting practice, we cobbled together a rotating game, of sorts, due to our lack of manpower. Dobbs was appointed to act as pitcher for both sides, and, as luck would have it, I was first to hit against him. His first victim.

Again, the boys all slavered in anticipation.

He threw me a hard one, which I took for a strike. It had good velocity, but I'd seen quicker from the wild-eyed farm boys of Pacheco. He threw me a curve, which I swung at and missed.

Billy Lawton, our shortstop, called out, "Throw him the fade-away!" but Dobbs demurred.

"Too hard on the old soup bone."

I ended up fouling out to Long John at first base, but still wasn't much impressed by what the Indian had thrown me. I began to wonder what all the damn hoopla was about. Then, it was Charlie Meyers's turn at the bat.

Hec Fernandez squatted down behind the plate to catch, and I took up a position behind him, as an umpire would. The better to assess the big Indian's abilities. Charlie took up Long John's new bat and swung it like a whip.

"Do your worst, Chiefie!" he called.

This was Charlie's second mistake.

Dobbs, obliging, went into a big wind-up, all arms and legs and flailing, much as Charlie had, but instead of changing-up on him, he uncorked what seemed a dart aimed straight at Charlie's left temple.

But just as Charlie went sprawling to avoid it, an amazing thing happened. The true velocity of the pitch became apparent, and I realized it was not a dart at all but just another cream puff, and one that curved down and away from Charlie and ended its flight by crossing right over the plate.

"Strike one!" I cried.

Hec came out of his catcher's squat, turned and looked at me in amazement. It was a pitch thrown by a left-handed pitcher that curved away from a right-handed batter.

"The fade-away," I said.

Charlie picked himself off the dirt.

"Sorry, Chucky," the big Indian called. "Didn't mean to scare you."

Visions of 'eighty-eight revenged danced in my head. Visions of Port Newton prosperous and happy again. Even visions of me playing ball, limber and strong as in the days of yore. Fantastic images. Glory, sunshine, green grass, and victory bewitched me. If I didn't know better, I'd say it was the devil's doing.

9

THE PORT NEWTON NEWS
Monday, April 23

TOWNE TOPICS

NEWTONS GORE BULLS 12-7
SEVERAL MEN INJURED BY ERRANT PITCHES

In the second joust of the new baseball season, held
yesterday, the brave lads of the Port Newton Athletic Club
came from behind to defeat Bulls Head Lumber, twelve
tallies to seven.

Charles "Icebox" Meyers, the Newton's veteran
pitcher, began the game with a case of nerves, surrendering
two hits and two walks, and personally misjudging a pop-fly,
all in the very first inning. After Meyers loaded the bases in
the third, the Newton's manager, Foghorn Murphy, shuffled
onto the field and passed the pitching chores along to one
Jack Poe Dobbs, the Washoe Indian that Constable Sheets
pulled from the Strait two weeks ago.

"I hated to take Charles out of the game," Foghorn
said, later. "He is my pitcher and so shall remain. But Mr.
Dobbs has been an exemplary fellow, practicing with the
club religiously, and in all fairness, deserved his chance."

Dobbs strode onstage in the proverbial pinch. The
sacks were jammed, none were out, and all eyes were upon
him by reason of his history as a professional ballplayer. But
hope dimmed rapidly when Dobbs' first pitch struck the first
batter to face him at the base of the neck where the head
joins the spine, knocking the man momentarily senseless and
forcing in a run. When the Chief, as he is sometimes called,
"beaned" the next batter also, a chorus of boos was brought
down upon the noble redskin's head, with many of the
Newtonians present advancing the theory that the only good
Indian was a dead one.

But baseball is a fickle thing, and the hoots soon
turned to hurrahs. For after seeing two more of their

comrades "dusted" in similar fashion, the Bull's batters seemed to grow more concerned with dodging the white orb than with hitting it. The side was retired without further incident and thus began a star-spangled performance in which Dobbs allowed no more runs over the next six innings.

After the game, L.F. Glease, Jr., player coach of the Bulls, expressed anger at Dobbs' performance. "A man shouldn't play like a savage, even if he is one."

But when your editor asked Dobbs if there had been intent behind the bean-balls he hurled, the Indian replied that nothing could be further from the truth.

"My wildness," he said, "grew solely from the fact that I hadn't pitched all spring. Be assured that there was no attempt on my part to injure any of my opponents."

In the fourth frame, Dobbs himself was struck by a pitch apparently hurled at him for the purpose of retaliation, but the Indian said he was not so much hurt by the incident as disturbed by it.

"Such tactics are one of the things that formed my disillusionment regarding the professional game, and I've had enough of it. I could be pitching for the Giants of New York right now, but I find Port Newton a much more convivial atmosphere."

When reminded that he could not, in fact, "be pitching for the Giants of New York right now" due to the fact that he was suspended from the National League for life in 1896, the Chief replied, "Suspended for life? What does that mean? How can you 'suspend' somebody 'for life.' It's idiotic."

As the innings rolled by and the Chief held the Bulls to naught, the Newtons seized the initiative, and a slow but steady comeback began. A walk, a stolen base, an errant throw, and a sacrifice fly became a run. A hit, an error, a wild pitch and two more Newtonians scored. A crashing blow off the bat of third-sacker Ernest Luciani into the endless depths of left-center field, a mad dash around the paths, and the Newtons had notched a homerun.

The culmination of these Herculean labors occurred in the penultimate inning when first baseman Long John Sheets lashed a ground-rule double over the much despised chicken wire screen in right field, drove in two runs, and gave the men of Port Newton the lead and the eventual victory.

After the game, buoyed by the team's first victory in human memory, players and spectators alike packed themselves into the Railroad Exchange Saloon, sated their hunger with hard-cooked eggs, and offered up libations to the gods of the ball yard.

Foghorn Murphy, for one, and Doctor Sam Fuller, for two, seem to be of the opinion that the big Indian has the capacity to restore the glory days of 'eighty-eight to Port Newton, but Dobbs himself held a more guarded opinion.

"These games must be played one at a time," he said, a proposition whose accuracy cannot be questioned.

CONSTABLE SHEETS KILLS A HOBO
RULED SELF DEFENSE BY JUDGE SCHMIDT

Last evening Constable John Sheets made his usual trip to the Southern Pacific Depot to meet the 6:45 train, and there saw two train hands struggling with a Negro of monstrous size and build. Long John dashed to their assistance just as the Negro broke free. The giant began to run, but Long John caught up with him, and in the struggle, the man bit Long John's hand badly before Long John was able to put him down with his billy club.

Long John then lodged the Negro in our ramshackle calaboose and paid a visit to Doc Fuller to tend his hand, on which a wound had been opened in the struggle. While Long John was still in Doc's office, Calvin Elwell, who helps Long John out upon occasion, came to Doctor Sam's saying that the prisoner was getting very violent and attempting to break down the door of the lockup.

The constable made his way back to the jail, and just as he was about to enter, the front door swung open and the prisoner emerged, running. Called upon to stop, the Negro instead came directly at Long John with the very same club the constable had used to subdue him. Long John drew his Colt Single Action Army revolver and shot the Negro dead through the heart.

The next morning, an inquest was held by coroner George P. Welsh, the jury ruling six to five with one abstention that the killing was unjustified. Long John was then charged with manslaughter in the court of Judge E.A. Schmidt. The judge, however, dismissed the case on the grounds that the killing was self-defense.

"It was an awful incident," said Long John, who appeared tired and haggard afterwards, "but if the Negro had stopped when ordered, none of it would ever have happened."

The incident points out the need for the Board of Trustees to authorize the building of a secure and modern jail in Port Newton.

Anyone who might have information regarding the identity of the dead man should report it to Coroner Welsh at his funeral parlor on Ferry Street.

LOCAL BREVITIES

The westbound freight on the Santa Fe line met with an accident at Bay Point last Saturday night. The engine and three box cars were thrown from the tracks, and the fireman and engineer narrowly escaped death.

Doctor Swain, of Martinez, offers painless tooth extraction using devitalized air. His crown and bridge work is warranted as first class.

The steamer *Hollandia*, which has been anchored in the Strait, was towed to San Francisco last Tuesday to be outfitted for the Klondike. It is thought that the recent dispatch of a division of Army Regulars to the Alaskan Territory will have a sanguinary effect on the lawlessness there and increase the swell of gold seekers all the more.

Boyd Elsworthy and Armando Cruz have each purchased a rubber-tired surrey. What next, boys? Automobiles?

Our library is in need of new books, but there is no money available for their purchase. A special meeting of the library board was held last Thursday and it voted to give an entertainment on the evening of Friday, May 18, at Pimental Hall, all proceeds to go to the book fund. The library is a sacred institution and it is the duty of all citizens to support it. By doing so, you are helping yourselves and each other.

One of the most romantic weddings to take place in Port Newton in many years occurred at St. Sebastian

Catholic Church, Sunday last, when Miss Isabella Tarpley, who graduated the Deaf Institute in Berkeley last year, and Mr. Pietro Lasell, who is also deaf and mute, were united in marriage by Father Noone. The two pledged their troth with silent love in a church that had been transmuted into a bower of roses and fragrant blossoms.

We congratulate Sheriff Ulshoter on the number of hobos now lodged in the Martinez jail. The court house grounds never looked cleaner.

Subscribe to the Port Newton News to keep yourself informed on local political matters.

Miss Peggy McCann, the daughter of John H. McCann who is the prominent owner of Del Hambre Farm, seems to have been poisoned Saturday morning by eating cooked rhubarb that had stood in a tin vessel overnight. Doctor Sam fears that her life is in jeopardy.

That noted penny-pincher Foghorn Murphy paid the second installment on his taxes on Saturday morning, just before they became delinquent. It pays to squeeze a dollar, eh Foghorn?

Lawyer Elwell reports that Mrs. Martha A. Rugg, of this city, has at last been awarded the government pension that is her rightful due. Her husband, Walter Rugg, was a private in the Ohio Heavy Artillery during the Civil War, and passed away last year. Since then, Mrs. Rugg and Lawyer Elwell have been forced to file a dozen affidavits to prove her marriage, her husband's service, and the disability he was afflicted with due to such service. We understand that Lawyer Elwell donated his services to Mrs. Rugg without charge, and his good work is to be commended.

The enterprising photographer Howard James, corner of Main and Park Streets, tells us he is selling some very pretty pictures of the Easter decorations at St. Sebastian's. He will be journeying to San Francisco on Saturday and will doubtless secure some fine views there.

MEETINGS AND EVENTS
Port Newton Athletic Club–Thursday

Foghorn Murphy wishes to remind all members of the Port Newton Athletic Club that an important meeting will take place Thursday evening in the P.N.A.C. clubroom, above the Railroad Exchange Saloon. Strategies for the young season will be discussed and new members will be voted on.

Fourth of July Committee–Friday Evening

The first meeting of this year's Fourth of July Committee will be held at Pimental Hall on Friday evening at eight o'clock. Mr. Joseph Griffin, chairman of the Standing Committee and owner of the Port Newton International Hotel, says that the formation of other committees, as necessary, will be discussed and their officers elected.

With an eye towards stimulating interest in the meeting and the event itself, the Standing Committee has convinced a colored troupe, The Mississippi Minstrels, currently appearing at Hoffmeister's Gardens in Benicia, to volunteer their services. The Minstrels will parade from the ferry slip to the hall and furnish entertainments once everyone is committeed out. Hot coffee and fresh doughnuts of the first order will be provided by Frank's German Bakery located at Main and Newton in our fair city.

10
SOPHIE FULLER
Senior, Port Newton Union High School

Dear Diary,

The Mother was in a perfect snit this afternoon.

I told her, "Daddy would let me use the telephone if it was him."

She said, "Sophie, that telephone is for doctor business not jabbering and silliness."

I *told* her McMillan's was having ice cream today. I *told* her I couldn't very well go unescorted. I *told* her Garnetta was being snooty about Mr. Travis saying she'd be perfect as Josephine Corcoran in *Pinafore*. I *told* her Calvin was playing sheriff with Constable Sheets, and it was silly for me to walk all the way downtown just to ask him if he wanted to go get ice cream when the constable's office has a telephone.

And do you know what the Mother said? "The walk will do you good, Sophie. Your legs are getting rather porcine, these days, or haven't you noticed?"

I'm a stranger in my own home.

Calvin was lounging around in the constable's office when I found him, and a dingy little place it is, all the way down at the end of the Front and surrounded by Chinamen and wash houses. When I walked in, Calvin was sitting behind Long John's desk, in Long John's chair, wishing he was Long John, no doubt. He was reading a copy of the *Police News,* the dirty boy.

"Why, Calvin Elwell," I said. "What on earth have you got there?"

He scrambled to get his filthy newspaper out of my sight. It was the issue that contained those stimulating photographs of Chocolate Jim, Diary dear, the Negro boxer.

"Long John went to Sacramento overnight," Calvin informed me. "And I'm holding down the fort."

"Aren't you just something?" I said, "Holding down the fort and all by yourself, too."

The jailhouse does seem to agree with him. Smelly it always is, from Long John's habitation in the back, and in

54

need of repair. The door to the lockup, the one that awful
Negro kicked down, was still in a shambles.

"And what on earth is Long John doing in
Sacramento?" I asked. "Hot on the trail of chicken thieves?"

"He's checking up on some things."

"What things?" I asked.

"It's confidential."

"You mean he didn't tell you?"

"Well, no," Calvin said.

Needless to say, it didn't take me long to bend
Calvin to my will and fort holding or no fort holding we
soon headed for McMillan's and ice cream. I do just love
McMillan's so. Smelling of alcohol, like Daddy's office, but
of sweet syrup, too, like a cherry orchard.

The jolly little bell on the door jingled above our
heads as we walked in. Mr. McMillan was way in the back,
inside his cage, like that of a bank teller. He looked stern and
determined as he mixed his elixirs. The shelves of potions
and powders rose from floor to the ceiling. The glass
counters were filled with perfumes and notions. By the door,
a family of travelers including two little ones drank
strawberry ice cream sodas at a little white table of curving
metal, passing the time while their train was shunted onto the
ferry.

I do set scenes, well, don't I? Even Mr. Meyers says
the best feature of my writing is the descriptions. It is a gift I
have, that of literature. Perhaps even more than my gift for
the stage, and I have almost completely decided that that will
be my life and love. Especially when one must contend with
idiotic directors like Mr. Travis. Why on earth would the
sailor yearn for "The Lass Who Loved a Sailor" in *Pinafore*
if the lass isn't even pretty?

But I have forgotten the most important part of the
scene, Diary dear, which is that Lily sat at a table in the
back, drinking one of those awful Lunks. I called a greeting
and waved.

"Yoohoo? Lily! Over here."

She looked up from her magazines, *Harper's* and
New Century. Lily is absolutely mad for magazines. She
pretended not to see me, and when she finally had no choice

but to acknowledge my presence, all she did was force a smile and go right back to her reading. Sometimes!

Calvin and I sat down at an empty table, and Billy Lawton, as ambitionless as Calvin, ambled on over to take our order. I asked him how long Lily had been there, bewildered, as it were, by her magazines.

"Oh, you know," he said. Lots of good that information.

I batted my eyes at him and tossed off the first thing that popped into my head.

"Tell me, Billy, that infield looked as hard as rocks, Sunday, and yet you scooped up every grounder hit to you as if the deplorable conditions did not matter at all."

"Weren't nothin'," Billy said.

"Why, just listen to him, Calvin. 'Weren't nothin'.'"

Men are so amusing, with their poses of false modesty. Like Nelson playing rounders at Eton as the Spanish Armada approached, or whatever it was.

"And tell me, too, Billy, how on earth do you ever manage strawberry ice cream at this early season?"

"Oh, it ain't fresh. Just preserves. Nothin' to it really. Why, I can make you peach or any kind you want as long as I got the preserves."

"Imagine that," I said to Calvin. "He can make any kind of ice cream he wants as long as he has the preserves. Isn't that fascinating?"

"No," Calvin said.

I'd made him jealous! And without even trying! Well, *hardly* trying.

As we ordered strawberry floats, the bell above the door jingled again, and who should waddle in but Garnetta McCoy, Port Newton's own little Josephine Corcoran. Talk about porcine.

I stood, and we embraced like sisters.

"Sophie, dear. I'm so sorry. It's just that there's so much singing in the part. And, well, literature is your forte, everyone knows that."

"Never fear, Garnetta. Pettiness is not a thing of my blood."

Then Garnetta saw Lily. "Lily. My heavens!" She waved. "Yoohoo!"

How gauche.

The moment she was safely down in her chair, Garnetta leaned her ample bulk towards me.

"It's terrible the way Lily spends so much time here. Lunks will rot your brain, and did you know she keeps a bottle of Nervina in her purse? Hanna Joost says she goes out into her yard and digs up a hundred dollars whenever she needs money."

"Don't be an idiot," I told her.

The door bell jingled once more, and *the savage walked in*. A fat cigar was stuck in his face, unlit. A derby hat, tilted to a rakish angle, was upon his head. I would suppose that in his younger days, he was a handsome buck, and he *is* well constructed, I admit that.

"Hey, sweetheart," he said to me. "Planted any kisses lately?"

"I should say not."

He gave Garnetta a big grin, took off his hat, and bowed as if she were the Queen of England.

"Don't think I've had the pleasure." He took her hand and kissed it.

"Oh, Mr. Dobbs."

My word.

He called to Billy Lawton, who was playing with his soda water machine.

"Hey kid. What's up? Got any coffee in this joint? Nice playing out there, by the way. Shortstop, ain't it? A credit to your race and all that."

He sat down with us. "Mind if I join you?"

I don't suppose I could have stopped him if I tried. I told him I'd witnessed Sunday's victory over those men from Bulls Head and congratulated him on his pitching. For all his rude ways, he was a spectacle out there. Daddy says he will be the salvation of us all.

But the savage, apparently, heard none of my observations. Instead, he pointed to the table where Lily was seated, hidden away behind her Lunks and her magazines.

"Why, that's Miss Newton, ain't it? The imperialist?"

"Anti-imperialist," I said. "And you know very well who it is."

"Funny," the savage retorted, "how your kiss wasn't enough to wake me, but Miss Newton's was. Like yours was impotent or some such."

"You're being obscene, Mr. Dobbs."

"Call me Jack," he said, grinning.

He lifted his arm, snapped his fingers at Billy Lawton and told him to bring a dish of strawberry ice cream to Lily's table. Then, straightening his jacket, he at last disposed of his unlit Havana and went straight back to see her.

I wanted to hear what he said to her, but Garnetta began jabbering away. "It's scandalous. Absolutely scandalous."

"Oh don't be silly. Hush up."

The savage sat right across from Lily, face to face and close at that little table.

"Whatever on earth could she be thinking?" Garnetta said.

"She's not thinking anything. It's ice cream day at McMillan's is all."

The savage was laughing and animated, and I supposed him to be telling a tale of New York, Boston, or some other far-flung and wonderful place. Lily's magazines were piled neatly. Her long gloves were cast aside, and they shared that one dish of strawberry ice cream, as if bound together by the magic of their kiss.

Later, Garnetta and I went down to the Parisian and had our hair washed.

11
DOCTOR SAM FULLER
President, Port Newton Athletic Club

"What will it profit us," Charlie Meyers began, "to gain the world but lose our souls?"

"Last week," Foghorn Murphy put in, "it profited us one hundred eighty-seven dollars."

It was the night we all gathered in our clubroom, up on the second floor of the Railroad Exchange, and voted on Jack Dobbs' membership in the P.N.A.C. Outside, train whistles spouted off, the great ferry *Benicia* churned the black waters of the Strait, and the channel buoys rolled and clanged. Inside, the cigar smoke was as thick as pea soup. Old team photographs hung from the walls 1878, 1879, 1880. A trophy case, mostly empty, stood by the front windows that overlooked the town.

"But don't you see," Charlie said, "this Indian isn't one of us and bringing in professionals is cheating."

He was right, but Foghorn was right too.

"Hell, Charlie," he said, "the Chief isn't a ringer. He's a bartender. Works for me. Lives in Port Newton. And hell, everyone cheats, don't they?"

I was at the officer's table, on the dais, wielding the president's gavel. Foghorn, being treasurer, sat on my left, picking his nails with a salad fork he'd swiped from Vinci's Italian. Cal Elwell, our secretary and parliamentarian, sat to my right, scribbling down Charlie's ramblings for posterity. Three blackballs were all that were needed to disqualify a man from membership, but my estimate was Dobbs would only draw one.

"Winning," Charlie said, "isn't what's important."

Foghorn growled. "The hell it isn't. We've been losing games for what?"

"Ten years," Hec Fernandez sang out.

"And I'm sick of it," Billy Lawton declared.

I called for order. "Charlie has the floor!"

I brought that gavel down, and the damn thing broke in two. The handle was left in my hand, but the rest of it, the head I suppose it's called, went flying in a high arc towards the right side of the room.

Father Noone called everyone off. "I got it! I got it!"

He cupped his hands, got right under that tumbling head, but muffed the catch and it hit the floor, a clean error.

"The *playing* of the games is what's important," Charlie went on. "Not the *winning* of them. What's important is for us to enjoy ourselves and have good fellowship."

Charlie was trying to pass himself off as our collective conscience, you see, but, in this godless world, it is self-interest that drives men. In Charlie's case, this meant preserving his status as starting pitcher, not to mention gaining revenge for that little set-to him and Dobbs had had at practice. High-sounding words are generally just politics, or so I've found.

"Teamwork and fair play," Charlie said. "Self-sacrifice. Grit, honor, determination. Those are the things that count in baseball."

"The only thing I can count is money," Foghorn cracked.

"You're a cynical son of a bitch."

"And you're a romantic idiot."

Charlie *was* a romantic idiot, by the way, and a devotee of Walter Scott's novels and Longfellow's poems.

"And what about chivalry? What about sportsmanship? That savage could have killed someone, throwing at those Bulls Head men the way he did. It wasn't baseball. It was a scalping raid."

"But it worked," Foghorn said. "And it was good to be pocketing prize money for a change, instead of shelling it out."

The men nodded their heads in agreement.

"I didn't mind it."

"I can always use a dollar or two."

Even Long John, who hardly ever spoke in our meetings, agreed. "Being constable doesn't pay much," he observed, from way in back, where he could sit with his long legs stretched out into the aisle.

I tried to reassure Charlie. "Just because Dobbs filled in for one game, it doesn't mean you'll never pitch again."

That was a lie, of course.

"We'll still need you in spots," I said. "The Indian will need relief, probably... well, maybe. And in the meantime, you could play other positions. Right field. We could use another good man out there."

"Right field?" Charlie said. "You might as well banish me to the salt mines."

And that, damn me all to Hell, was when I sprung the trap on Charlie.

"A moment ago," I said, pointing what was left of my gavel at him. "A moment ago you said teamwork and self-sacrifice were what counted in baseball, did you not?"

Charlie hesitated, sensed his blunder, bristled his fur, and arched his back.

"And what if I did?"

"Well, Charlie, here's your chance. Sacrifice yourself for the good of the team. Follow your own advice. Share right field with Father Noone. You can still pitch every now and again."

Charlie tried to recover. "It isn't fair."

"Nothin' is ever fair," Billy Lawton opined, and the boys all let out a cheer.

"Let's vote."

"Let's get it over with."

"I'm running out of beer."

There were two blackballs cast against Dobbs that night. One of them was obviously Charlie's, but I couldn't figure out who'd cast the other. The balloting was secret and well planned, proof against tampering. Each man was furnished with two balls–one white and one black–which he kept concealed until the time it came to slip one or the other into the ballot box.

I even wondered, when I found that second blackball, if Charlie had somehow managed to purloin an extra one and slipped it in. But if he'd done that, I thought, why hadn't he just purloined three and taken care of the matter once and for all?

61

After it was over, we all went clambering down the stairs to hoist a few Port Newton Steam Beers, as we always did. I didn't like what we'd done, what *I'd* done, to Charlie, but I did rather hope he'd be a man about it. Or at least realize that his pitching days were behind him and bury the goddamn hatchet, but it didn't work out that way.

Dobbs mingled among the railroaders and ferrymen, shaking hands, joking and being friendly. When he saw Charlie, Dobbs went over to him and invited him to shake hands, a generous offering of peace, I assumed–although it is always easier for winners to be magnanimous.

Charlie didn't take that hand but instead, did a military turn and headed for the exit.

"I don't speak with sons of bitches," he said, blowing right on by me, out through those swinging, batwing doors of the Railroad Exchange.

I went over to Dobbs, and told him he had to forgive Charlie. "He just doesn't like the idea of losing his position, is all."

"Don't worry, Doc. Hell, if I was him I'd have probably slugged me."

"Well, congratulations, at least, on becoming a member of the P.N.A.C."

"Hey, I'm honored."

It was a statement whose veracity I doubted coming as it did from a fellow who once boasted of peeing in the Roman coliseum, but it was a decent thing for him to say, nonetheless.

I told him, "We're looking forward to having you play with us this season," or some such drivel.

He slapped my back. "I been on the road too long, Doc, and you got a nice town here."

That seemed a sincere statement on his part, perhaps the only one I had yet heard him utter. But Foghorn came over, then, and that put an end to my hopes of actually getting to know the man.

"We'll show those Pacheco bastards a thing or two next Sunday, won't we, Chief?"

"They won't have a prayer."

Foghorn turned to me. "We got two hundred on the game so far," he told me, "not counting the purse, and I'll get at least another two hundred down by Sunday." He winked. "Before they know what's going on, eh, Doc?"

I nodded my head, as if in assent, but feeling rotten about the knife I'd stuck in Charlie's back. And that was when I looked up and saw Long John standing at the bar. He leaned against it, drinking coffee, not beer, but with one foot up on the brass rail, peering into the great mirror behind the bar. For a moment, I imagined the dirt and heat of the hay farm of his boyhood: his mother cooking breakfast before dawn–eggs, oatmeal, syrup, bacon. Her only relaxation, he'd once told me, was quilting, and I felt a twinge of guilt over the whole tawdry affair–sacrificing Charlie, bringing in a ringer, cheating.

Then, in the mirror and the cigar smoke and the laughter and jokes, Long John's eyes caught mine, and it came to me, that it was he who'd cast the second blackball against Dobbs that night.

12

BOX SCORE
The Port Newton News

```
PORT NEWTON                        PACHECO
NAME           AB   R  BH   E      NAME           AB   R  BH   E
Lawton ss       6   1   0   2      Valenzano       5   1   1   1
M Luicani lf    6   4   4   0      Burnett 3b      5   1   1   0
Sheets 1b       6   3   3   0      Easter cf       4   1   2   1
E Luciani 3b    5   2   2   0      Cruz  1b        3   2   1   0
Dobbs p-rf-p    5   0   1   0      Celas  rf       4   2   1   0
Fernandez c     5   1   2   0      Castro lf       5   1   1   0
Farrell cf      4   2   2   0      Bacon ss        5   1   1   1
Elwell 2b       5   1   2   2      Galindo c       4   0   3   1
Fr Noone rf     3   0   0   1      Hodges p        2   0   0   0
Meyers p-rf     2   1   1   0      Azevido p       2   0   0   0
TOTALS         47  15  17   5      TOTALS         39   9  11   4
```

```
RUNS BY INNING   1  2  3  4  5  6  7  8  9   TOTAL
--------------------------------------------------
PORT NEWTON      0  1  3  2  3  1  3  2  0    15
PACHECO          0  0  0  0  1  5  2  0  1     9
--------------------------------------------------
```

HOME RUNS: Sheets, Farrell; Cruz BASES ON BALLS:
Fernandez, Farrell; Cruz, Celas SACRIFICE HITS: Dobbs
STOLEN BASES: E Luciani, M Luciani 2; Burnett, Easter,
Bacon HIT BY PITCH: Cruz, Easter WINNING PITCHER: Dobbs
LOSING PITCHER: Hodges PASSED BALLS: Fernandez 3
NOTATIONS: Meyers pitched the 6th inning

UMPIRE: T.A. Alvarado TIME: 2:57

13
Calvin Elwell
Bartender and Second Baseman

The Chief was supposed to be a bartender, just like me, but he hardly ever did any real work. Bringing in business was his job. Mostly he just glad-handed the customers and acted friendly. Sometimes he'd be dealer when the boys played cards but mostly he'd just lean on the bar, drink beer and be, well, the Chief.

"Dutchmen make the best ballplayers," he'd say, and Foghorn would fall for it.

"In my book it's the Irish," Foghorn would reply, him being Irish and all.

"One thing for sure about the Micks," the Chief would say, "the unsportsmanlike play is on them. Mobbing the umpires, starting fights, all that."

Foghorn would fall for that one, too. "That's prejudice, pure and simple." Then the Chief would dig him again.

"I'm not saying that Micks are *naturally violent*, but it can't be denied that they're *natural drunks*."

"And I don't suppose redskins ever touch a drop."

I couldn't tell you why the Chief took a liking to me, but he did. One day he slid up to the bar, ordered another beer, and out of the blue said to me, "Hey kid, did you ever cruise the Barbary Coast?"

I asked him which one he meant; the one in Africa or the one in San Francisco.

"Hell, kid, don't be a jackass."

That was how it all started, me and the Chief raising a jollification in San Francisco. I was in my work clothes– white shirt, vest, bow tie. But the Chief didn't like that getup much.

"You aren't going with *me* dressed like *that*," he said. "Ain't you got nothing better to wear?"

I told him I sure did, but he just shook his head.

"I seen the clothes you got, kid, and none of them is fit for a pig."

After I got off work I went down to meet him at the Railroad Inn, just down the Front, where he was living by that time. It was where the sporting men lived, the gamblers, hustlers, and pimps. I found the Chief with the rest of them, lounging among the potted palms of the lobby. An unlit cigar was stuck in his mouth but a dime novel called *Deadwood Dick* commanded his attention.

It was May Day but drizzly. Bad luck for the children at the grammar school, all dressed in their finest, all set to dance around the May Pole, but with a drizzle coming down. Everything smelled of ocean, that day. The gulls were everywhere, coming in off the ocean like they do when there's a storm out there.

"Now let's get you dressed proper," the Chief said, when he saw me.

There was this Jew tailor just up Ferry Street off Railroad who sold suits of clothes which Long John always suspected were stolen. This tailor's back room was just full of them. More than you could count. But Long John could never prove anything.

"Gentlemen, gentlemen, come in. Come in." Grinning like the Cheshire cat, he was. "I got just the thing for you."

He showed us a suit which I thought just fine, but the Chief didn't like it, so I tried on suits all afternoon. The one he picked for me was much too bold, but I didn't have much choice in the matter.

"Put it on my tab, will you Hiram?"

"Yes, Mr. Dobbs. Surely. On your tab."

Imagine that. Credit from a Jew, and the fellow didn't even like baseball. Don't think his name was Hiram, either.

Later, the Chief said to me, "Never pay today if you can pay tomorrow." And I thought that very strange, for I'd always been taught to save and save for what I wanted, but the Chief didn't see it that way. I guess he was just ahead of his time; a dollar down and a dollar a week. Comes from us being godless, Doctor Sam says, but I don't recall seeing anything in the Ten Commandments regarding cash on the barrelhead.

Right after I got my new suit the Chief took me on down to Rampoldi, the barber, to get shaved. This was before safety razors became popular so if you didn't admire the possibility of cutting yourself, you'd go to Rampoldi's and have an expert shave you.

Doc is right, sometimes, about things being better back then. Mostly not, but sometimes, he's right. Getting shaved at Rampoldi's was one of the better things. Rampoldi's front window was filled up with racks and racks of shaving mugs. Each one was engraved with name of its owner: Long John, Doctor Sam, Charlie, Hec, Billy Lawton. All of 'em your friends and neighbors, and, we'd all sit around inside, talking and smoking and making jokes while Rampoldi shaved everybody. Nowadays, you stand all alone in front of your mirror with your Gillette and go to hacking.

"Hell," Rampoldi said when he saw me. "He's all peach fuzz."

"Shave him anyway," said the Chief.

It took about an hour to get from Port Newton to San Francisco, if you made connections right. First the train to Oakland, then the ferry from the Oakland Mole to the Ferry Building across the Bay.

The Ferry Building was brand, shiny new, in those days. Had a clock tower that looked like Big Ben in London, England. But our clock was bigger and better, free from the encumbrances of the Old World and just crawling with the vitality of the New. Ferryboats docked or cast off every few minutes–whistles blowing, children laughing, ladies bustling, pretty girls, old men, sailors, beggars. A lot like the Front in Port Newton but bigger and bolder and with even more snap to it.

Streetcars that took you anywhere you wanted to go swarmed the entrance on a maze of tracks. But it was only a few blocks to this restaurant the Chief knew about and we decided to foot it. He'd been a regular there a couple years back, when he'd played for the San Francisco Metros of the Pacific States League. Poppa's, it was called, and a strange place it was.

There was poetry written all over the walls and pictures of black cats running across the ceiling. There was a mural with goats and the devil and monks all cavorting with wine skins. And there was this young woman in a smock, looking as hard as any man, up on a ladder, painting away at it while everyone ate.

At first I was a little taken aback by the clientele, but then it came to me, that these were Sophie's Bohemians in the flesh, and now, I could lord it all over her.

Every single one of them seemed to know the Chief, too.

"Playing for the Wasps this season?"

"No, not this season. Probably going to head back East, sign on with the Giants, now that my arm's all right."

That was a lie, but telling lies didn't ever seem to trouble the Chief. In those days I used to think he was all show and no go; everything a false front, the bravado, the bullying, the playing to the grandstands. But I have since learned that the loudest fellow at the bar is usually the most afraid. I never did figure out exactly what it was the Chief was afraid of, but it was something.

Poppa, himself, the owner of the place, came out of the kitchen in back, all fat and sweaty.

"Chief. It's been too long."

"My credit still good?"

"It's always good, Chief."

We ordered the specialty of the house, which the Chief raved and raved about, much to Poppa's pleasure. It was as strange as the people. Chicken and rice and tomatoes but with *coconut meat* and all served in a *coconut shell.*

We drank dago red wine all through dinner and talked a lot about baseball, which was natural enough, and the Martinez game coming up, they being our main rivals outside of Benicia.

I was still Foghorn's spy at this time, and Foghorn was starting to get down some pretty big bets on our games. Meaning it was natural enough for Foghorn to have some interest in those stories about the Chief throwing all those games when he was in the National League, so I pressed him about it.

"You'd have done the same if you were me, kid. They used me. All of them. Stole from me. Put me on display like a sideshow freak. But I'd never throw a game for you fellows. You fellows treated me square."

68

He called to Poppa, "Bring us a knife. A good knife. The sharpest damn knife you got."

It was a little paring knife that Poppa brought, but he touched the edge with his thumb and nodded his head. Then the Chief took it and cut his right hand, on the palm, and grabbed my hand next.

"What the hell?" I said.

But that knife was so sharp and the Chief so quick I didn't feel a thing. He slapped our two hands together so the blood would mingle, just like in a dime novel, and looked me dead in the eye and held my eyes with his.

"Now we're blood brothers, kid, and all that, and we can never lie or cheat each other or prove false."

I still don't know if this is a thing real Indians do, or just a thing of fiction, emanating from the minds of writers. But, whatever the truth of it, the Chief seemed to believe it.

After our blood mingled, the Chief wrapped a napkin around his hand and did the same for me. He told me that since he was my brother, now, it was time to make a man of me, and I was just drunk enough to raise an objection.

"How do you know I'm not a man already? There's lots of girls in Port Newton. How do you know I haven't become a man with one of them?"

"Don't make me laugh, kid."

The Barbary Coast was just up the hill from Poppa's, on the borders of Chinatown, which was a maze of streets and alleys, overcrowded basements and opium dens– or so the stories said. Every now and again the politicians would rail against the Chinese, about them taking white men's jobs and such, and pass laws to try and stop them from coming into the country. But all such laws are foolish. People can't be stopped, even if they are Chinese, and once they got moving the Chinese couldn't be stopped by us white folks any more than us white folks could be stopped by the Chief's little Indian band up east in Nevada.

This was the time of the plague scare, so there was a quarantine of Chinatown on. There were cops and special deputies all about and barricades thrown up at DuPont Street. Health inspectors tossed trash and clothes and bedding into bonfires that burned in the street, while the Chinamen jabbered at them.

"No can do that!"

"That mine! Let go!"

We crossed the border then from Chinatown into the Barbary Coast which was another maze almost as bad. In the days of 'forty-nine, sailors used to get Shanghaied there, men got knocked upon the head and robbed, women were sold into white slavery. Sodom and Gomorrah, it was, back in 'forty-nine.

It was still rough enough when the Chief and I went there, but even so it was mostly just cheap dives, dancehalls, and shows. The blue noses passed laws and went to no end of trouble trying to close those down, but that couldn't be done either. You can't stop men from going to girlie shows any more than you can stop Chinamen from coming over here if they want.

"Watch 'em wiggle, gents! Watch 'em wiggle!"

"Step right in gents! Admission is free."

"Right this way. Hoochy-Coochy and the girls don't wear no underwear. Garn-teed."

I thought I'd seen a few things working at Foghorn's and along the Front in Port Newton–dancehalls, saloons, bar-fights–but I'd never seen anything like this place. Inside, there were electric lights strung all around and a regular band, not just a string band. There was a grand piano, trombones, drums, a bass fiddle, and more. One dark-eyed and ample girl was in the middle of the floor doing the Dance of the Seven Veils. Fatima, her name was.

There were waiter girls all about in skirts so short they almost didn't exist, but all wearing underwear. Some sold drinks and some danced with men on the dance floor. If you can call it dancing, that is. I don't know if this comes as much of a revelation to you, but men don't go to dancehalls to dance. They go there to squeeze the girls.

"Not so hard, baby," the girls would say.

A couple of tough looking ones caught sight of the Chief, and once they did, they were on him.

"Chiefie! It's been too long. Where you been keeping yourself, baby?"

"They love me, kid," he told me, as he passed out half-dollars. "As long as the money don't run out." He gave me a wink. "Story of my life."

But what really set this place apart from the dancehalls and dives in Port Newton was the rich people. Lots of them. Good looking women in great, huge hats and gentlemen in coats and vests, smoking cigars and all drunk as skunks. There was a special place for them, like a big veranda, three feet up from the floor with tables and chairs and a railing in front. From there they could watch the show, which now included me and the Chief as far as they were concerned. They had their own waiter girls and boys, too, and all of them were on opium for all I knew.

While I was studying these rich ones, figuring I'd boast all about them to Sophie–a somewhat weather-beaten waiter girl put one arm right around me. Before I knew it, she grabbed me where she shouldn't.

"You're a big boy, aren't you?"

The Chief introduced me to her, Natasha, and told her that he didn't pay for it himself anymore, but I probably would.

"And his daddy's rich, too."

That sealed it for Natasha. She got me down in a chair and hopped on my lap. She wasn't exactly light as a feather, either.

"Tipping is allowed," she said, and even I wasn't so green as to miss the meaning of that.

I started to shell out two bits, but right then, Fatima of the seven veils transfixed me with those big, black eyes of hers. She sashayed right over to me and rubbed her almost bare behind up against my newly shaved cheek. All I could think was, *I hope Rampoldi shaved me close enough.*

Pretty soon I was up and dancing with Natasha. "Not so hard, baby."

The Chief was pretty drunk himself by the time we sat down again, and he started rambling on about Moses in the bulrushes.

"I can't understand how Moses' mama could do that," he said. "Any mama. Give up her own baby boy. How could a woman do that?"

"You do what you gotta do," Natasha told him.

Two older men, pushing their way across the dance floor, both heavy set and in bowler hats, caught sight of us.

"Hey, Chief!" one of them called, with a wave and a smile.

This didn't suprise me one bit for by now I figured the Chief knew everybody in the world. What did suprise me was that the Chief called the both of them Chief, too. This, I learned when I got introduced, was because one was the chief of police and the other the fire chief.

"Meet my little brother," the Chief said.

"Hey, little brother," said one fat chief.

"Hey, little brother," said the other.

The two of them climbed up the short stairway to where the rich people sat and got showed to a table with some others. It struck me that, although maybe the Chief did know everyone in the world, he didn't have a true friend among them. Except maybe for me, his little blood brother.

All this time, police chief or no–Natasha, had kept whispering in my ear how she wanted to go upstairs with me. A hard working girl, she was, and I was tempted, I'll say. But it was Fatima who had my heart. Natasha had the better personality of the two, but Fatima was younger and prettier, and men are fools in such regards. Women are too, for that matter.

So when Fatima brushed by me again, that bare bottom of hers on my cheek, I took the plunge.

"Hi."

The negotiations started right after this, which the Chief handled, settling certain details of my coming tryst with Fatima: how much this cost and how much that and the other thing cost and how this or that was highway robbery.

"I don't do nothing unnatural," Fatima said.

"Like hell you don't," the Chief told her.

All this dickering took some of the romance out of things, but nevertheless, I went upstairs with Fatima. Five minutes later, I came back down again, feeling two dollars poorer but that was about all. The Chief was sitting at the same table where he'd been when I'd left.

"How was it, little brother?"

I figured I'd brazen it out, but that was when all that coconut meat I'd had at Poppa's began to have a disagreement with all the cheap wine I'd drunk, and I started feeling somewhat wobbly on my pins. Next thing I knew I was on all fours in an alley outback, sick as a dog, with passersby laughing at me the whole time.

"Now you're a man, little brother," the Chief said.

That son of a bitch took care of me all the way home, after I lent him his fare for the passage back, that is.

14

THE PORT NEWTON NEWS
Thursday, May 3

TOWNE TOPICS

THE CHIEF VISITS HIS RED BRETHREN

A mere three days after his magnificent pitching performance in the Athletic Club's victory over the Pacheco nine, Jack Dobbs–a full-blooded Washoe Indian–was feted at a clam chowder feed thrown by the Noble Brotherhood of Redskins at Vinci's Italian Restaurant in this city.

After the feast was over, the Redskins lit their peace pipes, and Dobbs, who was ironically the only man in the room not clad in feathers and war paint, regaled his audience with countless tales of his days not as a noble redskin, but as a highly paid baseball player in the National League.

Dobbs, according to his own account, was raised at the Washoe Indian School in Genoa, Nevada, where no one took much interest in him "until they saw I could stun a running jackass rabbit with a rock at fifty paces."

Following this, Dobbs says, he quickly became the star of the school's baseball team. At age fifteen, a turning point occurred in his life: the Indian School team journeyed to San Francisco to play a series of exhibition matches against several of the myriad clubs that inhabit that city, and Dobbs was given his chance to shine.

"We were a curiosity and much sought after," Dobbs said, "for it comforts the white man to see Injuns play baseball, and especially when the Injuns lose."

Although the Indian School was defeated by their white opponents in every game, Dobbs pitched so well that he was offered a contract to pitch for the Reliants of Oakland at a dollar a game.

"I jumped at the chance, but when the owner tried to rob me, I busted him one, paid myself off from his wallet, and departed in haste."

74

After that, Dobbs plied his trade in Denver and Omaha before finally gaining a tryout with the White Stockings of Chicago. He pitched successfully for three years with that club and then was sold to the Boston Beaneaters. There, he became a pitcher of the first magnitude and was wined and dined by princes, kings, and Back Bay aristocrats.

"The world was my oyster until I was betrayed in 'ninety-three," the big Indian told the Noble Redskins.

"Some numskull in the league office thought to boost attendance by increasing the scoring and so made us pitchers throw from further back. It was a travesty against the purity of the game and ruined the arms of me and a number of other fine men. What they said I did later is all on them."

The Chief took questions from the audience and, when asked what he thought of Port Newton's chances to claim their first championship since 'eighty-eight, he replied that they were good.

"I wouldn't place any bets against us," he said. "My elbow is as good as its ever been, and I can make most of the men around here look like clowns."

Later, when your reporter asked Dobbs what he thought of the policy of the Noble Brotherhood of Redskins to admit only white men as members, he could only shrug his shoulders.

"If I didn't speak with hypocrites, there wouldn't be no one left to speak with."

FOURTH OF JULY
COMMITTEE GIVES BIRTH TO MORE COMMITTEES

The Fourth of July Committee, which held its second meeting of the year at Pimental Hall on Tuesday, moved forward with plans for this year's celebration by establishing two new subcommittees.

The first subcommittee, headed by Mrs. John Glass and composed solely of women, will act as auxiliaries to the General Committee. The second new subcommittee, headed by Mr. Glass, will look into the voting irregularities that occurred in relation to the Goddess of Liberty contest last year and seek to avoid any reoccurrence of such unpleasantries.

"So exhalted a sinecure as that of the Goddess of Liberty," Mr. Glass said, "must be as free of opprobrium as would be the election of a pope or president."

In other business, Mr. Maxfield Travis, director of the Port Newton Dramatic Society, stated that with the permission of the Committee, the Society would stage its new production of *H.M.S. Pinafore* on the Glorious Fourth for the entertainment and enlightenment of the public.

His request was approved by unanimous vote and yet another subcommittee was formed, this to act as liaison between the Dramatic Society and the Fourth of July Committee itself.

All committees will meet again at Pimental Hall on Friday at eight p.m.

LOCAL BREVITIES

A team pulling a spring wagon set to running near Buck's Ranch on Saturday when Mr. Reese Hooper was on his way to Port Newton. Mr. Hooper says that the double tree became unfastened, the neck yoke slipped off the tongue, and the horses became unmanageable. He jumped the wagon when the horses first began to run and so was unhurt. When it was learned that Doctor G. W. Pawsey, our veterinarian, was away in Concord, Doctor Sam Fuller dressed the horses' wounds. Reports that Mr. Hooper was intoxicated are said to be false.

Last Thursday's heavy rains ruined a great portion of the county's cherry crop. Some damage to hay was also reported.

Constable Sheets was seen at McEwen's a few days ago trying on a new black worsted suit and his good looks seemed much enhanced by it. He wore it on May Day when he spoke at the grammar school, giving the little ones a dose of sound philosophy. He told some frightful tales of the immoral and degenerate specimens he has come across in his career as an officer of the law and demonstrated the pitfalls of dishonor to the children. He stressed, above all, the importance of law, duty, and honesty.

An impromptu punching contest was held at Archer's Saloon last Friday night between a Spaniard off the steamer *Golden Cross*, docked at the Sugar Wharf, and a red-blooded American who works for the Southern Pacific. Although we detest such exhibitions of violence, Mr. Archer tells us that the Spaniard was thoroughly in the wrong and was given exactly what he deserved.

If we all pull together, we can't be pulled apart.

After last month's explosion at the powder works in Hercules, an immense cloud of white smoke hung above the works for several hours. This cloud poisoned the breathing of all who inhaled it, and the acid from the destroyed buildings ran down the hillside for hundreds of yards killing every bit of vegetation in that once verdant glen.

For some time now, the men of the county have been discussing possible candidates for the Republican vice presidential nomination. About the only name that generates any enthusiasm is that of Governor Theodore Roosevelt of New York, but he has already said he is not interested in the office.

Sheriff Ulshoter of Martinez and a dozen deputies from Rio Vista raided a Chinese opium den in that city in search of the kidnapped white woman, Mamie Walbraith, who was allegedly being held there. The sheriff reports that he and his men found a room containing tiers of bunks filled with Chinamen, smoking pipes through short hoses that were attached to the pipes. Those that were not dreaming celestial dreams stared at them with vacant eyes. Miss Walbraith was not found.

White Hat O'Malley, the well-known politician, was in town yesterday, drinking with the boys at the bar in Foghorn Murphy's. White Hat says the story that he recently deposited a check for $20,000 in his bank is true but that the reporter who wrote it added too many zeros to the total.

"The check was only for $2,000," White Hat said.

Times are tough all around, eh, White Hat?

C.A. Orlando, of this city, has received the terrible news that his wife can live only a few days longer.

Hec Fernandez, who engineers one of the yard goats that loads the ferry, was left looking sheepish yesterday when he mistook a signal, nosed a dining car over the chokes, and left its prow teetering above the Strait. No one was hurt, but the diners who'd chose to stay aboard all decided to debark posthaste.

Our telephone number is Main 3. Don't forget us if you have a printing job that needs to be done.

MEETINGS AND EVENTS
County Medical Society–Thursday

The County Medical Society will meet at three o'clock on Thursday afternoon at the County Hospital in Martinez. Doctor Sam Fuller says that the miraculous workings of the X-ray and the Crookes tube will be demonstrated to those of the medical professional who care to attend.

May Day Dance–Saturday Night

The May Day Dance will be held at Pimental Hall on Saturday at 7 p.m. The proceeds will go to Port Newton Union High, which is in desperate straits due to the economic troubles that plague us. Waltz music, marches, and polkas will be provided by our own Silver Cornet Band, and Miss Hannah Joost will be crowned May Queen. To close the festivities, The Mississippi Minstrels, the colored troupe that is currently engaged at Hoffmeister's in Benicia, will sing Coon Songs and perform a Cakewalk.

Blessing of the Baseballs–Sunday

Father Noone informs us that the traditional Blessing of the Baseballs will occur at Newton Field on Sunday, noon, weather permitting. Although attendance for this event has been nothing short of sacrilegious in recent years, it is thought it will multiply fruitfully now, due to the improving fortunes of the team. After the ceremony, a challenge game will be held between our brave Newtonians and the Martinez nine.

78

15

SOPHIE FULLER
Senior, Port Newton Union High School

Dear Diary,

Lily looked absolutely stunning last night. She wore a simple black dress, but cut dangerously low, with a black cape to match and all set off by a hat of red roses she'd gotten when we went to San Francisco.

"Only a month out of Paris," the salesgirl told us.

Long John, too, had construed himself in a most dashing fashion, dashing for Long John, that is. He doesn't own any evening clothes, but he did put on a decent dark suit, and he even hired a carriage from Hackenschmidt's. And not just any carriage, either, but the old phaeton that was once Lily's father's with silver trim, leather dash, and two white horses! The very same phaeton I used to see the two of them riding around in looking so rich and admirable when I was a wide-eyed little girl.

It was a rather *odd* thing for Long John to do; I mean courting a girl in her daddy's carriage! But he isn't very sophisticated in such things, and neither is Lily, for that matter. Garnetta even thought Long John planned to pop the question. Lily Sheets? My word!

At supper, the four of us–me, Lily, Garnetta and Long John–ate lightly, minestrone and red wine at Vinci's. Lily drank too much and started asking Long John about that old witch Rosa Paredes.

"Doña Rosa?" he said. "Why on earth do you want to know about her?"

"No reason, Johnny. People are saying Judge Schmidt might have her locked up."

Long John shook his head. "There aren't any complaints against her. I think there'd have to be complaints, first. And then it would only be for her own good."

"Her own good, of course," Lily said.

After supper, when we climbed the stairs of Pimental Hall, the band was playing the Daisy song. Garnetta put her left arm in my right and as we climbed the two of us sang as one. "Daisy, Daisy give me your answer do." Then Lily put her arm in my left and started singing herself. "I'm half crazy, all for the love of you." And that is how the three of us, arm in arm, made our grand entrance, with Long John trailing behind.

Inside, the hall was lined with booths selling cakes and cookies. The smell of popcorn and caramel sweetened the air. Long John bought a grab bag for each of us and seemed quite pleased when we found that Lily's contained not only nuts and glazed fruits, but a tiny American flag as well.

"Cheers," she said, giving it a little wave.

Then, Hanna Joost, our so-called "Queen of the May," came out of the cloakroom.

"Oh my heavens," Garnetta squealed, "I can't believe it."

"Nor can I," I said.

We stood there, arm in arm, gaping in wonder. Hanna, for some mad reason, had dyed her hair *Titian bronze*.

"Oh Hanna, it's absolutely gorgeous," Garnetta told her.

What else can one girl to say to another at so frightful a moment?

I gave Hanna a big hug. "It's lovely, dear, yes, and so Bohemian."

"Bohemian?" Hanna said. "Don't say that. Papa already said he's going to kill me."

The band struck up a waltz and as always, there weren't enough boys to go around. You know how awful it is to have to dance with girls or old men, Diary dear, but Long John was an absolute jewel. He bowed to poor Hanna, perhaps to end her embarrassment and requested her hand.

"Miss Joost, may I have the honor of being first to dance with our Queen of Spring?"

Of course, she isn't the Queen of *Spring* at all but only the *May* Queen. I doubt anyone would have voted to make Hanna Joost queen of the *whole* spring. Still, it was a sweet thing for Long John to say, or to try to say.

Next I saw Mr. Calvin Elwell, who can't seem to stop bragging about his foolish little expedition to San Francisco with the savage. He emerged from the Forester's booth, which was gayly decorated with greenery and ivy as in a bower, and asked me to dance.

"Miss Sophie," he said, "would you do me the honor?"

I always do feel cruel about leading poor Calvin on, but I couldn't very well embarrass the boy right there in front of everyone, now, could I? And I hated to leave Garnetta standing all alone, but she said she didn't mind and so Calvin and I danced away.

As we waltzed, I determined I would test him. "And what do you think of poor Hanna's hair?"

"I think it's kind of pretty."

Can you believe that? Well, it was anything but *pretty*, so when our Silver Cornets struck up a two-step, I steered the boy into Garnetta's arms. I've always thought the two of them would go well together. But sadly she is short and squat and ill-suited to dance of any sort. The two of them looked terribly awkward on the dance floor. I still cannot believe that Mr. Travis wants her for Josephine Corcoran in *Pinafore*. Nor do I believe him to be as handsome as I once thought.

And that, Dear Diary, was when the coloreds arrived.

They were only the minstrels, but there seemed so many of them and they came so fast that everyone stopped and stared. The Silver Cornets stopped playing. The waltzers froze. Garnetta rushed to my side afraid that they would subjugate the entire hall.

"Fresh from the jungle, they look to be."

I told her not to worry. "Fellows like these know their place." But loud and raucous they were indeed. Absolutely overwhelming, and their leader was black as the ace of spades.

"Slip on your dancin' shoes," he called to his comrades. "We is goin' to a cakewalk to-nite."

There were over a dozen of them, four couples and a number of musicians. All were dressed in the most outrageous clothing; top hats, loud checkered suits, gowns of tasteless colors.

"Strike up dat ragtime music, boys!" their ebony-skinned leader called.

With that the colored musicians began to displace our Silver Cornets on the little stage, but very politely, I thought. After that little commotion, they began to play music such as I had never heard before.

The leader called out to one of his women, pretty and light skinned.

"Say Miss Liza Jane, you all think we can take deh cake at dis here ball?"

"I sure do, Rufus. These white folks, why, dey's polka people and not no cakewalkers."

That ruffled some Port Newton feathers, to be sure. Then Rufus approached Liza, much as Long John had approached Garnetta when requesting a dance. He made an exaggerated, sweeping bow, and it was clear that he was spoofing our own manners and more feathers ruffled.

But then, just as I began to feel trouble might ensue, Rufus fell flat on his face; a pratfall that broke the tension and caused laughter to reign again in Pimental Hall.

Once he regained his feet, Rufus cajoled, Liza relented, and the two began to promenade. As in a two-step, but hip to hip, rather than face to face, strutting with exaggerated pride, singing to each other and calling out mock insults.

"You is lucky you got a babe like me," Rufus called out. "Ain't nobody can strut like dis here coon."

"No sucha thing," Liza replied. She pointed at their ebony comrades. "Dey's dead swell coons, all of 'em."

"But can dey cakewalk and rag?"

This, apparently, was the signal for the rest of them to join in, and so they did, crying out phrases like "We sho' can!" and "You gots it, Rufus!"

All four couples now began to promenade like Rufus and Liza, making the most outrageous back bends and struts, whilst all the while calling out to each other and singing a song that made all other songs seem old hat.

"Ain't a gonna be any sleep at all. Ain't a gonna be any early call. Until the stars are gone; until the break of dawn, we're gonna dance at the Barber's Ball."

By the time their promenading and jesting drew to a conclusion, all of us—Garnetta, Calvin, Long John and even Lily—were in stitches. We were then asked to signal by our applause, the winner of "the cake" in this cakewalk. The loudest of the cheers and whistles, of course, came for Rufus and Liza.

Following much bowing and mock displays of surprise, Rufus took the stage with his musicians.

But listen, Diary dear, this was when the strangest thing happened. Garnetta and I were standing just off to the side of the stage, so that when Rufus turned his back to the audience and addressed his musicians, we were in a unique position to observe him.

He expelled a puff of air from his cheeks and, like a tired man, spoke to his band without the slightest trace of Negro dialect.

"Gentlemen, let's give the white folks a good show."

The musicians all nodded their heads as if his manner of speech was no surprise to them. Rufus said, "Hello My Baby," then wheeled around to face his audience and, like magic, the weary countenance disappeared, and he became, again, the grinning coon of the cakewalk. A curious people, these Negroes are.

Rufus began to pantomime the actions of a man cranking a telephone while Liza pantomimed those of a woman answering. Then he began to sing.

"Hello my baby, hello my honey, hello my ragtime gal. Send me a kiss by wire, oh baby my heart's on fire."

It was rather like a two-step but all the more. The most thrilling music I have ever heard in my life. Rufus and Liza began a dance, similar to the two-step, but without any skipping movements.

I heard a rude voice behind me.

"Hey, sweetie. Let's trip the light fantastic. What do you say?"

I turned and discerned that the source of this "invitation" was Mr. Jack Dobbs, the savage, but dressed in the finest of evening clothes–a black tail coat, a white shirt, and white tie. Never having been asked to dance in quite that manner, I hesitated momentarily, but Garnetta gave me a poke in the ribs.

"Go ahead," she said. "Your daddy's not here, is he?"

The savage said, "It won't kill you, sweetheart."

I tried to fend him off politely. "I've never danced that dance before."

"Ain't much to it. It's a rag is all. A one-step. All the rage in New York City. You pretty much just walk it but quick and with pep. Try not to bend your knees."

"My knees?" I told him. "Sir, I cannot walk without bending my knees."

He took me in his arms, as if to violate me, but began dancing vigorously, and I had no choice but to follow.

It was absolutely thrilling!

At first, beyond the coloreds, no one but the Indian and I had the courage to attempt this new and wonderful dance. There were raised eyebrows, Diary dear, I can tell you that! But I just lifted my nose to them–this *is* America, is it not?

When it was over I was exhausted from it and made a firm protest to the savage, demanding to rest. He, at last, relented, and we strolled off the dance floor to where Garnetta, Long John and Lily sat, like wallflowers, on some awful straight-backed chairs.

The savage called out, "Hey Long John. Shake a leg, why don't you?"

Long John managed a smile, but he didn't like it, I can tell you that. "I'll leave the cakewalking to you, Chief."

The savage grinned at Lily and, in an awful moment, it came to me that he was going to ask her to dance.

"Miss Newton. May I have the honor?"

At least he had the sense to be civilized about it; no talk of shaking legs or tripping the light fantastic.

Lily turned him down cold. "I'm already engaged."

Garnetta and I looked at each other and almost broke into giggles, wondering if Long John really had popped the question. Then, without the slightest hesitation, the savage turned to Garnetta.

"How 'bout you, sweets?"

Garnetta, who just doesn't know how to handle men, sprang to her feet without even pretending to show the slightest hesitation, and a moment later, the two were on the dance floor. But incredible as it may seem, Diary dear, Garnetta took to this new dance like a cat. Those stocky limbs of hers now seemed lithe, and she was quick, graceful, and laughing.

"My, my," Lily said. "Who'd have ever thought such a thing."

The dance ended very late and while the Negroes and the Silver Coronets were packing their instruments away, I came upon Lily and Long John in the cloakroom. I am not a snoop, Diary dear, but they seemed to be at odds over something so I stayed hidden for the sole reason of not wanting to embarrass them.

She said, "I don't want to talk about it anymore, Johnny."

He, "We have to. There are no such things."

"How do you know? You don't know *everything*."

"You were just dreaming."

"I know the difference between what I see in dreams and what I see right front of me in my bedroom."

He helped her with her cape from behind, then left his hands cupped on her shoulders very sweetly I thought, while she buttoned it in front.

"Sometimes it's just confusing," he said. "You know, when you're dreaming and you wake up sudden."

"I told you, Johnny. I don't want to talk about it anymore."

That was when Lily noticed me. It was one of those awful moments in which neither of us could admit to the truth; that I was there, and that she had seen me. So I stayed back among the coats and wraps and furs, as Lily changed the subject to that of her garden.

"Maybe I'll hire a couple of Chinamen," she said. "Dig up those old walnut trees."

"You know what I think about that," Long John said.

They left right after. I don't think he ever did ask her to marry him.

16
DOCTOR SAM FULLER
President, Port Newton Athletic Club

It is truly wonderful what the winning of a baseball game or two can do for a town. It put the zip back in everyone's step, and it became our preoccupation. In the saloons, the men, and in their sewing circles, the women speculated on batting orders and glove-work. Little boys followed Jack Dobbs around. People bought Long John drinks. We had pride again. We had a common bond. We were Newtonians, once more, and in the high clover.

By the Sunday of the Martinez game, our tumble-down grandstand up on Newton's Bluff was full for the first time in years and everybody in their Sunday best. The Silver Cornet Band, albeit a bit bedraggled from the May Day Dance the night before, kept up a stream of jolly tunes. Pretty girls in bright spring dresses filled the row behind our bench: Garnetta McCoy, Hanna Joost, Isabella Thayer, and the prettiest of all, my own darling daughter, Sophie.

We had new uniforms, too, so dark a green as to almost black and with a big, white "N" over the heart, just like the uniforms we wore in the year of the Stolen Championship. Everybody knew what that meant.

I had the shakes about my hands when infield practice began, but I don't suppose I was the only one. I hit grounders out to the boys, and they booted more than usual. I did what I could to encourage them.

"Pick it up, you damn jackass! Watch the ball all the way into your glove!"

Even Long John, at first, missed a couple.

"Christsakes, Long John. You look like a girl out there."

In the stands behind me, three cranky old men, George Orr, Ramon Landsberger, and Bill Marsh–men with rheumatic joints and aching hearts, men who could only long for youth and vitality–muttered that none of it was good enough for them.

"All they know how to do these days is swing from the heels."

"They don't look near as good as the boys of 'eighty-eight."

"Nowhere near."

Sophie, from under her parasol, taunted young Elwell without mercy.

"Yoohoo, Calvin! Don't let the ball go through your legs! Get down on it! Take it off your chest!"

When Dobbs walked to the pitcher's box and began his warm-ups, the crowd fell silent and just watched, all except a dozen or so "braves," members of the Noble Brotherhood of Redskins, that is. They perched in the highest rows, bare-chested, and spackled with war paint sporting turkey feathers in their hair and pounding on tom-toms.

"Here we go Big Chief, here we go." Boom. Boom.

Judge Schmidt, the same idiot of an umpire who'd let Tony Rossi come to the plate without a bat in the Benicia game, strode onto the field. His mustache was stiff and waxed, and an iron umpire's mask hung in his left hand. He called to me, Foghorn and Andy Boynton, captain of the Martinez nine.

"Your lineup cards and on the double!"

We met at the plate and shook each other's hands like we almost meant it. The judge took the cards.

"The rules are those that normally apply," he began.

I'd heard them a thousand times: over the chicken wire screen in right field was a ground-rule double and over the chicken wire and the rail fence both was a homerun. If a ball went into the juniper bushes in left, the fielder should stop, snap to attention and thrust his right arm on high.

"I'll rule such a hit a double," Judge Schmidt said, and, intending to be funny I suppose, he added, "No biting, no kicking, no gouging."

Foghorn put an arm around the judge's shoulders and laughed loud. "That's a good one, Judge. No biting. No kicking." Human beings can stoop ever so low when money is on the line.

We shook hands again like civilized men, then, Charlie Meyers came up to me.

"Right field, eh? Is that where you and Foghorn are going to put me? The salt mines?"

87

I put my arm around poor Charlie, just like Foghorn had done with the judge, and lied like a politician. "We need your glove out there, Charlie."

Willie, my son, a batboy now, with his own little uniform, dashed over.

"Mr. Murphy wants to know if it's all right to start the ceremony."

"Why ask me?"

"Because you're the president," he said.

Before Dobbs floated into town, we would have had to pay Willie, or any boy, to be our batboy. The job, you see, included searching the weeds and sticker bushes on the downward sloping hillside for foul balls, an unpleasant occupation for a lad. But now, with the Chief on our side, we'd had more boys inquire for the job then we could possibly use.

Jimmy Catlett had even offered to pay us cash money.

Willie dashed away, and when he got to Foghorn, Foghorn consulted his watch like a railroad conductor and made a big wave of his arm. Father Noone stepped out of the grandstand, wearing his vestments over his brand new baseball uniform and encircled by a gaggle of white-robed altar boys.

The crowd stood and bowed their heads. Foghorn walked out to home plate. "Ladies and gentlemen," he bellowed. "The Blessing of the Baseballs."

Father Noone, with his altar boys, began a progression towards the plate where Carrie Haskell waited. She was seven years old with a pink bow in her hair, and a straw basket overflowing with clean, white baseballs lay in her little arms. Father Noone stopped when he reached her, and stretched his arms out toward heaven.

"Eternal Father, we beseech thy grace. Let these balls fly fast and true."

In the pitcher's box, Dobbs removed his ball cap, crossed himself and knelt. Long John, at first base, bowed his head. Foghorn, seated on the bench with pencil and notebook in hand, toted up his wagers one more time.

Father Noone sprinkled holy water from his magic scepter. "Let no one be injured in our game today, Lord. But if such is your will, then let it be a member of the opposition who falls in pain, for we of Port Newton have lost too many games of late, and we've all been feeling mighty low."

The crowd cheered. The Silver Cornet Band struck up "The Stars and Stripes Forever." The Noble Brotherhood of Redskins beat their tom-toms.

"Amen," Father Noone said.

"Play ball!" Judge Schmidt shouted.

James A. Bagby Jr. of Martinez, a right-hander and the son of a blacksmith, stepped to the plate. He dug his cleats deep into Mother Earth, scowled at Dobbs, and in a show of ill-advised courage, pounded his bat upon the plate.

The big Indian wound up with that same excess flail in his arms and legs then let fly a ball that seemed aimed at poor Bagby's head. It looked just like that pitch Dobbs had thrown to Charlie Meyers at that first practice Dobbs had attended. Bagby, fooled just the same as Charlie had been, dove for cover.

The pitch curved a foot, and broke right over the plate–the fade-away.

"Strike one!" Judge Schmidt cried, and the crowd shrieked a benediction of their own.

Port Newton belonged to Jack Poe Dobbs.

A pitcher's duel, that game turned out to be, with few hits and few runs, at least when compared to most of our games. But in the sixth inning, the Martinez club tied the game at four apiece, due, in the main, to a booted grounder by Billy Lawton and a throwing error by Hec Fernandez.

But in the bottom of the inning Cal Elwell stepped to the plate, with Dobbs on third. There were two outs. Cal's knees wobbled. He tried to set his feet in the batter's box but couldn't get comfortable. The Martinez pitcher, Wilson B. Wyatt, a county supervisor no less, quick pitched him, hurling the ball before Cal was set.

It slipped straight over the plate, and the spectators all sighed as one. But Judge Schmidt, God bless him, tore off his mask, leaped up and waved his arms.

"No pitch," he cried.

He pointed a stern finger at the pitcher.

"You must give a man a fair chance to get ready, Mr. Wyatt. This is baseball, not anarchy."

In the ideal, I suppose young Elwell would have struck a mighty drive after that. But, in the reality of it, he sent a grounder skittering towards the pitcher. It slipped under Wyatt's glove, was missed by the diving second baseman, and trundled off into the outfield.

"Praise the Lord," Father Noone shouted, and Elwell was the hero of the moment.

We led by that one thin run, 5–4, until the top of the ninth, and that was when Dobbs tired and grew wild.

"Ball four," Judge Schmidt decreed, and the lead off batter trotted down to first.

"Ball four," he said, again, and moments later, the second batter walked too.

"What the hell was wrong with that one?" the Chief called to the judge.

"High and wide," Judge Schmidt replied.

The big Indian advanced towards him. "It was dead over."

The judge shook his head. Dobbs hurled his glove to the ground. "That pitch was a strike, and you're a goddamned idiot."

The men of Martinez rose up from their bench, shouting at Dobbs.

Now me, I want nothing to do with fighting under any circumstances, but when a brawl brews in baseball, honor does demand that a man come to the aid of his country. I began a slow shuffle towards home plate, the scene of the impending battle, hoping beyond hope that war would be averted.

By the time I got there, Dobbs and Judge Schmidt stood toe to toe. "Say another word, Chief, and you're out of this game."

"What?" Dobbs screamed, and that, apparently, was just the word the judge had warned him about.

"You're outta the game!" he shouted, waving his thumb.

"Me?" Dobbs said. "You can't eject *me*, you jackass. Hell, I eject *you*!"

"Me?" Judge Schmidt said. "You can't eject me, I'm the umpire."

"I can eject anybody I damn well please. You may be the judge, but I got the jury."

He pointed at the grandstand, where the fans stood and screamed, where tomahawks flashed, and war drums beat. Even my dear daughter, who had caught a dose of the bloodlust too, waved her fist at the judge.

"Kill the umpire!"

"Kill the son of a bitch!"

Dobbs turned towards Hec Fernandez, our catcher and the sergeant-at-arms of the P.N.A.C., then pointed at the judge. "Mr. Fernandez," Dobbs said, "is it Athletic Club policy to allow jackasses to wander around on our baseball field?"

Hec seized Judge Schmidt by the collar. "It is not, sir."

Andy Boynton, the Martinez captain, blew his stack. "If you think we're gonna play this game without an umpire then you're the one who's the goddamn jackass."

Dobbs, manufacturing an outward appearance of calm, responded: "You want an umpire? I'll get you a damn umpire."

He turned to Foghorn.

"Mr. Murphy. You're the umpire, now. What do you want us to do?"

Without hesitation, Foghorn called out, "Play ball!"

Captain Boynton turned to his men. "Pack your gear boys. We're going home." He grinned at Dobbs. "What do you think of that, redskin?"

Dobbs called again to Foghorn. "These boys refuse to play. Do your duty, Mr. Umpire."

"The game and all bets upon it," Foghorn declared, "are forfeit to Port Newton."

"You can't do that," Boynton screamed.

And that, as I recall, was when Billy "The Kid" Lawton, soda jerker, ice cream maker, and incendiary, went off like a pistol shot.

"He can do anything he damn well pleases!"

Billy took a swing at Boynton. Boynton tackled Billy. The men on the Martinez bench charged the field, and the Noble Brotherhood of Redskins charged out of the stands. In a moment, a writhing pile of otherwise sensible men struggled in the dust around home plate, and all because of ball four.

Long John tried to pull them off each other. Dobbs dove in head first. Foghorn, however, was reluctant.

"Hold me back, Doctor Sam," he said. "Otherwise, I just might hurt somebody."

Understanding Foghorn's true meaning at once, I seized him from behind and pretended to hold him back while he, at the same time, pretended to struggle.

"You know," he said. "There must be half a thousand souls in the grandstand today."

"Best crowd in years," I observed, placing my hands up behind his neck, in a halfhearted full nelson.

"Easy there, Doc," he said.

"Sorry."

"And, you know, if we keep on winning like this, we could easily draw more. And the summer will only grow hotter."

"Hotter?" I said, seeing no great revelation here. "The summer's always grow hotter around here."

"Do you know what I'm thinking, Doc?"

"I almost fear to hear it," I told him.

"We could sell beer," he said. "Twenty-five cents a bottle. What do you think of that?"

"Twenty-five cents a bottle. Why, that would be..."

"A five hundred percent profit," Foghorn said.

17

THE PORT NEWTON NEWS
Thursday, May 10

TOWNE TOPICS

FOURTH OF JULY CELEBRATION
TO BE THE BIGGEST EVER
ENTIRE COUNTY INVITED

The new spirit of self-assurance that seems to be revitalizing Port Newton of late put in another appearance at last night's meeting of the Fourth of July Committee. Mr. Gerald "Foghorn" Murphy proposed that, in honor of the new century, this year's celebration should be held on a grander scale then ever before.

"I don't know what inspired me," Mr. Murphy later told your editor. "The words tumbled out in such flood it was as if I could not stop them."

Mr. Murphy spoke extemporaneously and eloquently for twenty or more minutes. He brought tears to the eyes of many of the ladies present and even some of the gentlemen. At the end of his soliloquy, it was moved and carried by acclamation, that this year's celebration should not be limited to Port Newton alone, but that residents of every community along the Strait should be invited to the glorious occasion.

It was further suggested by Mr. Murphy that the celebration should span not just one day, but three, and should feature vaudeville shows, sailboat races, literary exercises, and barbecues, all culminating in a fireworks display and a Grand Masked Ball.

"And the cost be damned!" Murphy exclaimed, in an outburst uncharacteristic of the chronically frugal Foghorn. "This will be Port Newton's moment in the sun, and we should let it shine for all time."

He then suggested that a baseball tournament of epic proportions should also be held, spanning all three days of the celebration. Such an event, Murphy said, will firmly establish Port Newton as the preeminent baseball power along the Strait.

"There is a time when moping and defeatism must come to an end. It is team spirit and the enthusiasm of a team's supporters that drive it to victory, and now is the time for every Newtonian to support our team by his attendance. Only then will Port Newton emerge from its current darkness, and spring, full born, into the light of the new century."

Murphy's remarks were punctuated by cheers and outbursts of applause. A motion was made, seconded, and carried that the members of the Women's Auxiliary Subcommittee, chaired by Mrs. John Glass, be empowered to act as delegates to the various towns along the Strait and enlist their support for the tournament and the monster celebration.

It was also moved, seconded and carried that the Goddess of Liberty contest should be thrown open to every girl along the Strait this year, be she from Port Newton, Martinez, or even Benicia. Lastly, the work of securing orators for the Fourth was delegated to a subcommittee headed by Mrs. Grace Valentine who suggested "The Coming Age of Progress" as a theme.

Another meeting is scheduled for next week.

CONSTABLE SHEETS IN A SCRAPE
MADMAN SUBDUED AT "FLOATING PALACE"

On Tuesday last, Constable John Sheets of this city was summoned to Hogan's Saloon on the Front, where a murderous assault had just taken place.

Earlier, Weintraub McNabe, a brakeman on the Santa Fe, was eating his dinner at Hogan's when John P. Russell–an accordionist at Mother Mary's, a dancehall on one of the scows anchored in the tules–burst in in an agitated state.

"He flew in as if from nowhere," Paddy Hogan, the proprietor of Hogan's, stated. "Immediately, he began to rail against McNabe, accusing him of all sorts of foul acts."

Mr. McNabe is new on the Sacramento-Oakland division, and, thus, could not have been responsible for any of the crimes of passion of which Russell accused him. But when McNabe tried to tell Russell he must have mistaken him for someone else, Russell produced a razor, and the two went at it.

"They went to the floor scuffling," Paddy Hogan said, "and I came over the bar with a club."

Hogan struck Russell hard in the back, and Russell began to hightail it for home.

"When I looked down at McNabe," Hogan said, "there was blood all over and flowing. Then, I saw his ear. Russell had severed it with his razor, and it lay like a dead mackerel on the floor."

Constable Shects and Doctor Sam Fuller were quickly summoned and, after a brief investigation, Sheets made for Mother Mary's to hunt for Russell.

"These so-called 'floating palaces'," the Constable later said, "are nothing more than disorderly houses. There are a good dozen of these scows, lying in the tules between here and Antioch. They should all be burned, and the women who run them flogged out of town, in my opinion."

Upon arriving at Mother Mary's, Constable Sheets did not even need to inquire after Russell, for the man was drinking at the bar with Mary's guitarist and banjo player, as if nothing at all was amiss.

Sheets approached Russell who, upon seeing him, immediately raised his arms in surrender. Whether this was a ruse or not, we cannot say, but Sheets, mindful of the danger, drew his Colt and ordered Russell to throw away his razor and lay himself belly down upon the floor.

Russell did the former, but refused the later. "I don't prostrate myself for any man!" he screamed.

He came at Long John, who struck Russell down with the butt of his gun and subdued him after a brief struggle.

"Long John's courage never ceases to amaze me," Doctor Sam Fuller said later. "Happily, he will suffer no lasting ill effects from the wounds he received grappling with Russell. But as for McNabe, well, medical science may one day be capable of reconstituting a man's ear, but that day is not yet come."

LOCAL BREVITIES

The steam schooner *Cosmopolitan* docked at Martinez Wharf, yesterday, carrying 300,000 board feet of lumber. The unloading should provide work for several days.

On Tuesday and Wednesday, the Upper Bay Conference of the Congregational Church will hold its annual meeting at Crockett. The Port Newton Church will be represented by the Rev. Benjamin Crow and Mrs. Edith Fuller.

Mr. John P. Cummins, of Benicia, was killed while trying to cross the railroad tracks on Saturday. He had just debarked the two o'clock eastbound train and was attempting to get to the ferry when he was struck by an oil car, knocked down, drawn under, and dragged for some distance. The tragedy is compounded by the fact that Mr. Cummins had just been visiting his father, Jacob A. Cummins, also of Benicia, who is confined in San Francisco undergoing treatment for trichinosis. Mr. Cummins is said to have taken the news of his son's death very hard.

Chief Dobbs, Port Newton's newest hero, was given his first lesson in snipe hunting by Foghorn Murphy, Calvin Elwell, and a few of the boys the other night. We are told that the Chief held a sack open while the others beat the bushes for snipes. The Chief says that his lantern overturned and went out just as the frightened snipes began to fly from cover, so none were captured. Something tells us he will get another lesson soon.

Our postmistress, Mrs. Judge E.A. Schmidt, left for Calistoga early Monday and will remain there for a month, availing herself of the mud baths and healing waters. During her absence, Mrs. Josie Pimental will assume her duties.

The farmers of the Diablo Valley report that the annual plague of ground squirrels is particularly bad this year. Black Death Squirrel Poison is the recommended cure. A new shipment has just arrived at Brock's in Martinez.

The Board of Education's semiannual examination for prospective teachers will begin on June 11 in Martinez and will occupy the entire week. It should be noted that not a single applicant passed last December's series of tests, and some fear that the Board of Education has gone too far in attempting to prove to the legislature that state certification of teachers is unnecessary.

The new street cleaning wagon in Martinez was employed for the first time yesterday and the town never looked better. Port Newton would do well to follow our neighbor's example.

George Veale has decided to raise Belgian hares and has built a large pen in which to keep his stock. He also raises first-class pigeons including fan tails, ring doves, Jacobins, tumblers, and a large variety for which there do not appear to be names.

When asked about recent rumors, Lawyer Elwell tells us that he does not believe Concord's attempt to steal the county seat from the city of Martinez will amount to much even though the money of the proposed electric railroad is behind it.

"Concord is a good place to take a nap," he said, "but it is not even an incorporated city. As for the money, well, no one has seen the color of it as yet."

Why do women want rights when they have privileges?

Drop into McEwen's Clothing Emporium, at Main and Railroad Streets, and examine the excellent stock of merchandise the firm carries. McEwen's caters to the needs of gentlemen and can secure what any man wants at prices that are even lower than those of the San Francisco merchants. Do not go away to do your shopping. Keep the money at home.

MEETINGS AND EVENTS
Anti-Imperialist Society–Thursday
At eight p.m. tonight the Port Newton Anti-Imperialist Society will meet at the home of Mr. and Mrs. Henry Varney, 25 School Street. This month's meeting will feature Mr. Wilfred Tunney of the Martinez Democratic Club, who will expound on "Imperialism, Trusts, and the Republican Party."
Fire Department–Saturday

Finnis Hurley, G.B. Rocca, and Dudley Valentine, the leading men of the Fire Department Reformation Committee, have called a meeting to be held on Saturday afternoon, three p.m., at the International Hotel. Mr. Valentine tells us that there will be a vote on the purchase of a new chemical engine.

"The boys are all quite excited about the prospect," Mr. Valentine added. "These engines are efficient and effective, and should help protect us in event that the water pressure fails, as it did when Granger's Warehouse went up a few years ago."

He also says that since the Fire Department will remain a volunteer organization, the acquisition of the chemical engine hinges on subscriptions and on new members being recruited. This method of funding gives pause to those of us who feel that a professional organization, supported by property taxes, is all that is capable of defending a modern city from the ravages of fire.

Twentieth Century Club–Monday

A meeting of the Twentieth Century Club will be held Monday evening at 7 p.m. in the home of Mrs. Josie Pimental up Buck's Ranch Road. This month's meeting will feature a lively discussion of spiritualism. Father Noone of St. Sebastian Church and Professor David Drake of the University of California will debate the possibility of communication with those who dwell on the other side.

18

BOX SCORE
The Port Newton News

```
BLACK DIAMOND                    PORT NEWTON
NAME          AB   R   BH    E   NAME          AB   R   BH    E
Morgan cf      3   0   0     0   Lawton ss      4   3   2     1
Gwyn    2b     4   0   0     1   M Luciani lf   5   1   1     0
DeNina 3b      3   0   0     0   E Luciani 3b   4   2   2     0
Hinton 1b      4   1   1     0   Dobbs p        2   2   2     0
Llewelyn c     4   0   1     2   Sheets 1b      4   0   0     0
Iderstine lf   4   1   1     0   Fernandez c    5   1   1     1
Benedetto ss   3   0   1     0   Farrell cf     3   0   1     0
Frost  rf      4   1   1     1   Elwell 2b      3   1   1     1
Cruz   p       2   0   0     0   Fr Noone rf    2   0   0     1
Pagliuca p     1   0   0     0   Meyers rf      2   1   0     0
Vaughan  p     0   0   0     0

TOTALS        32   3   5     4   TOTALS        34  11  10     4

RUNS BY INNING  1  2  3  4  5  6  7  8  9   TOTAL
------------------------------------------------
BLACK DIAMOND   0  0  1  0  0  0  0  2  0     3
PORT NEWTON     0  0  0  0  1  4  2  4  x    11
------------------------------------------------
```

HOME RUNS: Hinton; E Luciani BASES ON BALLS: Lawton,
M Luciani, Dobbs 2, Farrell STOLEN BASES: Morgan;
E Luciani, Noone HIT BY PITCH: DeNina, Benedetto, Vaughn
Sheets, Elwell, Dobbs 2 WINNING PITCHER: Dobbs LOSING
PITCHER: Pagliuca PASSED BALLS Llewelyn 2; Fernandez

UMPIRE: T.A. Alvarado TIME: 2:42

19
DOCTOR SAM FULLER
President, Port Newton Athletic Club

It wasn't all crap, Foghorn's idea for the three-day Fourth of July celebration. It was mostly crap, but not all crap. Foghorn Murphy really did love this country. In his mind, these United States were the best hope of the world, and I couldn't disagree with him there. What it came down to was method.

"It's our duty to civilize those damn Filipinos," Foghorn would say.

"It's our duty to civilize ourselves," I'd tell him.

Foghorn's idea for the baseball tournament itself didn't spring from greed as much as you might think, but from an addiction, of sorts. This isn't to say that Foghorn was any less acquisitive than most men, but he always craved action and the more the better. A bigger purse, bigger bets, and the Railroad Exchange bustling at the very center of it all. Foghorn had it all figured out, or so he thought: Dobbs would out-pitch the opposition; Long John would out-hit them.

But as things fell out, it began to go sour almost from the beginning. Only a week after the Blessing of the Baseballs at the Martinez game, we played the Black Diamond club. Coal miners that bunch was, Italians and Welshmen from deep in the bowels of the earth. It wasn't much of a contest, on the whole. Dobbs' infamous elbow didn't seem to bother him–despite all the fade-aways and curveballs he threw. He mowed down those Black Diamonds one-two-three. He gave us confidence, too, and everybody was hitting a ton.

Everyone except for Long John, that is. For by this time Long John, who had previously been immune to such things due to his clarity of mind, had become mired in the muck of a batting slump.

As he slunk up to the plate, hitless in three attempts, Father Noone called out some dubious advice.

"Take two and go to right!"

After Long John had accomplished the first half of that couplet and taken two strikes he laid back with the bat. He tried to push the ball out to right field where some coolies Foghorn had hired were digging post-holes for a new fence. The result was a pop-up to second base, and Long John trotted back to the bench, head hung low.

"Good try," Foghorn sung out. But he muttered to me, "It was a shitty try. Jesus Christ, I don't believe it. We finally get a real pitcher and our best hitter goes belly up."

Foghorn spat tobacco juice onto the dirt at our feet, and I did the same. Everyone, even me, had started chewing the vile stuff by now. Not because anyone particularly liked it, but because Dobbs, a "real ballplayer," chewed it. Everybody, including me, wanted to look like a real ballplayer.

"I just hope it ain't contagious," Foghorn said. Spit. "The slump, I mean."

"Could be," I replied. Spit.

Back in 'ninety-six, Ernie Luciani had gone into a slump, and it had spread like plague. Father Noone even took to wearing an asafetida amulet around his neck to try and ward it off. Didn't work though, and the good Father went oh-for-ninety-six, as I recall.

Now, Long John plopped down on the bench right between the two of them, Ernie Luciani and Father Noone.

"Don't worry it," Ernie told him. "Worst thing you can do is think about it. Just go up there swinging."

Father Noone, offered the opposite advice. "You got to wait on that ball. You got to hold back, cleanse yourself of all temptation. Swing only at the last moment."

I called to him. "Over here, Long John," wanting to get him away from possible sources of contagion.

"I don't know what it is, Doc," he said, sitting down beside me.

"It's a mystery as deep as bad backs," I replied.

I didn't want to tell him the truth. Batting slumps are creations of the mind, and that is what makes them so devastating. A man knows that it's all in his head, you see, but he can't help himself. He starts to out-think himself. His swing becomes unnatural and, pretty soon, he's trying out an

101

endless succession of new bats or growing a beard and cutting his hair.

George Orr, Ramon Landsberger, and Bill Marsh, the three old men who always sat in the front row of the grandstand right behind our bench, began to offer their own ill-considered advice.

"You never think about bunting, do you?"

"Bunting will change your luck."

"Try bunting on 'em."

That's how it is in a batting slump. Even the dying and dead think they have the cure. It works on the mind and, in the end becomes, like Lily Newton's neurasthenia, an exhaustion of the nervous system.

Next time up, Long John tried to lay down that bunt the three old men had called for but only managed a foul pop to the catcher.

"Before you know it," Foghorn said. "Nobody'll be able to hit." Spit.

"Ain't an epidemic, yet," I told him. Spit.

After all our games, the team was in the habit of marching down to the Railroad Exchange to hoist a few Newton Steam Beers, win or lose. But these days we trooped down from Newton's Bluff victorious and, as victors, we were accompanied by scores and scores of beatitudinous Newtonians.

And now, as in Foghorn's dreams, the Railroad Exchange was packed with sporting men from the dancehalls, farm boys from the valley, painted ladies in abundance, and all looking to rub elbows with us masters of baseball. They crowded that mahogany bar and listened, entranced, while Hec Fernandez, our catcher, stood atop it, singing of his glorious exploits.

"Oh, yeah," he told the crowd. "The Chief shakes me off all the time."

A huge mug of Newton Steam was in his hand and, as he toasted Dobbs with it, laughter erupted from the happy little crowd. Dobbs, the hero of the moment, the hour, the day, toasted him back.

"Yeah," the Indian laughed. "I just don't trust the bum."

102

Everyone, even Hec, laughed at that. Everyone, that is, but Foghorn Murphy, the presiding genius and architect of it all. He, instead, dwelt like an evil dwarf at his table in back with a jealous heap of coins and bills, our winnings, piled on the table before him.

"Look at Fernandez," he said to me, pointing to Hec up on the bar.

"Look at him. Bragging like he won the game for us or some such. Why, men steal on him like he wasn't even there. Do you know how many times he's thrown the damn ball into center field this season?"

"I haven't been counting," I said.

"Don't you ever look at the scorebook?"

"Not since I stopped playing."

I asked him how much the heap of lucre in front of him amounted to, but Foghorn dodged the question.

"You know, Doc, I been thinking. Maybe we ought to add another bat to the lineup. Just to take the burden off Long John until he busts out of his slump. What do you say?"

"Another bat?" I said. "Who? And where would he play?"

"Well, I don't know. Maybe somebody who could help Hec out with the catching. Hadn't thought about it all that much. But business is booming. More customers coming into the Exchange all the time. I'm selling more beer than ever."

"I don't follow, Foghorn."

"I'm just saying maybe I could use another bartender, that's all. And, well, the Chief knows this fellow in Oakland, Neptune Beach to be exact."

As I look back now, I figure that was when I should have put my foot down. I knew Charlie Meyers was right, at least in theory–cheating is wrong and the team should be for us Newtons, not paid professionals. But what about the town's newfound confidence? What about the Fourth of July, the greatest baseball tournament ever and Port Newton's moment in the sun? What was right? What was wrong? Did such considerations even matter?

"I don't know, Foghorn," was all I said.

"Just a thought," he told me. "That's all. Just a thought."

I looked over at that mahogany bar of Foghorn's about then; the one he'd salvaged off the wreck of the *Delta Princess*. The boys were all gathered alongside, joyously swapping stories about the game. Long John, tall and lean, drank a beer and ate his roast beef sandwich. He laughed and tried to mix in, but failed in the attempt. Batting slumps are things of the mind, and the mind can work upon a man. The evil humors multiply.

20
SOPHIE FULLER
Senior, Port Newton Union High School

Dear Diary,

Lily and the savage!

It all started with school leaving me absolutely exhausted. First, in Mr. Meyers's class, we had to listen to hours and hours of commencement speeches. Everybody had to write one, or was supposed to.

"We, the graduating class of June 1900, are the hope of the nation and the future..."

Garnetta and I sat way in the back and kept breaking into fits of laughter.

To make matters worse, Mr. Travis rebuffed my labors on the dialogue in *Pinafore*. He says my version is much better than the original, which is obvious. But he says that the original is what audiences expect, so the original is what they should get. As if he couldn't have told me this before I broke my back slaving over that manuscript, and, to add insult, he says the only part he has for me is as one of the First Lord's *sisters*.

I am *not* a chorus girl, Diary dear.

Thus, when school at last adjourned and my daily trial was ended, I hurried away. Returning home, I found no one there excepting Willie, who, since the Mother was still away in Crockett at the church meeting, was setting fire to his toy boats in the backyard.

"You're a monster, Wilhelm."

"Same to you but more of it."

Needing human companionship, no matter how lowly, I made the determination to stroll downtown and visit Mr. William Lawton at McMillan's soda fountain. I passed down the hill, expecting to find Lily sweating like a Chinaman amongst her hydrangeas or whatever they are, but she was not and, all the more intriguing, that same stirring music the Negroes played at the May Dance was coming from her gramophone inside.

My first thought was that Lily had gone shopping in San Francisco without me, which angered me desperately.

Especially because she'd dragged me to that awful debate at the Twentieth Century Club about spirits and ghosts. I stormed up on the front steps and gave her doorbell a couple of good twists. A foolish act, since the doorbell has not worked since that awful day the Savings Association collapsed, and those low creatures of the town besieged poor Lily in her own home.

I heard laughter coming from inside, Lily and a man. I, of course, assumed this to be her "Johnny", Long John that is. I banged on the door with the big iron knocker. This, falling like a smith's hammer, seemed to contain the power to cause both laughter and music to stop. There was silence. Then voices. Then the door swung open and there was Lily.

"Sophie," she said. "Hello." She straightened her hair which was all mussed and bothered. She was breathless, and her forehead glowed with perspiration.

I chided her immediately. "What's this I hear coming from your gramophone? You've bought new recordings and not said a word to me about it? Did you go to San Francisco without me, your best friend on earth?"

She said, "I would have asked you if I could. It just happened, you know? I was downtown, and Jack came in."

By Jack she meant the savage, I realized, for that was when I heard him. "Hey, sweetie, let her in. The more, the merrier."

I pushed right past her into the hall to see what I could see and there he was, as big as life in the front parlor– on the love seat in the window bay that looks out on the Strait. His suit jacket and collar were *off* and the top button of his shirt was *undone*. On the table next to the love seat were two glasses and a bottle of that awful Vin Mariani. The savage offered me some. Of course, I declined; then that barbaric grin of his swept over his face.

"Hey, sweetheart. Wanna see a Turkey Trot?"

I told him I despised the creatures, excepting on Thanksgiving, and Lily went into stitches. "It's a dance, silly. Jack's been teaching me all the latest dances."

"It just got invented," the savage told me. "The Turkey Trot, I mean. At the Bohemia in San Francisco. It's so new it's still ragged."

"The Bohemia?" I said. I'd read the stories that circulate in the press about the Bohemia including white slavery, opium, and free love. Then I realized all at once that *Lily had been there.*

She is so much like me, craving for the world but trapped in a peasant village. Long ago, before I knew you, Diary dear, Lily almost escaped it. She was going to be a June bride, and I was going to be a bridesmaid, even though I was only thirteen. I would have been the youngest bridesmaid in the history of Port Newton, Daddy said.

We were all to have organdy dresses, and the boy was rich. A Belmont from Nob Hill in the city and, oh, Lily would have loved that so much. Nob Hill, I mean, and living in the city, if not the boy, himself.

Her wedding was going to be in the city with the reception in the ballroom of the Palace Hotel. All the best people, and pretty little Sophie in her organdy dress! Lily was not exactly left standing at the altar but almost so. The boy, or his family more than likely, broke it off right after the trouble, the Savings Association trouble that is. Calling the marriage off was all about money, but isn't everything? I mean, what would things be about if they weren't about money? Which brings me back to love, Lily, and the savage.

She hurried to the table where the gramophone sat, procured a record suitable for a Turkey Trot and placed it on the turntable. The savage made a little circling motion with one finger as if to dance with me. I declined, but I did feel reinvigorated from the wine which he had absolutely *forced* me to drink. So when Lily mocked me, "Oh Sophie, what would Daddy say?" I considered myself dared.

There was nothing wrong in it, really. I mean, this is America, after all, and the savage is so *swarthy* I could not resist.

Halfway through the dance Lily took hold of the both of us and, soon, we were all dancing. All three of us at once, forgetting the need for partners whatsoever. It was all so very free, and we spun and laughed and stumbled all over each other until, at last, we all fell back onto that love seat. The three of us were having the gayest of times.

"They got places in the city that can't be touched out here in the sticks," the savage said. "Cakewalks, raggy music. You name it. They got it."

"And that club you mentioned?" I asked, just dying to know if it was true about the white slavery.

"The Bohemia? Yeah. And there's the Dog and the Nouveau, too. Poppa's for eats. Ain't a bad city, all together. Can't hold a candle to New York, though."

Lily said, "Jack's been telling me about Paris and Rome."

The Indian shook his head, and then, perhaps the wine taking him, too, began to ramble. About how they cheated him back East. About how they'd robbed him. About how his elbow went bad.

Then he said, "But a man can't cry over spilt milk. I did what I did, and I am what I am."

"I suppose everyone is that, Mr. Dobbs," I said.

But my jest sailed right over his head and, as if pondering his entire future, he said, "I been thinking about quitting."

"Quitting what?" I asked.

"Pitching, of course."

I asked him whatever else he would do if he didn't pitch. "Go back to the reservation?"

"That ain't funny, sweetie."

"I did not intend it to be, sir."

Then he told us he was thinking of opening a cigar store!

"Me." He laughed. "A cigar store Indian."

He went on all the more about how, even though McMillan's and the mercantile sold them, there were no true cigar stores in Port Newton.

"If a fellow wants some selection, why, he's got to go all the way to Martinez."

He had it all planned out, it seemed: glass display cases, polished walnut shelving on the walls. He'd sell coffee and magazines and newspapers.

"The Eastern papers," he said. "And there'd be tables and chairs where the men could sit and smoke."

His enthusiasm seemed genuine for this idiotic project, but Lily did not appreciate the idea.

"Why on earth would you want to settle in Port Newton?"

"I seen worse places," the savage replied. But Lily, wanting nothing to do with him, now, got up off the love seat, and moved purposely away. She fell into the huge easy chair that had been her father's and sank into it and one of her moods.

21

THE PORT NEWTON NEWS
Monday, May 21

TOWNE TOPICS

MONSTER CROWD EXPECTED FOR FOURTH OF JULY
CELEBRATION TO LAST THREE DAYS
GREATEST BASEBALL TOURNAMENT EVER

Pimental Hall was crowded to suffocation last night as the General Committee for the Fourth of July celebration was joined by enthusiastic representatives from the various Fourth of July committees along the Strait.

All except the Benicians, it seems, have approved of and made clear their intention to attend the giant celebration that will take place in this city on the Grand and Glorious Fourth. It is thought that we will cater to the largest crowd ever seen in these parts and, withal, the Southern Pacific and Santa Fe Railroads have agreed to put on special trains to bring in the thousands from all over the county.

The following tentative schedule of events was proffered by the Women's Special Auxiliary Subcommittee, which seems to have done at least as much work as the committee made up of men, if not more.

Monday, July 2, will begin with the firing of the National Salute and the crowning of the Goddess of Liberty, who will reign over all three days of celebration. The coronation will be followed by orations, bicycle races, trap shooting, an open-air vaudeville show, and the beginning of the greatest baseball tournament ever witnessed east of Oakland and west of the Mississippi.

Tuesday, July 3, will feature boat racing, literary exercises, the semifinals of the baseball tournament, foot races, and a greased pig contest. In the evening the day will be topped off by a production of Gilbert and Sullivan's musical play *H.M.S. Pinafore* courtesy of Mr. Maxfield Travis and the Port Newton Dramatic Society.

Wednesday, the Glorious Fourth itself, will begin with the Procession of the Floats up Main Street, followed by the Championship Baseball Game, a barbecue of epic proportions, and a massive fireworks display. The whole three days will culminate with a Grand Masked Ball to be held all throughout streets of Port Newton.

Parties wishing to bid for the ice cream and lemonade stand at Pimental Hall should give their written bids to Mr. Glass of the General Committee no later than next week.

NEWTONS EDGE BENICIA
LONG JOHN'S SLUMP
ROSSI'S REWARD

Our Port Newton boys journeyed to Benicia Sunday afternoon and bested the louts, 4–3, in a tense pitcher's duel.

It was initially thought that this game would feature some heavy hitting by Rossi and Sheets, the two leading first basemen along the Strait. The odds ran at even for most of the week. But Long John Sheets, as is well known to all Newtonians, has not hit well of late, and by the day of the affair, the sporting element had lengthened the odds to three to two, in favor of the Benicians. Mr. Foghorn Murphy, manager of the Newtons, remained undaunted, however.

"This is not a team built upon the shoulders of any one man," he said prior to the contest. "It is a true team, and as a true team we shall rise or fall."

Murphy put his money where his mouth was, laying on bets heavily. His sagacity was adequately proven not long after when Benicia's premier slugger, Anthony Rossi, was felled by an unforeseeable injury.

In the top of the first, with two runners on the paths, Port Newton's favorite native son, Jack P. Dobbs, stepped to the plate. Despite the fact that two were out, Dobbs attempted to surprise the vaunted Benician defense by laying down a bunt along the first base line.

"I gambled," the Chief later said, "that I could catch them napping, but I did not reckon with the catlike quickness of Mr. Rossi at first base. What happened next proved an unfortunate incident which I truly lament."

What happened next was a collision between the aforementioned Dobbs, thundering up the base path, and Big Tony, lumbering down it. The two met, halfway between home and first, became entangled, and as Rossi fell, Dobbs somehow spiked his opponent high up on the ankle and the blood flowed.

"It was a nasty gash," said Doctor Sam Fuller, president of the Port Newton Athletic Club. "I'd have stitched him up free of charge, but Rossi was adamant on only being treated by a Benician."

Big Tony was carried from the field of honor by his fellows as a Viking carried off on his shield. But after the game, he revealed his true nature to your editor.

"That red devil of yours did it on purpose. If he ever gives me the chance, you'll see he's a coward at heart."

After Rossi, Viking or otherwise, was dispatched from the fray, the game quickly devolved into the aforementioned duel of pitchers. And, as such, the advantage swung back to Dobbs and the Newtons.

In the fifth frame, shortstop Billy Lawton stole second base and scored on a ringing double by the eldest of the two Luciani brothers, Ernest. Dobbs himself delivered a single, and that was enough to put the Newtons in the lead, 4–2.

There was an anxious moment in the bottom of the final frame. Two passed balls, committed by Newton's catcher Hector Fernandez, allowed one Benician to score and the tying run to advance to third. Dobbs, however, fanned the final batter on a pitch that flew towards the plate on a straight trajectory until a shower of water, or some other substance, seemed to fly off it, and the ball tumbled earthwards miraculously, as if falling off the edge of a table.

After the game, when asked about his catcher's defensive lapses, Dobbs said, "My good friend Hector does a yeoman's job behind the plate, and I have complete confidence in him. But any catcher faced with the brilliant assortment of curves, fade-aways, and drops that I can deliver is always in for a rough go."

LOCAL BREVITIES

Miss Eva Dunkell, who has been, until now, a volunteer nurse with the Red Cross in the Philippines, returned home last week. Miss Dunkell, whose fiancé was killed in the fighting there, says that conditions are difficult in the extreme and that our soldiers suffer much from typhoid and dysentery.

"It is sometimes so hot," she told your reporter, "that it is painful to be in the sun."

Miss Dunkell said that the work at the hospital is hard and that the hours are long. She further states that the clean sheets and nightshirts sent by the people of the county at Christmas were especially appreciated and that the men in her care found the homemade jellies to be exceptional.

Doctor Sam Fuller informs us that an epidemic of the whooping cough threatens the town of Crockett.

The entertainment given for the benefit of the library fund on Friday night was well attended and profitable. Miss Garnetta McCoy was in perfect register singing several selections from the Messrs. Gilbert and Sullivan. Mrs. Eloise Hay and Miss Valentina Picoli favored the audience with an exhibition of the dances of Spain, and Judge E.A. Schmidt delighted everyone in attendance by sawing our May Queen, Miss Hanna Joost, in half.

Mrs. Rosa Paredes has been in the habit of wandering the streets speaking jibberish of late. Yesterday, a complaint was lodged against her by the merchants of Port Newton and, on Friday, a hearing will be held before Judge Schmidt to determine whether Doña Rosa should be committed to the asylum in Stockton where she could be properly cared for.

About seventy-five men will be put to work at the Tulloch Chemical Company in Hercules next week. Another schooner load of lumber was received at the L.F. Glease Company of Bulls Head yesterday. The old flour mill in Pacheco has been taken over by the Bank of Martinez.

Constable Sheets seems to be getting quite expert at using the new bicycle he recently acquired from the shop of that noted wheelman Patch McKenzie, located at Escobar and Ferry Streets in Martinez.

The Republicans of the Second Congressional District met last Thursday and adopted a concise and comprehensive platform that cannot be improved upon. They stand for McKinley, prosperity, an honest dollar, free competition, no surrender to the trusts, and a patriotic nation that will defend its interests at home and abroad.

No one can hold back the march of progress.

Last week, one of the San Francisco papers published an article that claimed there is a conspiracy to import cheap Chinese labor into this county. It should be remembered that the editor of that paper is Democratic and everything he says should be taken with a grain of salt.

IMPROVING OUR FAIR CITY

Foghorn Murphy, secretary-treasurer of the Port Newton Athletic Club, announced that the work being done on the old ball-yard up on Newton Bluff will make it the finest along the Strait.

"The grandstand is being repaired, expanded, and painted a benign and lovely green," Foghorn remarked. "Not only will refreshment stands be constructed, but professional waiters will be employed to distribute cold drinks to those who find the action so thrilling that they prefer not to leave their seats. It will be just like a park in the Eastern leagues."

Mr. Murphy also noted that proper fences will be erected.

"The rail fence and chicken wire screen in right field have long been a source of embarrassment to Port Newton. They are a danger to outfielders and children alike, and the new barrier will also serve to keep the riffraff out."

The Newtons' fans, however, may not be pleased by the fact that, for the first time, the Athletic Club will charge an admission fee of fifty cents, twenty-five for children under twelve.

"These monies," Murphy added, "will only be used to defray the immense costs involved and, once these are paid, the charge will doubtless be dropped entirely or at least reduced."

MEETINGS AND EVENTS
"The Last Loaf"–Friday

The popular two-act drama entitled "The Last Loaf," which attempts to show that true charity will gain heavenly reward, is to be played for the benefit of the Concord Christian Church at seven p.m. on Friday in the Concord Odd Fellows hall. The talent is said to be Concord's very best, which means they could doubtless use some help from Miss Garnetta McCoy and the thespians of Port Newton.

22
Calvin Elwell
Bartender and Second Baseman

With the Chief, I never knew if anything he said was ever genuine. With Doc and Long John, you always knew they were being straight with you. Sophie was almost always devious, but was so bad at it that it generally turned out harmless enough. The Chief was another kettle of fish altogether.

The day after the Benicia game, where he cut Tony Rossi's leg real bad, the Chief stepped up to the bar where I stood in my bow tie and white shirt. I was getting the free lunch ready, most likely. He made his voice low and conspiratorial.

"We're blood brothers, kid. You know what that means, don't you?"

"I suppose," I said, although I did not.

He asked me if I'd do him a service and I told him I'd do whatever he wanted, within reason. He told me to meet him in his room at the Railroad Inn after my shift was over, and I said I would, so I did.

The upshot was this: He wanted me to go into Oakland for him, and go to a certain pharmacy there and buy him a jar of leeches.

"Leeches?" I said.

"For my elbow, kid. It's killing me."

I told him he ought to see Doc about it, but he said doctors didn't understand about leeches. "Only Injuns and Chinamen understand leeches."

Besides that, he said, he didn't want it spread all over town that his elbow was hurting. "Don't tell Doc. And whatever you do, don't tell that sweetheart of yours."

"I don't have a sweetheart."

"Well, don't tell her, anyway."

When my shift was over, I took the train to Oakland and, after getting lost among the maze of streets downtown, managed to find the so-called "pharmacy" that had the leeches. It was in Oakland's Chinatown, where there wasn't supposed to be any plague, but I scurried along quick as I could, trying to hold my breath as much as possible. It took me a while to find the pharmacy, which was all full of Chinamen, and even longer to get the Chinaman there understanding what I wanted. But once that was done, there it was–a glass bottle filled with water and a whole score of the creatures.

It was a sickening sight, but the Chinaman wrapped the jar in newspaper, so I didn't have to look at the leeches on the train. Once back home, I found the Chief in his room, reading one of his dime Westerns, and swigging at a bottle of bourbon whiskey but using his right hand for it. His shirt was off and his left elbow looked all swollen and blue and disagreeable.

He offered me the whiskey and, even though I didn't really want any, I didn't want to look like a baby, either. So I took it. He got up, went over to the wash basin and scrubbed his elbow, wincing all the time from the pain of just touching it. Then he got an empty jar he had and a pair of tweezers, came back to the bed again, sat on it and opened the leech jar. He took one of them out with the tweezers. It was a horse leech, black with brown stripes. He laid it on his elbow.

"Okay you son of a bitch," he said. "There," he said, when the little sucker bit into him.

He did that three or four times with three or four leeches, placing them all over his elbow, then took a hand mirror and looked at them, all sucking his blood.

"Just like them damn owners," he laughed, meaning baseball team owners.

He started rambling on about the owners again and how they bought and sold a man like a slave. Then he asked me if I trusted Foghorn, and I told him what Foghorn had done for me–taking me in when my father disowned me and all.

"He likes a dollar though, doesn't he?" the Chief asked, and I told him he sure did.

"Sometimes he acts devious," I said, "but he's a good man at heart."

"Like Long John?" he asked.

"In a different way," I said.

Then, he told me all about the cigar store he was planning to open, which I already knew about from Sophie. Seemed he figured he could win enough money betting on our ballgames to get the venture started.

"Foghorn might lend me some, too, and once it gets going I'll just watch the dollars roll in, maybe even take a wife."

"Who?" I asked, as if the whole town didn't know who he had in mind by now, but he just shrugged his shoulders.

"Anyone that'll have me, kid."

When one of the leeches finished its meal and unhooked itself, the Chief took the tweezers, picked it off himself and dropped it in an empty jar. Then he asked me if I could read to him from the Western he had, and I said I would.

I read all of it aloud while the leeches sucked him. It was about this Indian princess rescuing this white man from her people just before they burned him at the stake. When I finished it, we both agreed it was a good one, for it had a clever twist, as usually it is the hero who rescues the princess and not the other way around.

I've wondered in the years gone by how much of these dime Westerns the Chief actually believed. For me Westerns are like Santa Claus. Everyone agrees to pretend they are true and so we do, but in our hearts, we know they are not. There are no fat men who come down chimneys at Christmas and no heroes who rescue princesses or vice versa.

I can't really say if that's how the Chief felt about Westerns. But he must have known things hadn't been like that. There were plenty of such books about baseball, too. About handsome young men who played ball honorably, like Knights of the Table Round. What the Chief had seen, though, was men beating him up, spiking their opponents, and cheating for money. No princes in baseball. No fair-haired and incorruptible pitchers, either. Except maybe Mathewson, or so people say.

When the leeches were all done, the Chief sealed up both jars, wrapped his elbow in linen and put on his shirt and coat.

"Got to keep it warm," he said. "But we can still have some fun."

He got that little knife-gun of his and grabbed the whiskey and the jar that had the used leeches in it.

"Don't want to hold onto these things," he said.

Making a long story short, we went out back, onto the docks behind the Railroad Inn. The same docks where the *Esmeralda* had tied up the night Long John rescued him. The Chief threw that jar out into the water, but with his right arm, not his left. Then he commenced to take pot shots at it with that little thirty-two.

There was only a quarter moon, I recall, and though the lights from the Front helped some, it was pretty hard to see that jar, much less hit it. We fired off all the chambers and reloaded, drank whiskey, and stood there taking pot shots for sometime.

"What the hell are you boys doing?"

Long John came up on us from behind, his revolver, a big Colt, drawn and at the ready.

"Put the gun down!"

The Chief did that, quick as thought, laying it on the dock, and put his hands up high without even being asked. I did the same.

"Now back away from the thing!"

I acted the craven coward, I'm ashamed to say. "We didn't mean a thing Long John. Just, well... taking some target practice."

"You been drinking, Cal?"

"Yes sir."

"You too, Chief?"

"Not a drop."

Long John holstered his own gun, picked up the thirty-two, unloaded it, and said we could put our hands down.

"It's illegal to discharge a firearm in the town limits, and anybody as drunk as you two shouldn't be playing with guns on any account."

The Chief said, "I guess you know all about firearms in your line of work."

"I guess I know more than a baseball player," Long John said.

Long John was about the nearest thing I ever knew to that Western hero who rescued princesses and tussled with Jesse James and Billy the Kid. Those fellows never seemed to think twice about it, but I fear Long John did.

Maybe he'd have been better off if he'd become a lawman in Concord or Clayton or Danville, where farm boys were about all he would have had to deal with. But Port Newton could be a rough place in those days, and that Negro he'd killed a few weeks before had disturbed him, I think. He'd tried for a long time to find out who the Negro was, but all we ever knew was that he was just a hobo on a train who busted out of jail and died on the railroad tracks just down the Front.

"You boys swear on your honor you won't do this no more?"

"Yes, sir," I said.

"I ain't got no honor," the Chief told him.

It was more than just Lily Newton between them, I figure. Partly it was the way the Chief played ball. How he cheated to win and didn't even feel bad about it; how giving his word didn't mean a thing to him. Long John had been poor all his days. He'd raised himself up from farm boy to constable, and here was this fellow who wasn't even white, but who had seen the sights of the world and tossed money away like it was nothing and just because chance had blessed him with a left arm that could throw a baseball.

"I probably ought to let you two sleep it off in the calaboose," Long John said, "but I suspect I'll give you a break."

"I make my own breaks," the Chief said.

"I guess you do," Long John said.

To the Chief, Long John must have seemed like just another white man giving him orders. Just another pip-squeak desk clerk or waiter who made him come around to the back door to get a goddamn ham sandwich. Two dogs growling was what they were.

23
DOCTOR SAM FULLER
President, Port Newton Athletic Club

I kept my medical offices in my home in those days, practical and civilized. We were up Buck's Ranch Road, of course, just beyond the Newton mansion. The Elwells and the Pimentals were below us, too, we being the last to build.

What I'm getting at is that being situated near the top of the hill allowed me to devise a signaling system of which I was very proud. I erected a flagpole in the front yard, had some Chinamen do it rather, in a spot where the tip of it could be seen from just about anywhere in town. Old Glory flew at the top, and a signal pennant flew below that, generally a green one. But if I wasn't home, and a patient came, or for any other cause she might deem appropriate, my wife would hoist a red or yellow pennant. I, upon seeing its flutter, would find one of the few telephones that existed and give her a call.

Pretty damn clever, I always thought.

I was down on Main Street tending little Flora Randall, daughter of Thomas Randall of the Randall and Fischer Meat Market, on the day Long John came to see me. The Randalls lived up above their store, as many did, and Flora was always ill with nose and throat problems–from the fumes of the carcasses in the ice room and the bloody sawdust on the floor, I always supposed.

At any rate, I did what I could for little Flora. Medical magic was limited in those days. Then I bade my goodbyes, went down Randall's back stairs, and walked around to Main Street. I looked up the hill, as I habitually did, and saw a yellow pennant snapping away on my flag pole. This meant that, although no emergency was in the offing, there was a patient waiting.

I slipped into McMillan's pharmacy–where I saw Lily Newton, reading her magazines and drinking magical potions of another sort, and gave my wife a holler over McMillan's telephone. An incredible miracle those things were, talking wires. Who could have ever imagined such a thing?

"It's Long John," Edith said, her voice sounding clear enough for the purpose at hand. "I don't suppose it's anything serious, but he says he's been having headaches."

"How's Willie?" I asked. Our son had stayed home from school that morning, complaining of a stomach ache.

"You baby him too much."

"Probably so."

I told her I was down at McMillan's, and that I'd be home before she knew it, which I was, more or less. She greeted me at the door with a peck on the cheek.

"Long John's in your office," she said.

She'd been in the kitchen all day, doing the ironing—which necessitated heating the irons on the stove—and was now sawing down bars of soap, each of which was about a foot long to begin with. She looked a bit worn down from it all, and I prescribed an afternoon nap for her.

"You work too hard," I told her.

"I don't suppose you could get your daughter to help me every now and again."

"Fat chance of that."

Then Willie, the little faker, went chugging right on through.

"Toot, toot! I'm a steam engine!"

My wife looked at me, and I at her.

"You heard him," I said. "He's a steam engine."

Inside my office, Long John was perched on the examining table with his shirt already off.

"Hiya, Doc."

Long John was a fit man—physically at any rate. The muscles of his upper body were trim and well-defined, the only flaws being various scars on his upper arms and chest. Occupational hazards, he always called them. I asked him about the headaches.

"They aren't too terrible. But I've been getting them for the last month or so and almost every day, now."

I poked and prodded him. Looked in his ears, up his nose, down his throat, all that.

"That scuffle with the guitar player at Mother Mary's you had a couple of weeks ago..."

Long John corrected me. "Accordionist."

"Accordionist, yes. You didn't get hit in the head, did you?"

"Probably," he told me. "It wouldn't be the first time."

I asked him if he'd experienced any nausea or vomiting, and he told me he hadn't.

"I'm fine, otherwise," he said. "Just a headache every day."

"Every day?"

"Almost. And my neck and shoulders have been awful stiff as well."

"Been sleeping all right?"

"Fretful."

I had him open wide. "Grind your teeth when you sleep do you?"

"I don't think so."

"Appetite all right?"

"I can always eat."

"Been forgetting things? Anything like that?"

"I don't think so." He shook his head then laughed and made the same joke that everyone made when I asked that question. "If I have been forgetting things, I don't recall it... Say, Doc. You remember the night we fished Dobbs out of the Strait?"

I cut him short. "You don't suppose these headaches have anything to do with him, do you?"

"Naw," he said. "They're just headaches."

"Dobbs could cause any man a headache."

"The night we pulled him out of the drink," Long John went on, "did you get a good look at the wound on his head? Almost exactly in the back, wasn't it?"

"As I recall, yes. There was blood. Most of it washed away in the water, of course. But the bleeding was stopped by the time we put him on the bar."

"Did it look to you like someone conked him? He says he must have hit it when he fell, and I'm wondering if you could say which it was. A blow or a fall?"

"Well, no, I don't suppose I could. There's really no way to know."

"The ferrymen say there were some men playing craps on deck. I figure it was Dobbs with those loaded dice of his. You saw those, didn't you?"

I told him I had. "The ones that always came up seven. How could I forget? You're sure these headaches aren't about him?"

"Look, Doc. I did some investigating and the fellow's a liar. He said he played for Sacramento, last year, but he didn't. He played a while for Watsonville but even they cut him halfway through the season."

"So he told a few white lies. A fellow like Dobbs, why, what a blow to his pride to have to admit that no team wanted him."

"As far as I can tell, he was on his way to Oakland to drink himself to death with his old baseball buddies. And look what he's doing to young Cal, getting him drunk all the time."

"It isn't all the time," I said.

"Why, I almost arrested them the other night, and that boy never used to do such things. What kind of example is that to be setting?"

I thought I understood it all. And worse, I thought like Foghorn, that I could control things. "Look, Long John. Romance doesn't always last, you know."

"She's not right," he said, meaning Lily. "Do you know what she thinks?"

"Long John, things don't always go the way we want them to. If Lily's chosen someone else, well, there's nothing you can do about it. Worrying won't help. Stop worrying and try to enjoy life."

I asked him if he'd tried wintergreen oil. I was busy, you see, there were patients in town I had to visit, a meeting of the County Medical Society to attend.

"Wintergreen oil," he said. "No. Haven't tried that. Got some morphine tablets from McMillan, though."

"Cut those damn things out first. They might be doing more harm than good. Something like a hangover. Cut out the drinking and smoking for a few days, too. Cut out the coffee. You drink too much of that damn stuff."

"I can't cut out the coffee."

"Well try. And get more sleep. Get some wintergreen oil from McMillan. Put it in boiling water, put a towel over your head, and inhale the vapors."

I put my hand on his bare back and guided him down off the examination table. "It's up to Lily, not you or me. We don't always get what we want in this life, remember. Try to relax. Try to enjoy things. Don't dwell on unpleasantries. Try the wintergreen oil. You might even start hitting better."

Some goddamn doctor I was.

24

SOPHIE FULLER
Senior, Port Newton Union High School

Dear Diary,

Stabbed in the back and by my so-called best friend. Everything was fine. Mr. Murphy and I had an unspoken agreement. Then Garnetta got scared and blabbed it all to the parents. It was *my* idea, she said. *I* was the one who tempted *her*. But it was *her* idea as much as *mine*, Diary dear.

We had been planning on going shopping in Oakland from the start, then I–then *we*–saw the advertisement in the papers that Gentleman Jim Corbett was going to be at Neptune Beach. I just couldn't bear to live anymore if I missed seeing *him*.

All I did was suggest to Garnetta that we take the train all the way to Alameda, *first*, then go back to downtown Oakland and do our shopping *afterwards*. She was a jellyfish about it, needless to say.

"I don't know," Garnetta said. "I mean, prize fighting? Do they even allow girls to attend such a thing?"

"It isn't prize fighting," I told her. "It's an exhibition of the manly art of self-defense."

We first saw Gentleman Jim coming out of the Hotel Napoli, where all the boxers stay when they're training, and there wasn't a mark on him even after those tragic twenty-three rounds against Jeffries. He walked through Napoli Gardens like a king, as his admirers thronged around him– and not just a few desperate women either.

"Well, he *is* handsome," Garnetta said.

"I'm glad you're perceptive enough to see that, at least."

Jim is slender and tall and, even in a suit and tie, you can see how athletic and well wrought he is. Not an ounce of fat but only muscle and, as we later saw, a stomach as hard as iron.

"And he does seem to be," Garnetta said, "well, a gentleman."

Sometimes, Garnetta.

With that I seized her by the arm and hurried her off towards the beach. She has no sophistication at all in such matters, but I had in mind the perfect place from which to view the exhibition. I knew that the sand around the ring would be jammed with unpleasant people, as it was. There were a thousand more under the awnings, in the dance pavilion, and on the steps. But we arrived perfectly in time to be at the railing on the promenade which overlooks the plunge and the beach.

The swimmers and divers were out in force and there were many fine specimens among them. But the creature they brought out to spar with Jim was a gorilla; short, squat, and hairy. He was announced as being named James McDowell, but I have since learned from Mr. Foghorn Murphy as I will reveal in due course, that he is most usually called "Plugly," because he is, in fact just that, "plug-ugly."

"My heavens," Garnetta said, upon seeing the beast. "I hope he doesn't hurt Mr. Corbett."

I told her I doubted it possible that anyone, especially a creature like this McDowell, could truly hurt the great Corbett. He is, after all, the most wonderful champion ever. And that was when he came out of his dressing room, just across from the ring, accompanied by a huge entourage, guiding him, caring for him, absolutely worshipping him as he trudged through the sand, all business. Swimmers stopped swimming, divers stopped diving, and all crowded towards him cheering, applauding, and issuing words of encouragement.

"You're still number one in my book, Champ."

"When's the rematch, Jim?"

The ring was set on a raised platform in the middle of the beach. Jim's attendants helped him through the ropes and then stripped him of his robe, revealing that incredible physique of his. He danced about for a moment, waving to his admirers, then began shadow boxing and throwing punches in rapid succession. Once at the gorilla's corner, he shook the man's gloved hand between his own two gloves, in a wonderful exhibition of sportsmanship.

And it was then that I saw them. Mr. Foghorn Murphy and Jack Dobbs, the savage, were standing in the sand, directly behind McDowell. Mr. Murphy chanced to

127

look up, saw the two of us at the railing of the promenade and, after some hesitating, tipped his hat.

"Oh my heavens," Garnetta said. "Father will kill me. Let's get out of here."

"Come now, Garnetta. Be cool and calm. Smile and wave back as if you are doing nothing wrong... Yoohoo, Mr. Murphy. Yoohoo, Mr. Dobbs."

The two of them put their heads together. Some low words were passed. Then, all smiles, they turned and waved as if they were ever so happy to see us, and I understood immediately that something was rotten in Denmark.

A moment later, the exhibition began. A bell rang. The two contestants touched gloves in the middle of the ring. Gentleman Jim danced again, not even putting up his hands, much less throwing a punch, but allowing this plug-ugly fellow to swing at will.

A great roar went up when Jim threw his first blow. It made an awful sound as it struck, a crunch of flesh and bone in McDowell's abdomen. Jim then flicked a left at his opponent's chin that snapped back the head as if it were that of a rag doll.

But I will say this for Mr. Plugly McDowell: while he may be an unskilled brute, he is no coward or sissy. He took blow after blow from the great Corbett, each falling with the sickening power of a woodsman's ax. In the sixth round, he crashed to earth like a great tree falling, then lay heaving upon the canvas.

Garnetta turned her eyes away and foolishly said that the whole affair was inhuman and that prize fighting should be banned forever.

I chided her. "It's the natural order of things, Garnetta dear. As you gain experience you will understand that. The fit survive. The weak perish. One must decide which of the two one will be and then be it."

"The world is not made up solely of brutes," she said.

"Of course it is," I told her, but by then the time had come for us to meet the lion in his den and brazen it out. "Come Garnetta, we must go say hello to Mr. Murphy and the savage, and we must behave as if we had just seen them at a Sunday picnic in Founder's Park."

128

We made our way down to the sandy beach and proceeded towards the ring, where the gorilla sat sprawled on a milking stool. His arms and head lolled against the ropes, mouth open, tongue bloody and swollen. The savage squeezed water from a sponge atop the gorilla's head. His only attendant, an unshaven fellow whose belly hung over his pants, removed his gloves.

The savage was uncouth, as always. "Hey, darling," he said to me.

Mr. Murphy was clearly embarrassed to see us. He tipped his hat, "Miss Sophie. Miss Garnetta." Then he craned his neck to survey the crowd and asked if *Daddy* was with us.

"No, not today," I told him. "Garnetta and I just decided to come to the beach and there was this awful fight going on."

Then Mr. Murphy lied through his teeth. "The same with us. We came for some fresh air and, well, amusement. This being an amusement park and all. Only to discover that Mr. McDowell here, is an old friend of Mr. Dobbs."

With that, the gorilla, Plugly McDowell–still slumped on his stool–pointed in my direction.

"I remember you." He slurred as if drunken. "We used to pitch her high and tight, didn't we, Chief?"

The savage fanned him with a towel. "She's a girl Plugly. What the hell? We didn't play against girls."

"Oh," the gorilla said.

But that let the cat from the sack, indeed, and pretty little Sophie Fuller understood at once. Long John's batting slump, Hector Fernandez' throwing errors, the survival of the fittest.

"You were a catcher, I presume, Mr. McDowell?"

"Look at my hands," he said, holding them out to me, battered and bruised, covered with knobs like walnuts. "That's all I got to show for twenty years of it. Hands like these."

"And will you be joining our Athletic Club?" I asked.

He looked at Mr. Murphy. "Sure, I suppose. What's it pay?"

That was when Mr. Murphy truly lost his composure, some poker player he is. He said it was all perfectly proper. He said he needed another bartender was all, "To give Cal a little relief." As if that could sway me.

"And what could be more natural," I asked, "then to go looking for a bartender in a boxing ring at Neptune Beach?"

"You won't tell your father about this, will you, Miss Sophie?" A whipped dog, he was.

"Of course not, Mr. Murphy. I won't say a word to Daddy if you don't."

I reached out my hand to him, like one of his barroom cronies, and the bargain was sealed.

25

THE PORT NEWTON NEWS
Monday, May 28

TOWNE TOPICS

THE FOURTH OF JULY
THE MONSTER CELEBRATION
CIVIC IMPROVEMENTS TO DAZZLE VISITORS

Every day the Fourth of July Committee receives word from more of the cities along the Strait that they intend to join Port Newton in celebrating the arrival of the new century. Countless fraternal organizations have also agreed to take part in the monster celebration and the great parade to be held on the Fourth; the Odd Fellows, the Woodmen of the World, the Native Sons, and many more. The Noble Brotherhood of Redskins has already promised that they will appear *en masse* and on horseback in their colorful attire.

The sugar refinery in Crockett has announced its intention to close for all three days of the celebration so its workers may place themselves in attendance. Mr. P.R. Levine of the Nitro-King Works of Hercules has offered to furnish all the powder needed for the firing of the National Salutes, and a number of acts for the open-air vaudeville shows have already been secured by the Entertainment Committee: the Mississippi Minstrels; Hazel Fontaine, world-renowned ventriloquist; trapeze artists The Flying Floyds; and J.H. Clarence, the fancy dancer and banjo comedian.

There will be floats and gaily decorated rigs in abundance and, now, news of the most fantastic variety has reached the ears of your editor. It has long been rumored that the new Sierra & Bay Electric Company had intentions of running a line from Solano County, across the Strait and into Port Newton–a feat that would guarantee us cheap power almost without end. As has been reported before, this rumor bore fruit two weeks ago when Mr. P.G. Bristol, general manager of the company and one of the largest stockholders, met with the supervisors of the county and was granted a special franchise for this very purpose.

Now, Mr. Bristol has announced the intentions of the company to hasten along with their plans to such an extent that they will erect temporary electric street lights in Port Newton in time for the Fourth of July Celebration. This glorious news means that darkness will be banished forever on that night of nights, and that the Grand Masked Ball and the climactic fireworks display will take place in a shining, electric city, marching forward into the bountiful future.

But all is not well in the world, as M. Voltaire once observed, and at the last meeting of the Fourth of July Committee, there was much disputing as to the form the baseball tournament should take. Objections were first raised by Judge T.A. Marsh of Martinez, who questioned the inclusion of the city of Concord in the first place.

"This current attempt of theirs to take the county seat away from us," he said, "is nothing short of piracy. They don't even have a sewer system, do they?"

Mr. Foghorn Murphy, of Port Newton, who suggested the three-day tournament in the first place, now says that a schedule that grueling will exhaust the teams and make for poor play, and that the games should be played over the course of an entire week.

"That's a pack of hooey," declared Anthony J. Rossi, captain and guiding light of the Benicia club. "That redskin of Murphy's has got a bad elbow, and that's all there is to it. He can't pitch three days straight, and without his red nigger, Murphy knows he's as good as lost."

Despite Mr. Murphy's and Judge Marsh's objections, it was voted and carried that each team would play three games in three days, and that eight cities would contest for the championship: Port Newton, Benicia, Martinez, Concord, Hercules, Pacheco, Crockett, and Black Diamond.

NEWTONS DRILL HERCULES
NEW CATCHER SPARKS VICTORY
Our brave Newtons taught the Hercules boys a lesson they won't soon forget in a 12–3 drubbing yesterday.

The contest was marked by the sterling play of Port Newton's latest citizen, James F. McDowell, who is usually referred to as "Plugly," and not for his good looks, either.

McDowell recently took a position as a bartender at Foghorn Murphy's Railroad Exchange Saloon, and says that it is a complex job but that he will do his best.

"Foghorn keeps a bat hid under the bar," he said, "and if any man causes trouble, I'm to let him have it."

Suspicions concerning Mr. McDowell's sudden move to our city, following on the heels of poor play by the Athletic Club's catcher, Hec Fernandez, were greeted with guffaws by Mr. Murphy, manager of the ball team.

"I would call it a great good fortune that Mr. McDowell has moved here, and I think even Mr. Fernandez will join in welcoming an experienced man to aid him at his position."

Indeed, the Newton's new catcher asserted his powers early in the game. One rather slender Herculean, on an ill-conceived dash towards the plate, attempted to bowl over McDowell, who is built along the lines of a brewery horse, but the plug-ugly one blocked the plate with consummate skill.

"The man bounced off him like a child's ball off brick wall," a bemused Foghorn Murphy later commented. "Not many will make it past McDowell when it counts."

McDowell also exhibited a rifle arm in gunning down three men upon the base paths. It could have been more, but after the early showing he made, the Hercules boys gave up on the fleet-footed game entirely. He also exhibited good prowess with his stick work and hit safely in three of five attempts.

But all is not as it appears at the Athletic Club. For one thing, McDowell's membership was unanimously approved in an unusual Wednesday afternoon meeting of the P.N.A.C. that was held in the saloon itself rather than the clubhouse. A source who asked not to be named claims that McDowell is a professional athlete most recently employed at Neptune Beach in Alameda as a part-time pugilist, strongman, and wrestler.

"What will it profit us," our source added, "to gain the world but lose our souls?"

LOCAL BREVITIES

The bark *Blackberry* from Shield, England, docked at the smelter last Friday with a load of coke after a trip of 355 horrible days. Her captain reports that she was beaten back five times by rough weather as she attempted to round Cape Horn. He says the crew suffered from a shortage of provisions and underwent a great many hardships. This awful journey points out the desperate need of our country and the world for a canal across either Nicaragua or the isthmus of Panama. The French have failed in this undertaking, and it is time for America to put things right.

Charles "Icebox" Meyers tells us that his wife and children are enjoying a camping excursion to the Yosemite Valley.

Coal miners are wanted at Tesla, Alameda County. Apply to the superintendent of the mine. He says that good pay will be offered to good miners.

Lawyer Elwell and the trustees of the school district are jubilant over the sale of bonds to the Oakland Bank of Savings last week. Twenty-five bonds were sold, each in the denomination of $500 and bearing interest at the rate of eight percent.

Roy Burdett, who hauls ice for Mr. Jay McBride, was felled by cramps at the depot last night. His life was feared for, but owing to the prompt attention of Doctor Sam Fuller, he pulled through. Doctor Sam says that Burdett went to sleep on a load of ice after being overheated from work and became so chilled he began to suffer spasms.

Hec Fernandez' brother, Anton, had his leg broken when he was working a hay press in Pacheco last week.

Father Noone of St. Sebastian Church was recently afflicted with an abscess of the ear. Doctor Sam Fuller performed a surgical operation and tells us that the good Father is improving daily.

A German man, Paul Beale, met with an accident and died from injuries when the wagon he was driving up Buck's Road overturned and Beale was thrown over the precipice into the canyon below. It is irony, indeed, that Beale, who had been in this country but a few months, recently received word of the death of a wealthy relative in the old country, which had made him heir to a fortune.

Rudolph and Bertha Schofield are pleased to announce the engagement of their daughter, Annie, to Mr. Ernest Luciani. The marriage has been set for September. After honeymooning in the Santa Cruz mountains, the newlyweds will return to Port Newton, where Annie will continue to operate the millinery department at Schofield Mercantile while Ernest begins learning the business. Ernest's brother, Mike, will be best man, and Miss Isabella Thayer of Crockett will be maid of honor.

When the 9:20 train went through on Friday night, many people reported seeing what appeared to be flashes of lightning behind it and thought a meteor or some other phenomenon was traveling directly behind the train. The mystery was solved today when it was learned that Constable Sheets was engaged in a foot race with two fleeing hobos at the time of the reported incident and that the light he carried was apparently flashing about in an unpredictable manner. Long John reports that one of the hobos was caught and subdued, which makes a total of six of these troublesome vagrants that are now lodged in Sheriff Ulshoter's jail in Martinez.

White Hat O'Malley, the well-known politician, is leaving with his niece for a three-month holiday in Europe, which will include a lengthy visit to the International Exposition in Paris. White Hat says that the American exhibits of moving sidewalks and stairways, of wireless telegraphy, and of the most powerful telescope ever built should convince the world that Americanization will be of great benefit to all. He also says that neither he nor his niece have any concern for their personal safety despite the recent bombings and the attempt on the life of the Prince of Wales.

Last night, your editor awoke with severe pains about the chest and lungs, but he took a goodly dose of Electric Bitters, available at McMillan's Pharmacy and Fountain, corner of Main and Railroad, and his pains were instantly relieved.

GODDESS OF LIBERTY
MISS THAYER IN THE LEAD

The balloting began only four or five days ago to elect a Goddess of Liberty, who will preside over the Fourth of July festivities, but the contest is already as hot as a firecracker. In past years, each community elected its own goddess but, in honor of the new century and the unprecedented nature of our gigantic celebration, only one supreme goddess will be elected this year and, already, two large ballot boxes have been received from the town of Crockett. We give, below, the leading candidates so far.

Isabella Thayer (Crockett)	426
Genevieve Hurley (Martinez)	237
Hanna Joost (Port Newton)	125
Sophie Fuller (Port Newton)	115
Josie Castro (Concord)	102

A message was received from the city of Benicia late last night to the effect that their candidate is of such charm that she will sweep the contest hands down. But as the identity of this lovely of lovelies is being kept secret it is difficult for your editor to venture an opinion on the subject.

MEETINGS AND EVENTS
Fire Department–Friday
The Fire Department Reformation Committee will meet again Friday evening, seven p.m., at the International Hotel to discuss the failure of new and honorary subscriptions to raise enough money for the purchase of a chemical engine. Mr. Dudley Valentine, chairman of the committee, says that other methods of funding the purchase will be discussed.

"It has also come to our attention," Valentine said, "that, if the men are expected to turn out in force to parade on the Fourth of July, new uniforms should be procured." The old ones, Valentine said, are an embarrassment to all concerned. Red uniforms with black helmets are said to be favored, but this seems to us a misguided use of funds. Fires are fought with modern engines, not epaulets and brass buttons.

DOCTOR SAM FULLER
President, Port Newton Athletic Club

Decoration Day was always melancholy in Port Newton, and the heat was oppressive in the year Jack Dobbs pitched for us. We'd already had several days of the stuff, the first bad stretch just before summer. It began at eight in the morning and continued unceasingly. No fog. No relief. Not even a breeze.

So we drove up Park Street to the cemetery early that day–Sophie, Willie, Edith, and me. Others had the same idea, an early visit to eternity: Judge Schmidt and his son; Garnetta McCoy with her parents and siblings; the Lucianis and the Schofields, bound together, now, by the engagement of Ernie and Annie–all of us, dressed in our Sunday best, despite the heat.

Our dear little daughter Mattie, who'd died the day she was born, was laid away in that cemetery. My father also rested there. He'd been a true pioneer physician, the founder of the County Medical Society. My mother lies next to him. She was a hard worker, like my wife, and a strong Congregationalist too. My little brother, John, was there, and almost all of Edith's people; uncles and aunts and cousins beyond number.

I always supposed we would all dwell there one day, me and Edith, with poor little Mattie between us. Someday, Willie and Sophie and everyone else we knew and loved would be there too–the Elwells, the Pimentals, the Meyers.

But there is no permanence anymore. Nothing is fixed. Not even the stars. God is dead, and there is no way for a person to know who they are, or why they are, in a world that is ordered by random.

Afterwards, Willie wanted to take the picnic boat up the Strait. But Sophie had planned to go to San Francisco with Garnetta McCoy, and Edith–as always, it seemed–had work to do around the house. Me, I figured I'd spend a classic afternoon at the Railroad Exchange, talking baseball and drinking beer, anesthetized against the heat and cares of the world. So Willie, left out in the cold as it were, asked permission to go swimming in the Strait.

"We're gonna dive for Old Man Newton's treasure under the wharf."

"There's no treasure, Willie, you know that. And it's too dangerous."

"Aw, Pa. It's hot."

Later, I walked downtown. The flags were all at half mast. All the businesses, except Archer's Saloon, had closed their doors in honor of the holiday. Bill Marsh, Ramon Landsberger, and George Orr sat in their usual chairs on the plank sidewalk in front of LeRoy's Mercantile, shaded by its canopies. The hitching posts were empty. The watering troughs were dry. A black cat slept in the sun on the dusty steps of Newton Savings–old Port Newton, at the *fin de siecle*: the end of an age, the beginning of eternity.

All the boys were at the Railroad Exchange, drinking beer to cool them and make them forget. Foghorn sat at that old poker table in back, all alone, dealing out hands and betting each one himself. His jacket was off, his sleeves were rolled up. He drank lemonade and, in honor of the day, the player piano was silent for once. Cal stood behind the bar teaching Plugly McDowell the mixologist's art, or trying to.

"Never pour a jigger quite full. You can short 'em a little if you use the jigger proper. It all adds up, in time, a drop or two here another there... Beer, Doctor Sam?"

"With a whiskey up front," I told him.

"Hot today, eh?"

"Sure is."

I drank down my shot and asked McDowell how he was.

"If I'd known how hot it got out here," he said, "I'd have asked for more money."

McDowell had played well in his first game, making my same old predicament–right versus wrong; theory versus practicality–all the more difficult. And, now, rumors about Dobbs' elbow had started flying. In the last innings of the Bay Point game it had looked to me like he was trying to short-arm his throws–as if he were a shot-putter not a pitcher. So I scooped my beer mug off the bar and grabbed a fistful of peanuts, foolishly thinking I might learn something about the elbow from Foghorn. I went back to the poker table where he sat, still dealing out hands.

"Looks like you're a few players short," I said. I put down my beer and shelled a nut.

"That fellow," Foghorn said. He pointed at one of his imagined card players. "Pulled tens back to back, but he's been losing bad and losing his nerve along with his money."

"That fellow..." He swung his finger towards the imaginary player to the left of the first imaginary player. "He's got a queen showing, and is inclined to bluff. Care to run his hand, Doc? You probably need the practice."

I ruffled at that, but didn't show it. I plopped down behind the queen, peeked at the hole card, and asked him if he remembered the night Long John pulled Dobbs out of the drink.

"How could I forget?" he said.

"Do you remember the hand we were playing? When I had the three jacks showing?"

"I was entitled to that pot," he said, becoming antagonistic. "You left so I took it. You never called my bet. If you had..."

I cut him short. "I don't care about that. All I want to know is if you had that third king in the hole?"

"You know I can't divulge such a thing, Doc. That wouldn't be poker. It wouldn't be ethical."

"Ethical?" I said. "When did you ever care about ethical? And what's this crap I hear about Dobbs' elbow?"

"I don't know. What is it you hear?"

"That he's using leeches on the damn thing."

"Who told you that?"

"Sophie," I said. "Is he using leeches on himself or not?"

"Whatever he's doing, it's working. You see how he's pitching, don't you? Hell, Doc, maybe you ought to leech some of your patients, too."

"This is the twentieth century," I said. "And I don't use leeches on people. He ought to at least have me look at that elbow. It's embarrassing that he doesn't."

"Injuns don't care about doctors. He told me he's thinking of settling down here."

"Don't try to change the subject."

"I'm not trying to change the subject. He's thinking of settling down here."

"You haven't been leading him on, have you?"

Foghorn dealt the cards then shrugged his shoulders. "Who can say what the future holds. Except Doña Rosa, maybe... Hey, Doc. Pair o' queens showing. I'd bet that if I were you."

I should have told him right then and there that the future might hold a crippled arm for Jack Dobbs if he kept using it up like he was. But I hesitated, and the moment passed, as moments are inclined to do. A Chinese boy from one of the wash houses dashed in through those old batwing doors.

Foghorn yelled at him.

"Hey. Chop. Chop. No Chinks."

He gave the boy the old thumb, just like an umpire. "Out!"

But the kid didn't run. He looked at me, raised a finger and pointed west, towards Newton Wharf & Warehouse.

"Long John want you."

"Long John?" I said.

"You come quick. Boy drowned. Swimming in Strait."

"A boy?" I said.

Church bells began to ring–Congregationalist, Catholic, church bells all over town. In a flash, I realized that, permission or not, the temptation to go diving off Newton's Wharf, would be more than a boy like Willie could stand in heat like this.

"Who is it?"

"Maybe two boy," the kid said.

Again, I went running, just as on the night Dobbs floated into town, and again Foghorn, that blessed old son of a bitch, was right behind me.

There was a crowd on Newton's Wharf, still sweltering even in the dying afternoon sun. Railroad men, ferrymen, Carlo Rampoldi and the customers from his

140

barbershop, the sports and gamblers from the Railroad Inn, Doña Rosa Paredes–the whole town, damn near.

A half dozen rowboats stood just off the pier. Captain Alvarado was in one of them. Dobbs, elbow or no elbow, was in the water, clinging to the gunwales of the boat, catching his breath. He sucked in a lung full of air and dived again into the cold waters of the Strait.

John McMillan, the pharmacist, came towards us at the quick, still in his white smock. Lily Newton trailed behind him, elegant, even in her poverty–a cool blue dress, long and sweeping, a huge hat, and parasol to shield her from the hot sun.

McMillan said, "My God, Sam. Who is it?"

"We don't know. A boy," I told him. "Maybe two."

Doña Rosa shook her head. "Only one," she said, pointing towards the empty air above the Strait. "Only one spirit flying."

Lily came up behind Doña Rosa and put her hand on her arm. "Can you really see ghosts?"

"You mean you can't?" Doña Rosa said.

Only the week before I'd barely managed to talk Judge Schmidt out of committing her to the asylum in Stockton. It flashed through my mind that maybe I'd been wrong, but then, at the end of the pier, I saw Long John lift a boy out of a boat.

"Who is it?" I called, starting towards them.

Long John looked up. "Jimmy Catlett. His luck's run out."

Jimmy was Willie's best friend. The same boy who'd offered to pay to be a batboy on the ball team. He lived up School Street and he and Willie played together all the time.

"What about Willie?" I asked.

Long John said he didn't know. He laid the boy on the wharf. "I think Jimmy's the only one."

I'd brought Jimmy into this world with my own two hands. Now, I got down on him and tried to pump the water out and the air in, but he was already gone.

I'd told so many people–fathers who'd lost sons, wives who'd lost husbands or children–how life goes on and that you must bear up under the weight of the horror of death and live for the living. But one never thinks, one never imagines, that it might be their turn. And all of it, like Long John had said, was nothing but luck. Jimmy Catlett. Aged twelve years, seven months and sixteen days. Just another floater from the Strait, a water baby, cold, wet, dead.

27

BOX SCORE
The Port Newton News

```
PORT NEWTON                                  HERCULES
NAME            AB    R   BH    E   NAME            AB    R   BH    E
Lawton ss        5    0    3    1   Foskett 2b       3    1    1    1
M Luciani lf     5    0    1    0   Boyd cf          3    1    0    0
Sheets 1b        5    1    1    0   Botts 3b         4    0    0    0
E Luciani 3b     5    1    2    1   Mahoney ss       4    0    2    2
Dobbs p          4    3    2    0   Ivey 1b          4    0    1    0
McDowell c       3    1    2    0   Borba lf         4    0    0    0
Fernandez c      2    0    1    0   Sperry c         4    1    2    0
Farrell cf       4    1    2    0   Brknridge rf     4    0    0    0
Elwell 2b        5    2    1    1   Rogers p         0    0    0    0
Fr Noone rf      2    0    0    1   Klein p          1    0    0    0
Meyers rf        2    0    0    0   Elsen p          1    0    0    0

TOTALS          42    9   15    4   TOTALS          32    3    6    3

RUNS BY INNING   1   2   3   4   5   6   7   8   9   TOTAL
-----------------------------------------------------------
PORT NEWTON      0   3   4   0   0   1   1   0   0     9
HERCULES         1   1   0   0   1   0   0   0   0     3
-----------------------------------------------------------
```

HOME RUNS: Farrell BASES ON BALLS: M Luciani, Sheets,
Dobbs, Elwell, Noone; Boyd, Rogers STOLEN BASES: Lawton,
Sheets HIT BY PITCH: Lawton WINNING PITCHER: Dobbs
LOSING PITCHER: Rogers NOTATIONS: Foskett, first base on
catcher interference; Farrell, out for cutting second;
Fr. Noone, ejected for kicking

UMPIRE: Sheriff Ulshoter TIME: 2:12

28
SOPHIE FULLER
Senior, Port Union High School

Dear Diary,

Its been over a week since Jimmy Catlett drowned. Thank God dear little Wilhelm was rescued, and all, but Daddy's been moping around the house the whole time, and *life goes on, Daddy.*

We'd been planning all week on going to the Anti-Imperialist meeting, but then Daddy said maybe we shouldn't because of Jimmy. And I do worry about the poor dear. A doctor, dealing with death everyday, must steel himself to the vicissitudes of life. And besides, Professor Drake was going to give a *magic lantern show* at the Anti-Imperialist meeting, and I thought it might cheer Daddy up.

"Oh, you go if you want," he told me.

He just sat there, in his chair in the parlor, drinking his whiskey sodas. Not even reading the newspaper or petting the cat or anything. He just sat there, looking out the window like he was a thousand years old and pickled in brine. The Mother was on my side for once.

"Going to Lily's will do you good," she told him. Then she said she'd heard that Millicent Hodapp and some other old bags were going to boycott the meeting because of the nasty rumors about Lily and the savage, and ordered Daddy to go downtown and get himself shaved.

"And don't stop at the Railroad Exchange, either. You spend so much time there, people are going to start thinking you're a sot."

Daddy just shook his head, so Mother went right over to him and, just like she does to Wilhelm, pinched his ear and pulled him to his feet.

"You know what I think about the intermingling of the races, but Lily needs us and we are going!"

Wilhelm ran away and hid somewhere, but the rest of us went. Me in my pretty new shirtwaist and Daddy all clean shaven. An even more exciting prospect than the magic lantern show was that *Eva Dunkel* was going to speak. Eva's the nurse who just got back from the Philippines. She was absolutely the smartest girl in town. I was only about fourteen when she left for college, but I remember her perfectly. She went to some school back East, and that was where she met the love of her life. They wrote each other poems about God and life and love and *everything*. Then he joined up to go fight the Spaniards, as any red-blooded man should, contrary to what Daddy and Lily say.

But instead of going to liberate Cuba the poor boy ended up getting sent to the Philippines. Eva just couldn't stand being away from him, so she joined the Red Cross to be a nurse and got sent over on purpose. It's ever so romantic.

Lily stood in the reception hall, greeting her guests when we arrived. Despite the ravages that gardening in the hot sun has worked upon her, she looked absolutely radiant; a glow that never presented itself when Long John was courting her. It was as if her skin had become a source of light, and I asked what magical potion she had discovered.

"Amour," she said.

The savage was standing next to her in the receiving line. Everyone in town gossips about them and yet everyone still cheers him for winning their baseball games, the hypocrites.

But Mother was right, for once, because hardly anyone came. The Heywards and the Varneys were there, but they're the founders of the Anti-Imperialist Society and so they *had* to come. Mother kept telling Lily that more people would, too, but Lily only laughed and said she didn't care a whit. That is a healthy enough attitude for a girl, but I'm not sure she truly believes it herself.

When Riley Towne shook her hand she said to him, "You're not going to write about this are you?" Meaning write about how people were boycotting the meeting.

"Write about what?" Mr. Towne said, meaning, I believe, that he would not.

"You're looking pretty tonight, Miss Sophie," he said to me.

"Why thank you, Mr. Towne. And have you voted in the Goddess of Liberty contest as of yet?"

"It's a secret ballot, miss."

"But you are going to vote for me, aren't you?"

"I plan to vote for the young lady who best epitomizes the spirit of liberty."

Can you believe that, Diary dear? And then there is the matter of his hands. I enjoy the smell of a man's cigar, but Mr. Towne reeks of cigarette smoke and his fingers are as yellow as a Chinaman's.

When I finally saw Eva Dunkel I could hardly keep from bursting into tears. She is still dressed in the black of mourning after all these months.

"Hello, Eva," I said to her. "Remember me?"

"Why, Sophie, of course I remember you. And you're looking absolutely lovely. A regular woman, now, aren't you?"

I gave her an embrace, for words alone could not tell the depths of my sorrow for her. Bravely, she patted my back as if I were the one who needed comforting.

"There, there. You'll have to come over and have tea one day."

Later, she spoke to the Society about the horrors of the Philippines–the festering machete wounds and the disease. Our boys must eat spoiled food and as many have died from that as have died from the depredations of the guerillas. Our government should be ashamed.

Professor Drake showed Eva's slides of Manila Bay, where Admiral Dewey sank the Spaniards, and slides of the jungles, too, where the guerrillas murder our boys. There was an awful picture of a dead boy in the trenches and even one of Aguinaldo himself. Daddy says Aguinaldo is a hero to his people, but Riley Towne says he is an ambitious coward, and he's right about that, stinky cigarettes not withstanding.

After Eva's presentation was done, Professor Drake turned the operation of the magic lantern over to Calvin, and I knew that would end in disaster. The magic lantern is a monstrous thing of polished mahogany, brass and sizzling light, and Calvin means well, I know, but he is just not of a modern mind.

Professor Drake showed us slides of the fantastic world of tomorrow: "Buildings a hundred stories high, at the peaks of which, dirigibles will dock... Trains will rocket across the land... New medicines will increase life spans

until men are as immortal as gods.... War will be banished...
All men will be as rich as kings."

And that was when the magic lantern caught fire.

"Holy Christ!" Calvin yelled, useless young man
that he is.

Smoke poured out of the thing and Mrs. Heyward
screamed.

"It's going to explode!"

All Calvin could do was fan the machine like an
idiot, but Professor Drake was cool throughout. Such are the
benefits of sophistication.

"Nothing to be concerned about, folks."

He had brought a chemical extinguisher with him in
case of just such an occurrence and, knowing precisely what
to do, the professor dashed quickly to the scene, hoisted up
the extinguisher and let fly with a blast aimed directly at his
infernal lantern.

"Thank God," Mrs. Heyward said, as the flames
were quashed.

"Thank science," Professor Drake replied.

Afterwards, Lily's house was absolutely full up with
smoke. Everyone started coughing and choking and Daddy
started making motions for the door and home, but Mother
would have none of it.

"We came for Lily," she told him, "and for Lily we
shall stay."

Almost everyone left after that, including Calvin and
the professor and Eva. The few of us that were left went out
on the veranda to escape the smoke–me, Riley Town,
Mother and Daddy. Lily and the savage sat side by side on
the swing. It was fine enough outside, in the warm night with
the crickets chirping. We gazed at the dark beauty of Lily's
yard for a pleasant time. At least until Mother, who doesn't
understand the loveliness of silence, and started chattering
about the wonders of the new century.

"Do you really suppose we'll have buildings a
hundred stories high in Port Newton?"

Daddy said that if anyone had them, Port Newton
would.

Poor Daddy. He loves this old, stinky town so much
he can't see the truth of it. Port Newton is dying, and it isn't

because of Old Man Newton, either. The fit survive, the weak perish, and Port Newton is passé.

After that we talked about the war. Professor Drake had prophesied, too, that there wouldn't be any wars in the new century because they'd be too expensive. But they've always been expensive, haven't they? And there's always been war, hasn't there?

Then, the crickets on the hill fell silent and, a moment later, the gate creaked. We heard footsteps across the veranda, and there was Long John, all decked out in his Sunday best.

"Sorry I'm late," he told Lily, his head slightly bowed, his hat in hand. He is a nice man and our protector and all that, but he sometimes seems to be afraid of his own shadow.

He said he would have got there sooner but that there was some trouble down at the Front. "Sailors. Nobody hurt, though."

Daddy sighed. "Thank God for that."

Lily said, "You didn't have to come, Johnny," which I thought very cruel of her.

"Oh, no trouble," he said.

I do not think even Long John is such a bumpkin that he failed to comprehend Lily's remark. But, whatever the case, he plopped down on the porch swing, right next to the savage.

"Hope you don't mind," he said.

"Mind what?" the savage asked.

I half expected the two of them to go after each other, with hidden knives like in *Carmen*, which is the lowest, most immoral opera ever. Lily and I went to see it last year in San Francisco without telling anybody and nobody would have known if Garnetta hadn't spread it all over town.

Long John turned his hat in circles in his hands. "All this of the Fourth," he said. "The crowds. I bet we'll have fights aplenty on the Fourth."

"Human nature," Riley Towne said. "We're all savages, deep down, eh Dobbs?"

"Speak for yourself," the Indian said.

Long John then commenced to recite a litany of the fears he held regarding the Fourth: the undesirables that would infest the town, the inadequate manpower Sheriff Ulshoter had allotted him, even the firecrackers the little boys would shoot off.

"Sometimes I wonder why the hell I even bother," he said.

Mother tried to move the topic to safer ground but ended up making things worse, as usual. She told him about how Professor Drake had said we won't have any need for officers of the law in the coming century since we shall all be so rich, crime will be banished.

"Oh," Long John said. "There will always be criminals. I don't suppose I'll ever be out of a job."

The savage laughed. "There'll always be drunks and sailors, eh, Long John?"

"Yeah. Sometimes I wonder why I don't chuck it all and go play baseball for a living."

"You wouldn't last a day playing professional ball," Dobbs said. "Not with a swing like yours."

The savage began to take Long John to task for standing so far from the plate when he batted. Lily said she needed to make some more coffee, and got up and went to the kitchen. But there was plenty of coffee. She'd made pots and pots of it for the meeting.

"You afraid of the ball, Johnny?" the savage said. "Is that it?"

"I ain't afraid of nothing."

"You think so, eh?"

"I think so, eh."

If it ever came down to fists, Diary dear, which of them would fortune favor? The scientific boxer, as I suppose Long John would be, or the savage, bar-room brawler. The fittest, of course, would survive, and that, I should image, would be he of the white race, our constable, who fights on the side of justice and civilization.

29

THE PORT NEWTON NEWS
Monday, June 11

TOWNE TOPICS

THE INDIAN SCALPED
BIGGEST CROWD EVER
THE BOOS RAIN DOWN

The citizens of Port Newton showed up in happy droves at Newton Field Sunday but ended up showering hoots and hollers down upon our boys as the ball team of the Concord Athenian Club defeated them, 12–9.

When the contest commenced, an air of joy and jollity filled the newly rebuilt ballpark. Burly waiters struggled through the jam-packed grandstand hunched under the weight of bins filled with iced-down bottles of Newton Steam Beer. The fans waved flags and sang lullabies to the Concords. The Noble Brotherhood of Redskins waved their tomahawks and whooped their war-whoops.

In short, every soul present expected the beloved lads of the Port Newton Athletic Club to make short work of the Concords, and such seemed to be the case in the early innings. The Newtons tallied two in the third, three in the fourth, and four more in the fifth, while newcomer Plugly McDowell gunned down any base runner who dared contemplate thievery. So great did the rout appear to be, that the Newtons, fans and players alike, openly taunted the Concords, not only the ball team, but that primitive city itself.

"You don't even got sewers!"

"Come back when you got sewers!"

But, alas, the Newton's ace pitcher Jack "Chief" Dobbs began to labor in the sixth and, when errors by Lawton and Elwell betrayed the big Indian, the taunts that rang down from the grandstand were no longer aimed at the opposition, but at Dobbs himself.

"Get a white man out there!"

Later, George Orr, who remembers the championship days of old and was among the loudest of the hooters, complained that players today just don't understand the game anymore.

"Heart is what makes a ballplayer," Orr went on. "But I doubt these fellows could tell heart from tongue if it was served up on a silver platter."

Afterwards, Dobbs denied that injuries to his elbow, past or present, had anything to do with the defeat.

"Anyone can have one bad day, can't they? Go ask Sheets if you want to know about bad days. He came up with runners on the sacks more than once and couldn't even put the ball in play. Ask Sheets if you want to know about bad days."

Indeed, a chance to put the issue completely to rest in the early frames came a-cropper when the once potent constable went down on strikes with the bat still on his shoulders.

Still, Long John refused to say he was in a batting slump.

"Yes, I know such things exist, but remember, those Concord boys have a fine team and the way baseball is set up, one team must win and the other must lose. There is no getting around it."

Despite all these woes, the Newtons still appeared to have a chance at victory in the ninth frame. But with two out and runners on first and third, Captain Cuyler Edwards of the Concords called time out and trotted from his position at third base to the mound.

Edwards spoke a few low words to pitcher A.P. Nelson, proprietor of Concord Mercantile, corner of Galindo and Main in Concord, then called to first-sacker Rube Reid, to join the conference. Again, words were whispered, and only when Judge Schmidt, the umpire for the game, demanded that the colloquium conclude did the players return to their respective positions.

Now, pitcher Nelson makes his windup. Calvin Elwell edges off first base. Nelson poses in the stretch and a hush of anticipation descends upon the crowd. Suddenly, third baseman Edwards shouts out, "Hey, Schmidty!" and at

151

the precise instant when Umpire Schmidt instinctively turns towards the sound of his name, first baseman Reid shoves runner Elwell to the ground, and pitcher Nelson whirls and fires the ball to first.

"You're out!" Judge Schmidt cried, turning back to the play just in time to see Elwell tagged, but not the foul that preceded it.

A rhubarb of spectacular proportions, punctuated by boos, curses and the heaving of beer bottles, delayed the progress of play for a good fifteen minutes, but availed the Newtons nothing.

"I saw what I saw," Judge Schmidt later said, "and I call what I see."

"We just took a leaf out of your Newtons' book," said Captain Edwards of the Concords. "You fellows have turned into bushwhacking redskins. Why shouldn't we?"

Foghorn Murphy, who is thought to have lost heavily in betting on the game, said that dirty play such as the Concords exhibited has no place in the friendly brand of baseball played along the Strait.

"It is the worst case of outright cheating I have seen since the Stolen Championship of 1888. Those men should be whipped as dogs and driven into the desert to starve."

When your reporter repeated Captain Edwards' charge that just such underhanded tactics seem to be a reason for Port Newton's baseball resurgence of late, Murphy said that nothing could be further from the truth.

"Above all things, the Port Newton Athletic Club stands for fair play and reason."

When your reporter further ventured that the beer the Athletic Club has begun selling at the park seemed unreasonably priced, Murphy retorted that certain charges, of necessity, need apply.

"You don't think those waiters work free, do you?"

Perhaps the only happy circumstance for the Newtons on a day marked by catcalls and boos, was the performance of pitcher Charles "Icebox" Meyers, who relieved Dobbs in the eighth, and allowed but one run in pitching the last two innings.

"I believe I have at last regained my form," Meyers said. "And if Mr. Dobbs should falter again, I shall be ready to stand at the very center of things."

THE FOURTH OF JULY
A CELEBRATION FOR THE AGES
THE PERFIDY OF THE BENICIANS

The preparations for the great holiday spectacle scheduled to play itself out in the streets of Port Newton on the second, third, and fourth days of July proceeds apace. One thing is certain: the town will be a mass of red, white, and blue bunting and brightly lit, at that. For already, the posts and electrical wires that will turn the night into day are being erected along Railroad Avenue and Main Street all the way up to School.

The redoubtable David Drake, professor of science at the University of California, has agreed to attempt a balloon ascension over Port Newton during the holiday. This feat, he says, will be a fitting way to usher in a century when the skies will be filled with just such aerial ships. The professor states that an accident, such as the one that almost resulted in the destruction of the International Hotel in 1894, is no longer to be feared on account of advances in the design and construction of "aeronautical chariots" such as his.

But with only a month remaining before the Grand and Glorious Fourth, our friends the Benicians have demanded that the sailboat race, scheduled for the second day of festivities, be conducted from their shores.

As of now, the race is slated to begin and end in Port Newton, and this is the only thing that makes any sense at all. Port Newton is where the crowds will be. Port Newton is where the barbecue, scheduled for noon that same day, will take place. The open-air vaudeville show, following the race, is likewise to be held on these southern and more commodious shores of the Strait.

"You people already got all the ball games and the trap shoot," Mr. Anthony Rossi of Benicia stated. "Why not let us have the boat race? Without it, we might just keep ourselves to home."

153

Faced with such demands, the Committee on Venues has gone into deep deliberation.

LOCAL BREVITIES

Wilbur Dean of Martinez met with an untimely end Saturday evening. His brother, Watson, had just returned home from a visit to Walnut Creek and was taking his pistol out of his pocket when it somehow became caught in the fabric. When Watson gave the pistol a jerk to remove it, it went off, and the bullet struck Wilbur in the right eye, killing him instantly. Sheriff Ulshoter says an inquest will be held later this week.

Billy Lawton and Cal Elwell had a set-to in the Railroad Exchange after the ballgame on Sunday. The fists flew, but no damage was done. We can understand this of Billy, but what's got into you lately, Cal? Is a certain doctor's daughter spending too much time at a certain soda fountain?

The Young Men's Institutes of Port Newton, Martinez, and Benicia are sponsoring a picnic excursion to Laurel Grove at Point Tiburon in Marin County on Sunday. A steamer will leave Martinez wharf at 7 a.m., and pick up passengers in Port Newton and Benicia before getting underway for Tiburon. The Y.M.I. expects over a thousand picnickers. Round-trip tickets are priced at $4 for adults and $.50 for children.

There is much discontent among the stevedores on Grangers Wharf at present. They charge that Mr. Hurley Sullivan has been hiring men on as warehousemen and having them do stevedore work instead. This action causes men who formerly made $20 per ship to have to settle for only $10.

The hot weather does not bother us as much as do the mosquitoes.

The students of Mr. Charles Meyers at Newton Union High School have given him a gold mounted fountain pen as a token of their esteem.

The excursion rates offered by the Southern Pacific Railroad were too tempting for W.F. McMillan, Ernest Lucas, and Joe Soto, who took the train north to Shasta to do some fishing.

The ladies of the Catholic and Congregationalist churches have interested themselves in the children of Mr. Jerry O'Connor, who was an employee of the Newton Wharf & Warehouse Company before it shut down three years ago. The children, two in number, have been in desperate straits since Mr. O'Connor passed from consumption. They will live with Mr. and Mrs. Erskine until further notice. Anyone who feels inclined to donate clothes or money should contact Mrs. Edith Fuller. The Red Cross Society, led by Mrs. Evelyn Lasalle, is also taking up a collection.

Alex Tierny is having trouble with his eyes and Dr. Sam Fuller has ordered a treatment of eyewashes in an attempt to save his sight.

A large crowd was present at the Rebekah Lodge's social on Monday evening. Ice cream was furnished and all agreed that it was a pleasant evening.

Mrs. Nellie Buck of Buck's Ranch has sent your editor a box of Royal Ann cherries. The fruit is very ample and of the finest quality for either eating or canning.

GODDESS OF LIBERTY

Votes in the Goddess of Liberty contest, to determine which of the Strait's lovelies will reign over our gigantic three-day Fourth of July celebration, are pouring in, and the contest seems to have resolved itself into a tight, four-filly race. We give the latest totals below.

Isabella Thayer (Crockett)	1,872
Hanna Joost (Port Newton)	1,745
Genevieve Hurley (Martinez)	1,505
Bessie Swift (Benicia)	1,434
Sophie Fuller (Port Newton)	762
Pearl Lowell (Walnut Creek)	517
Connie Garibaldi (Pacheco)	175

MEETINGS AND EVENTS

Beyond the various and numerous meetings of the various and numerous Fourth of July Committees, there seem to be no further chats, colloquies, conferences, or caucuses scheduled this week, making it both particular and curious.

DOCTOR SAM FULLER
President, Port Newton Athletic Club

It was a Monday morning, eleven days after Jimmy Catlett's death. I was in my office with my medical books, my filing cards, and the old skeleton that hung in the closet, still trying to make sense of the senseless.

My wife knocked on the door, opened it, and stuck her head in.

"Are you seeing patients today, Doctor Sam? It's Riley Towne."

"Of course I'm seeing patients. Why the hell else would I be here if I weren't seeing patients?"

"Whatever you say."

She opened the door wider, and Riley came in, clad in a checkered suit that was about as loud as John Philip Sousa. I could tell the old son of a bitch had had a few by the smell of his breath, but I was no man to judge. I stood up, shook his hand, and asked him how things were going down at the newspaper.

"Well enough," he told me. "I've been getting more job printing, lately. Hell on the fingernails, though."

They were black from the ink, the cuticles torn.

"I suppose," he said, "that if I'd wanted to get rich, I'd have been a doctor."

"What the hell do you mean by that?"

"Oh, you seem to have it pretty good. A good wife, a family. Plenty of time to sit around and drink boilermakers."

I pointed at the coffee cup in front of me. "Does that look like a boilermaker?"

"Don't get touchy now."

"Look, Riley. You were the one who came to see me, not the other way around. What's the problem?"

"The cough," he said. "It seems a bit worse, these days."

"Of course it's worse. It's the damn cigarettes. I've told you and told you. Those things'll kill you one day. Go back to cigars. That's my advice."

I told him to take off his coat so I could have a listen at his chest. There was a fifth of something called "Doctor King's New Discovery Elixir" in his coat pocket. I pulled it out and perused the label.

"What are you doing with this crap?" I said. "For one thing, it's for female problems."

"Yes, but it works on coughs, too." He took a swig and offered me one. "Works on everything, actually. Cures what ails you. It's magic, McMillan says."

I tried it–cherry syrup, alcohol, codeine probably, or some sort of opiate derivative. Magic, indeed.

"Not bad," I said.

I took another swig and got my stethoscope.

Riley Towne was forty-five years old, a little stove up in the chest and abdomen, but not the worst specimen I'd ever seen. I had a listen at his lungs, but they didn't seem any worse than usual. Some wheezing. Some congestion. But the heart seemed strong and regular.

"Bringing up lots of phlegm?" I asked.

"In the mornings," he said. "But that's all."

I listened again and had him breathe. I didn't detect anything new, but I figured I was on to him.

"Is there something else I can help you with?" I asked.

"What do you mean?"

"Sometimes people come in here and tell me they've got one problem, but they really don't. It's really something else, but for some reason they're afraid to tell me. I end up having to dig it out of them."

He took another shot of Doctor King's Elixir.

"It's the whole thing," he said.

"What whole thing?"

"You know. The Indian and all."

"You came to see me about the Indian?"

"It's crap, Doc. You know it. I know it. Everyone knows it. In their hearts, at least. You're just too caught up in the whole thing to admit it."

"And what the hell am I supposed to admit? There's no harm in us winning a few ballgames is there? Look what it's done for the town."

"First it was the Indian. Then this McDowell fellow. Now you're charging admission and selling beer."

I shrugged him off. "The improvements cost a lot. The ballpark, you know."

"It's not good for the children."

"When the hell did you ever care about the children? I'm the one who cares about the damn children."

"You've seen how the little boys follow Dobbs around. Why, it was like he was president of the United States or something. It's not right, Doc."

"I don't see any harm in it."

"And now you're going to bench Billy Lawton. Hell, Sam, the ball team is Billy's life."

"Billy Lawton? I don't know anything about Billy Lawton getting benched. Why would we bench Billy?"

"Too many errors. Foghorn wants to bring in another fellow from Oakland, or so my sources tell me. But this isn't the professional leagues, Doc, this is good, old friendly Port Newton. Or it was once, before all this started."

"What the hell do you want me to do about it?"

"You're the damn president of the damn P.N.A.C., aren't you?" He passed me the elixir. "Here, have some liquid courage."

The blood rushed to my head, hot and steamy, and my lid blew right off.

"You don't come in here and give me any crap about courage. I had a boy drown last week. I birthed him with my own hands. Two months ago, Long John and I pulled Ida Mencken and her babies out of a goddamn well, and there was little Peggy McCann, poisoned from eating bad rhubarb, and so on and so on and so on. It's death I'm dealing with, not baseball. And don't you see? It's not some future, unimaginable death by cigarettes. It's death in the present tense."

There was a dreadful silence following my tirade, which gave me enough time to regret it all.

"I'm sorry," I said.

Riley started to put his shirt back on. "I suppose I'd better go."

"So what do you want me to do, go bust Foghorn in the nose?"

"Well, at least he'd have a busted nose, then." He slid into his coat, grabbed his hat and stepped to the door.

"I'll leave you the elixir," he said. "I think you need it more than I do."

"To hell with you," I told him, and the door slammed, shutting me in.

I swigged on that elixir and muttered to that skeleton of a once-living man that hung in my closet. "The goddamn nerve of him."

I swigged again, then again, and by the time I finished the bottle, I thought that what I needed was more–or perhaps one of those awful Lunks that Lily Newton drank. The place to get both was McMillan's so I stumbled out of the office, and reeled down the hall, bouncing off the left wall, then rebounding off the right.

"Doctor Sam?" my wife said, watching in wonder as I lurched down the front steps.

"I'm going downtown," I told her.

"Oh no you're not. You're drunk, in no condition to go anywhere, and I won't have you replacing poor Lily as the talk of the town."

"I am not a child," I told her.

"You and Willie," Edith replied, but I just kept going.

I staggered down the hill, past Lily's, past the schoolyard where just a few days before Jimmy Catlett and Peggy McCann played. Then, looking back over my shoulder, I saw the Chief, coming down the hill behind me– from Lily's, I supposed–and the boys in the schoolyard saw him, too. They surged towards him, surrounding him and hurling question after question at him.

"Are you gonna win next Sunday, Chief?"

"Probably."

"How's the old soup bone, Chief?"

"Fine. Just fine."

I stopped and waited, realized that I was swaying in the breeze and steadied myself against an old gnarled, mother oak. When Dobbs reached me, and the two of us were both surrounded by little boys in all varieties–dirty, clean and neat, shoeless, rich, poor. I told Dobbs that I'd heard he was a bad influence on our youth.

"Hell," he said. "It's their fault I'm like this in the first place. I figure they're a bad influence on me... Hitting the sauce a little early, ain't you Doc? A little hair of the dog? Is that it?"

"A little hair of the hare," I replied, something that seemed pretty damned funny to me at the time–as senseless as everything else, now.

"I'm not drunk" I said, "just elixired."

"What's that supposed to mean?"

"It means I'm going to bust Foghorn in the nose."

"Glad to see you're letting your hair down, Doc. I always figured you for wound too tight. Like a cheap clock."

"I'm not cheap," I protested. "I just have neurasthenia, like everyone else."

We began to walk. Port Newton was as it always was–the three old men in front of the mercantile, the buggies laboring up Main, the Beehive Cafe, half empty. A Mexican boy sold copies of the newspaper at the corner of Main and Park. Doña Rosa Paredes wandered along the street talking to herself, not in English or even Spanish, from what I could tell. Latin, maybe. The old girl was getting worse.

In McMillan's, Dobbs and I found two pretty little white chairs at one of those pretty little white tables. I almost slipped right off mine as I sat, and demanded Lunks from Billy Lawton.

"I hear Foghorn's going to bench you," I said to Billy. "Bring in a fellow from Oakland to take your place."

"Not me," Billy said. "It's Cal that's benched. I'm just moving over to second. Foghorn convinced Cal to sacrifice himself for the team."

"The son of a bitch," I said.

"Which son of a bitch?" Billy asked.

"He can't bench everybody."

Dobbs pointed at me and said to Billy, "He's gonna bust old Foggy in the nose."

"Really?" Billy asked. "When?"

"Just as soon as I get my Lunk," I said. "And that reminds me," I told Dobbs. "You ought to let me look at your elbow, and I mean that, Chief. Leeches or no leeches. Lunks or no Lunks."

"It'll be fine by Sunday."

160

"You just might end your days a cripple if you keep using it up like you do."

"Everybody's a cripple. Look at you. Look at Lily."

"I'm no cripple," I said.

"Yeah, right."

"At the game yesterday," I told him, "somebody threw a goddamn beer bottle at me."

Dobbs shrugged as if it were nothing. "The sons of bitches paid their money, so they got a right, you know?"

"John Varney threw it."

"Who?"

"John Varney. President of the Anti-Imperialist Society."

The Chief shook his head. "Ironic, ain't it? Hey, when one of those things hits you, it really hurts."

Right after that, Billy Lawton took a break from work so he could "see the show," and together the three of us climbed the pedestrian bridge over the railroad tracks. The little switch engine that tended the ferry belched smoke and sparks, and amidst all that we descended towards the Front: the beaneries, the billiard parlors, the cheap hotels, the wash houses, and saloons.

Inside the Railroad Exchange, we climbed the back stairs to the Athletic Club clubroom. We knocked the secret knock, and the spy hole in the door slid open. A single, bloodshot eye greeted me.

"What's the password?"

"For christsakes, Foghorn, open up. It's me and Dobbs and Billy."

He opened the door and we stepped in. Plugly McDowell and another fellow, who bore an ugly resemblance to him, lounged on two of the old easy chairs that lay heavy in the clubroom.

"Doc," Foghorn said. "You're just in time to shake hands with the newest member of the P.N.A.C."

The fellow lifted his glass in an easy *salud*–a shot glass full of whiskey it was.

"Meet Booger McDowell," Foghorn said. "Plugly's brother."

I took a swing at Foghorn, missed, lost my balance and almost fell on my face. I don't remember much about whatever happened next.

31

BOX SCORE
The Port Newton News

```
Port Newton                  Martinez
NAME           AB  R  BH   E  NAME           AB   R   BH   E
B McDwl ss-3b   5  1  2    0  Bockley lf      5   0   0    1
Lawton 2b-ss    4  1  2    0  Green 1b        4   0   0    0
M Luciani 3b    2  1  1    1  Ward ss         4   1   1    0
Elwell 2b       1  0  0    0  Chavez 3b       4   2   2    0
E Luciani lf    4  0  0    0  Boynton rf      3   1   1    0
Fernandez rf    1  0  0    1  Warren c        2   0   0    1
Dobbs p         4  1  2    0  Wyatt p         4   0   2    0
Sheets 1b       5  1  0    0  Mellus 2b       4   0   0    0
P McDowell c    4  0  2    0  Talbart cf      3   0   0    0
Farrell cf      4  1  1    0
F Noone rf-lf   4  1  1    1

TOTALS         38  7  11   3  TOTALS         33   4   6    2

RUNS BY INNING  1  2  3  4  5  6  7  8  9   TOTAL
-----------------------------------------------
PORT NEWTON     4  0  0  0  3  0  0  0  0     7
MARTINEZ        0  2  0  0  0  0  2  0  0     4
-----------------------------------------------
```

BASES ON BALLS: M Luciani, Elwell 2, Sheets; Boynton,
Warren STOLEN BASES: Lawton, Farrell, B McDowell HIT
BY PITCH: Warren WINNING PITCHER: Dobbs LOSING PITCHER:
PASSED BALLS: Warren NOTATIONS: M Luciani, ejected for
tripping; E Luciani, ejected for fighting; Manager
Murphy, ejected for foul language in the 7th

UMPIRE: Judge Schmidt TIME: 2:43

32
Calvin Elwell
Bartender and Second Baseman

It was June, I remember–midsummer's eve–or almost so, and there we were, me and Sophie, the Chief and Lily, skittering our way across the railroad tracks down by the ferry, heading for Benicia. Most times people took the local train at the depot and rode over in that on the ferry, getting off at the depot in Benicia. But, that night, Lily was feeling her oats, and so we'd decided to embark the ferry this cheaper, but more dangerous way, running across the tracks, dodging the yard goats and switchers.

There was a Shakespeare play over in Benicia and Sophie wanted to see it because she was thinking of quitting the Port Newton Dramatic Society and joining the Benicia Thespians.

The Chief was all for it. "If they pay more, jump. That's what I'd do."

Sophie fell for it hook, line and sinker. "They don't pay us at all."

"They don't?" the Chief exclaimed in mock surprise. "What the hell do you do it for, then?"

Lily, who was feeling oatty, like I said, punched him in the arm. "Shame on you!"

I always did walk on eggs around Lily, jolly or not, for I never knew where her mercurial nature might take her. But she laughed a lot, that night, which was good to see. So there we were, dancing across those tracks, dodging those steam engines that were hot as tea kettles.

I was all thumbs when it came to Sophie in those days, she still teases me about it. And when I tripped on the tracks, and almost went sprawling, she let me have it.

"My word, Calvin! No wonder Mr. Murphy benched you."

Sophie was all aflutter that evening, speculating on how she figured the Chief was going to ask Lily to marry him that night.

"It's amour," she kept saying to me. Whispering and excited. "Their fates intertwined the moment she woke him with her kiss."

Sophie was strong on amour and kisses in those days, and the two of them, Lily and the Chief, were acting very lovey-dovey, indeed.

Once we boarded, we sat down in the little lunchroom they had on the ferry mainly for the passengers who wished to debark their trains while they rode across. But a redskin and a white woman together drew so many looks that Lily got to feeling uncomfortable.

"I can't stand it in here anymore." Too stuffy, she said it was.

I feared her mood would take a dark turn with that, but once we were out on deck the air seemed to cheer her, and all four of us ended up standing by the rail looking out into the waters of the Strait. It wasn't unpleasant as the air was warm, it being midsummer and all.

It's gone now, but that ferry really was a giant. It could hold two whole trains and more. Two big side-wheels on it. Four sets of tracks from side to side. All muscle and clank and smoke. Sometimes, when Doc had a few too many, he'd lament, "Everything is for the machines, these days."

Him and Foghorn used to debate that and everything else too, sitting at Foghorn's poker table or elbows on the bar, a foot up on that brass rail.

"Machines are the natural order of things," Foghorn would say.

No wonder Doc took that swing at him.

It was only a mile or so across to Benicia, and the railroad boys were so good breaking up and loading those trains that the trip didn't take long at all. We look back with nostalgia on those horse-and-buggy days now, but time always sells at a premium and so it did, even then.

The play we were going to see was outdoors, in the park, just up Benicia's main street, which they called First instead of Main. Benicia was pretty rough around the waterfront, like Port Newton, but not so bad, I think. Sophie, the little fool, didn't mind the stares from the rough types at all, and displayed herself as proud as could be.

165

"You'll protect me, won't you Calvin?"

I didn't say anything to that, being a coward at heart, and, though she was hard on me at times, I didn't hold it against her. Most nice girls, you see, wouldn't even dare be seen with a fellow like me, a bartender, that is, since it would be bad for their reputations. But Sophie didn't care about such things, wore me like a medal she did. No wonder I ended up stuck with her.

Lily and the Chief drew a few remarks when we passed the saloons. But she just put her arm inside the Chief's, kept her eyes down and quickened her pace.

"Look at the squaw!"

"Some buck she's got there."

I feared that the Chief would take umbrage to such comments. It is an unfortunate fact that disputes between men always come down to violence, or at least the threat of it. But so it has always been, and so it shall always be. I figured he probably had that little thirty-two strapped to his calf, and I didn't want any part of such shenanigans.

"Let 'em talk," was all he said as we hurried by.

Up in the park it was very pleasant. The trees were all hung with red and green and blue Chinese lanterns. The summer air was warm and fragrant and little black squirrels skittered along over the tree roots bulging up from the ground just as we had skittered across the railroad tracks.

I never was much for Shakespeare. Try as I might, I just can't follow the words. And more, I never understood why the players always speak them so quickly. I don't suppose people ever spoke so quick in Shakespeare's day any more than they do now, so why speak the lines like that? Especially since they're so hard to follow in the first place?

Sophie told me, "They must go 'trippingly off the tongue,'" but I don't think she understood them any more than me.

I will give Shakespeare this, however: He usually filled his plays with lots of war and blood and sword fights, like in a dime novel or Western movie. But the particular one we saw that night was all laughter and jokes and people in love with the wrong people. But it gets straightened out by magic at the end, so everything was put right.

166

"If we lived in the city," Lily said to the Chief, "we could go see plays all the time."

When I heard that, I thought maybe Sophie was right after all, and that the Chief really was going to ask her to marry him. But then the Chief said, "I like it here, fine," so I guessed he wasn't interested in wedding bells, at least not that night.

Afterwards, Sophie couldn't stop talking about how wonderful the play was. The Chief said he'd seen better productions of it back East even though I figured him not much for Shakespeare, either. Lily said she liked happy endings, which I thought ironic, even then.

"I'm starved," she said, still in a jolly mood. "Let's go to Hoffmeister's Gardens."

This was the Sunday night following our second game against Martinez, I forgot to say, and the Chief's elbow was killing him, though he didn't show it. We won the game, but it hadn't been quick work. At first it looked like we would win in a breeze. But they didn't quit and it wasn't easy holding them off. The boys got a little desperate and that was when the dirty play really got started: the tripping and fighting and intimidating. Foghorn got kicked out of the game when he spit on Judge Schmidt. I never would have gotten to play, myself, if Mike Luciani hadn't got kicked out, too.

Worse, more and more of the boys were becoming disaffected with the whole thing. Charlie Meyers always had been unhappy with the arrangements, all that of "gain the world but lose your soul." And Hec Fernandez hadn't been pleased when Plugly McDowell had taken his spot. Nor I when Booger had taken mine, and left me warming the bench.

After the game, the Chief had spent the whole afternoon with his elbow in a bucket of ice. I helped him leech himself a couple of days after, which was when I complained and asked him what I could do to get into the games more.

He said, "Play better, kid," and that was the end of that.

167

But I'm getting ahead of myself for I was going to tell you about what happened at Hoffmeister's Gardens the night we all went to Benicia.

Hoffmeister's was filled with people, everyone sitting at long tables, drinking beer and lifting their glasses. The same Negroes who'd put on such a good show at the May Day Dance, the Mississippi Minstrels, were entertaining there. They had always just fascinated Sophie. When they came out, dancing and yelling, Sophie tried to tell some story about how the leader of them really talked like a white man, but it was very loud in there and Sophie didn't always make sense when she told stories.

The Chief looked a little askance at the whole situation but said, "I guess we'll be all right." I realized then, that for all his bravado, the Chief had learned to be a cautious man. Especially when being with a white woman in a place where white men were doing some heavy drinking.

Lily was still very jolly and eating sausages like they were going out of style. She said, "Oh, nothing will happen," but that didn't do much to ease my mind.

The minstrels had just finished doing an act and everybody was laughing and applauding. Rufus, the leader of these darkies, went around shaking hands with people and being friendly, which no one seemed to mind. What shouldn't have surprised me, but did, was that he seemed to know the Chief.

"Say there, Jack," he said, talking just like a white man as Sophie had said.

We were sitting at one of those long tables, up at one end of it, a little away from most of the others, not exactly shunned, but not exactly in the midst of the revel, either.

Rufus asked the Chief what he was up to these days.

The Chief shrugged his shoulders. "Just trying to survive."

I didn't realize it at the time, but this wasn't just some casual expression the Chief was using, that about just wanting to survive. Later on, after all that happened happened, we got Father Noone drunk on cheap red wine and coaxed him into what amounts to breaking his vows and spilling the beans about what the Chief had told him in the confessional, right after Long John fished him out of the Strait.

It seems the Chief hadn't just slipped off the deck of the ferry or been mugged or gotten into a fight over a dice game like we all thought. The truth was that the Chief had tried to do himself in. He'd come out on deck broke, drunk, hungry, friendless, and forlorn. He looked into those cold waters and figured he'd nothing left to lose and so he'd decided to take the gamble, roll the dice on going to heaven, that is. And so he did. He jumped over the side, hit his head, got sucked under by the driving wheels of the ferry, and had a vision of hellfire and brimstone so nasty he figured it was real.

But I'm getting ahead of myself again for none of us knew any of that on the night we rode the ferry to Benicia, and saw *A Midsummer Night's Dream*, and quaffed a few beers at Hoffmeister's Gardens.

Rufus, the darky, came over to us in Hoffmeister's. Him and the Chief said hello, for the Chief knew absolutely everybody in the world, it seemed. Lily told Rufus how much we'd liked his show, he thanked her, and that was about all there was to it. Him and the Chief shook hands and then Rufus was off, grinning and talking it up while people all applauded and shook his hand.

"Oh yas suh, we do loves to dance... Yas, ma'm. We got a natural talent for it... Yas suh."

Later on, Rufus got beat up bad over in Port Newton, during the Fourth of July celebration, and Doc was extremely upset. But then, I'm getting ahead of myself again.

Tony Rossi, of all people, came over to us, there in Hoffmeister's, a great mug of beer in his hand and a beer glow on his face. I thought, "Oh-oh, this is trouble," for I didn't figure he'd exactly forgotten about how the Chief had spiked him and gashed his ankle when we'd beat them a month or so before.

But Big Tony was as smooth as Rufus. I'd never known him beyond playing ball against him, and this experience puzzled me for a time.

"How's that leg of yours?" the Chief asked. "Sorry I had to do that."

"Hell, Chief, it's baseball, is all."

Now that I think about it, I realize he was one of those fellows, like Billy Lawton, who change completely when they play ball. Dr. Jekyll to Mr. Hyde. They throw their bat against the backstop when they strike out, curse and start fights. Liquor also does that to men, and women, too, when a few drinks can turn them from beauties into beasties.

For that reason I once thought Prohibition, which is the law as I write this, would be a good thing. But I do not think so now. Alcohol makes for more wife beatings, fights and killings–of which I saw all three when I tended bar–but if people want a thing they will find a way to get it. Just like the girlie shows of the Barbary Coast. Just like the Chinamen coming over. The people cannot be stopped, and especially not by politicians and blue noses.

That was about all that passed that night in Benicia, but for one more thing. We said our goodbyes to Big Tony about then, who was all love and kisses. But then he eyed Sophie and Lily from behind as we walked out and said something to his companions, and they all laughed. I couldn't hear what it was, but I don't suppose it was very complimentary. That was when I knew for certain that Big Tony was a man who couldn't be trusted.

We walked back down towards the ferry, and all was jolly once again until we again came to the saloons and dives of Benicia's waterfront. We braced ourselves to walk the gauntlet again, and for more taunts and insults.

"Just keep going," the Chief advised, as we got nearer. "Don't let 'em know they're getting your goat."

There were the same men, on the same plank sidewalks, lounging in front of the same saloons, holding up the walls, you might say, but this time it was different. This time, they began to sing.

"Daisy, Daisy, give me your answer do..."

"Just keep going," the Chief said. "Just keep going and smile."

There wasn't any more trouble after that, and we rode home on the *Benicia*, standing quietly at the rail watching the dark waters, the same ones the Chief had jumped into when he'd tried to end it all but like I said, I didn't know about that then.

33
SOPHIE FULLER
Senior, Port Newton Union High School

Dear Diary,

You'll never guess. I'm to be a Handmaiden of the Goddess!

Today was the last day of school, the last ever in my life, and Mr. Meyers finally gave me back my story, the one about love among the Bohemians.

"I like how you keep things in order in this one," he said, adding that too many writers allow their thoughts to run away with them and get all jumbled up. "But *you* don't. Not here at least. It's all in the right order."

Recognition at last! And the poor man, saddled with that awful wife of his.

But that was today, Diary dear, and yesterday is my concern here, the Commencement Dinner. It was at Pimental Hall, of course. Same old bunting. Same old ribbons. Same old people. Spaghetti from Vinci's! How gauche!

What was odd was that Hanna Joost made a huge point of wanting to sit next to me. We have not exactly been friendly of late because of the Goddess of Liberty contest, and I still can't understand how anyone, even a man, could vote for a girl with Titian bronze hair.

Halfway through the spaghetti slurping, Hanna leaned close to me and said, "I've got to talk with you, Sophie."

It seemed awfully stupid, since she was sitting right next to me and all. So I said, "Well, go ahead and talk."

"It's confidential. I'll talk with you later. Just don't forget."

"How could I possibly?"

Then, for the next hour, our fate was a maze of tangled spaghetti and pokey speeches.

"We venture forth into a vibrant and auspicious century..."

"We are the new hope of a new age..."

"We will be called upon to accomplish great deeds..."

Afterward, those of us who hadn't died of boredom had to help pull back the tables *ourselves* for the dance. And we "the promise of the future." Indeed!

The dance was fine with a string band from Walnut Creek, and for once, at least, there were enough boys to go around; although most are afraid of pretty girls. I could have danced with any boy I chose, whatsoever, but I stayed mostly with poor Calvin because he is so pitiful.

"Do you like me, Sophie?"

"Well of course I like you, Calvin. I wouldn't dance with you if I didn't like you."

"I mean, do you *really* like me?"

The poor boy.

Hanna Joost asked me if I wanted to dance with her during a slow waltz because we'd be able to talk, and I said I would. I insisted on leading, as Hanna is incapable of doing so, and as we glided along she said to me, "You know what's going to happen, don't you?"

I said I most certainly did not.

She said, "We're splitting the Port Newton vote. Isabella Thayer is going to win the Goddess contest if we don't do something to stop her."

I told her it mattered little to me. "I suppose I could have won easily if I'd tramped all over town making a spectacle of myself."

"Look, Sophie. Don't be stupid."

"Me?" I said. "You're the one with the Titian bronze hair."

"Listen for once. If I win, I'll make you one of my Handmaidens. I promise."

I was much surprised to say the least. The Handmaidens get to ride on the Goddess's float right along with her and wave to the crowd, just like the Goddess. The Goddess has to read the Declaration of Independence aloud from the reviewing stand on the Fourth, but the Handmaidens don't have to do *anything*. Everyone exalts them almost as much as they do the Goddess, and last year, the Handmaidens got their pictures in the San Francisco papers right alongside the Goddess.

I was truly touched and told her so, but just as I suspected her motives were not all so pure.

172

"Don't let it go to your head," she said. "I've got to win first, and here's what you have to do. Withdraw from the contest and tell all your supporters to vote for me."

I told her it was a very interesting proposition, but most of the votes were already in.

"I've talked to Mr. Glass, on the committee," she said. "And he's going to take care of it."

"Take care of what?"

"Just leave it to him."

Then I remembered that Mr. Glass is *the man who counts the votes*. "And who will be your other Handmaiden of Honor?" I asked.

"My sister," she said.

I thought for a moment. "Why, Margo's nice and all. And loyalty is a fine trait in a goddess. But what about Garnetta McCoy?"

"Don't push it, Sophie."

"I'm not pushing anything. But Garnetta, well, you know. She isn't the prettiest girl in the world, and that means the two of us will look all the prettier. By comparison, I mean."

For once, Hanna used the brain God gave her, and when she agreed, I promised I would withdraw first thing. So, good to my word, right after school today, and right after Mr. Meyers showered me with praise for my story, I went downtown and told Mr. Glass of my decision.

"Sophie," he said, "you've made the adult choice."

"Well, of course," I told him.

As I walked back home, up the hill, I decided I ought to tell Lily about my good fortune. I expected she'd be out in her yard laboring away, but she wasn't, so I went right on up the steps and knocked on the door. I am not a snoop, Diary dear, but when she didn't answer I tried the door and *it was open*.

"Yoohoo, Lily?" I called, sticking my head inside.

Then I thought I heard voices coming from somewhere and called and called but no one answered and by now I was worried, so I went bravely in.

"Yoohoo."

She wasn't in the parlor or the sitting room or on the veranda, and I even stuck my head in the kitchen, which was

absolutely filthy. I went up the back stairs and remembered
how, when I was little, Lily and I would play ghosts when it
was dark and rainy and especially when there was thunder
and lightning. One time, I got lost among the halls and
rooms and balconies upstairs. The air was all electric and
there he was, all of a sudden, in a lightning flash, Old Man
Newton.

"Who are *you*, little girl?"

He scared the living daylights out of me. He had that
long white beard like Santa's, but he wasn't fat and jolly at
all. Lean and hungry he was, like in Shakespeare, and with
breath that smelled musty, like old money.

"What are *you* doing up *here*?"

I ran, of course. It was all my fault, getting lost and
disturbing him, but the Old Man got horribly angry with
poor Lily. I don't know what on earth he thought she'd done
wrong except she said, later, that she was responsible for her
actions and that everyone had to own up to their
responsibilities.

Now, the rooms upstairs are almost as filthy as the
kitchen, and the savage's clothing–a vest, a coat, even
pants–were strewn about in Lily's bedroom. Still, I went
bravely on, and that was when I found another dark stairway.

"Yoohoo?"

I never wavered in my purpose, all the way up those
awful stairs–dark, narrow, twisted–and I realized those were
the stairs where Old Man Newton appeared so long ago. As I
advanced up them, the voices grew more and more
intelligible and, at last, I found myself in the Old Man's
office, just below the roof. Lily was in his swivel chair at the
his desk in the dormer window where his spyglass still
watches Port Newton.

"I can feel him," she was saying. "Can't you? He's
all around. I can smell him."

Rosa Paredes was with her. She sat in an old leather
easy chair that was cracked, like her skin, by age and
neglect.

"*Un fantasma*," the old witch said.

Lily saw me and started. "Sophie! My God! What
are you doing here?" Without warning or reason, she began

to chastise me. "Do you just let yourself into people's houses these days? My God, Sophie!"

"Nobody was about," I told her, "and the door was open."

"You can't just break into another person's house."

I defended myself with vigor. "I heard voices. I was worried about you and here you are with this... this woman."

The old witch was eating something–bread with butter and jam and chewing with her mouth open.

"And why on earth," I said to Lily, "would you ever invite such a creature as this into your home? Just look at her! My God!"

"It's my business who I invite into my home."

That awful little gun of the savage's was beside Lily on the Old Man's desk, and when I saw it, Lily realized that I had and began to make excuses.

"He's already accosted me twice," she said. "Once down at McMillan's. Once here. He came right to the door."

"Your father?" I said.

Lily shook her head. "No, no. Johnny. He hides up in the trees, at night, in the eucalyptus, watching the house."

"Long John? I don't believe it."

"Don't tell me what I've seen and what I haven't. And you still haven't apologized for breaking in."

I was tired of her self-righteous accusations by then. "So are you going to shoot me with your little gun if I don't?"

"Oh my God, Sophie. Don't be such a fool." She picked up the gun. "It isn't even loaded."

"I suppose a girl knows when her company isn't welcome."

Lily's mood turned again. "Oh Sophie. Promise me you won't tell anyone about this. About Long John, about any of this."

"Have no fear," I promised. "My lips are sealed." So I am only confiding in you, Diary dear, and, of course, Garnetta.

34

THE PORT NEWTON NEWS
Monday, June 25

TOWNE TOPICS

PACHECO PUMMELED
NEWTONS PLANT PLOW BOYS

The baseball team of the Port Newton Athletic Club crushed the Pacheco nine yesterday, 18–6, in a game decided not by righteousness, hard work and team play, but by Port Newton's newest residents: Jack "Chief" Dobbs, James F. "Plugly" McDowell, and McDowell's younger brother, Matthew, also known as "Booger."

Although Dobbs tired late in the game, he began it by pitching with the uncanny pace and accuracy we have come to expect of him, fanning farm boy after farm boy. The few who actually gained first base were kept pinned upon it by the powerful throwing arm of the elder McDowell, Plugly, while his fleet-footed brother, Booger, ran the opposition to distraction.

Better, or perhaps worse, was the batting exhibition put on by Port Newton's newest resident, center fielder Juan Caballero, or so he calls himself.

Señor Caballero, although black as the heart of the devil, is not a Negro, or so Mr. Foghorn Murphy of the Athletic Club assures us. Instead, Caballero is a full-blooded Cuban, newly arrived in this country and born of an aristocratic family on a sugar cane plantation near Havana.

"We were all real appreciative of you sending your boys over to free us from the Spaniards," said Caballero, who speaks perfect English. "Without them, my people would still be oppressed and enslaved."

It strikes your editor as truly wonderful that these four gentlemen, and all professional baseballers no less, have decided to make Port Newton their home. Even more so, it amazes us that all have found employ at the saloon of Mr. Foghorn Murphy–two as mixologists, one as a bouncer and, in the case of Mr. Caballero, as a virtuoso of the Spanish guitar.

When asked about this singular coincidence, Doctor Sam Fuller, President of the Athletic Club only said, "Ask Foghorn."

Murphy himself offered this explanation.

"Most would, I suppose, consider our good fortune unusual, but Port Newton is such a fine place to put down roots, it wouldn't surprise me to see a veritable plethora of new emigrations here."

At least until after the Fourth of July Tournament, eh Foghorn?

As for the game itself, the Newtons, propelled by the form and grace of these talented, if ignoble, beasts, quickly ran up a lead of a dozen runs as the crowd–fifty cents a head for adults, twenty-five for children–went through spasms of delight similar in nature to those exhibited by rich little boys at Christmas.

Once Murphy deemed the lead sufficient, the starting players relinquished the stage to some of our less accomplished citizens–Calvin Elwell, Charles "Icebox" Meyers, Father Noone and the rest. Over the last three innings they scored three more runs, whilst surrendering only two to the opposition.

THE CELEBRATION A WEEK AWAY
CONSTABLE SHEETS' WORRIES

At last, the arrangements for the several bicycle races to be held on the second day of the Grand Fourth of July Celebration have been finalized. The course will be from the railroad depot, up Main Street, then up School Street all the way to Buck's Ranch, and returning to the depot via Buck's Ranch Road. Besides the various men's races, a race for novices has been scheduled and also a race for ladies.

The prize monies for the many and varied competitions–the Foot Races, the Trap Shoot, the Tug of War and so on–have not yet been settled on, but it is guaranteed that they will be generous. As is traditional, the prize in the Greased Pig Contest will be the pig.

The Committee on Events has also announced that, on the second day of the festival, the volunteer fire brigades of the various cities along the Strait will hold a tournament featuring hose cart races through the streets of Port Newton. They will also put on various displays of the fireman's art at the new ballpark between the games of the baseball tournament.

A few words of caution are in order, however. For one, in light of the many equestrian companies taking part, Constable Sheets has ordered that no fireworks of any kind be exploded on the streets during the Grand Parade. The law will not look with favor on anyone caught perpetrating such acts.

The heat is also expected to be tremendous in the afternoon hours and, because of this, the constable will have many barrels containing ice water placed at convenient points in the town. Spectators should inform themselves of their placement at an early hour.

The constable also expressed hopes that the merchants of the town will not take advantage of the situation to raise prices beyond reason and reminded us that things are not as they once were in an earlier day. Such events as the Fourth of July, he warns, are liable to bring in bunco steerers and tinhorn gamblers from less civilized parts of the state. Most dangerous among these fakirs, Sheets tells us, are those who pretend to have lost an arm or a leg and, even worse, are those who offer to sell a person a "photograph of the future."

Such things are not yet possible.

LOCAL BREVITIES

The new uniforms for the members of the Volunteer Fire Department arrived last Thursday and the lads do look sharp. It is supposed by your editor that all that spit and polish is intended to make a fire sit up and take notice.

Foghorn Murphy is putting a new coat of paint on the Railroad Exchange in preparation for the coming holiday celebration, and it is reported that even Foghorn has been seen up on the scaffolding, elbow deep in the stuff.

Mrs. Alexa Avenzino, just returned from the hot springs at Calistoga, was robbed of her jewelry at knife point on the very streets of Port Newton last Thursday. The perpetrator of the crime was Homer Rexwroth who was, at one time, a noncommissioned officer in the First California Regiment and is a veteran of the Philippine Insurrection. Since doing honorable service with his regiment and returning from Manilla, however, Rexwroth has subsisted by taking odd jobs in saloons and other places. No one is certain of his address. He was found sitting on the steps of LeRoy's Mercantile a full hour after the attack and surrendered without resistance. Judge Schmidt is now interviewing him to see if he should be admitted to the Stockton Asylum for the Insane.

In the list of promotions at the Port Newton School that we printed last week, we inadvertently omitted the name of Lucy T. Miller. Lucy was indeed promoted, from the sixth grade to the seventh, and we apologize for the error.

Dr. Sam Fuller reports that little Ruthie Pavolini, the child whose skull was partly crushed when she and her mother were struck by a train two months ago, will be released from County Hospital today. Doctor Sam says it is a miracle that little Ruthie survived at all, but sadly reports that she will never again have the use of her legs.

Ernie Luciani has notified us that with every fifty-cent purchase of firecrackers at Schofield Mercantile, a chance will be given for a drawing on a watch, to be held after the Grand Parade on the Glorious Fourth.

We congratulate the Republican delegates in Philadelphia for having the perspicacity to have nominated the hero of San Juan Hill for the vice presidency. He is a man who can get things done.

Father Noone and several of the ladies of St. Sebastian Church will take a dozen children camping in Placer County near Auburn in August. "It will be a good way to escape the heat," the good Father says, "and also educate the children about the glorious days of 'forty-nine."

Mrs. Meyers and Mrs. Fernandez drove up to the cemetery on Tuesday to place flowers on the graves of the men who drowned when the *Zeelandia* went down in the Strait last year.

It has come to the attention of Lawyer Elwell of the Port Newton Board of Trustees that a certain officer of the county has been paying a monthly sum to a certain official of the Democratic Party in order to keep his job. Lawyer Elwell says he will ask for the immediate resignation of each and that charges will be filed.

The body of Benedict Rossi, who passed away at French Hospital in San Francisco on Thursday, was returned to Benicia on Friday. The body was laid to rest in St. Dominic's Cemetery in Benicia. Afterwards, a reception was held at the Benicia Odd Fellows Lodge of which Mr. Rossi was a member. Our sincere condolences to the entire family. Your father was a fine man, Anthony.

Supervisor Wyatt of Martinez is distressed over the reports he reads of Boxers slaughtering Christians in China. His niece and nephew are missionaries, six hundred miles into the interior. He says he does not believe the rebellion has reached them as of yet, but communication is impossible.

Another incident of a horse being driven to death has reached our ears. The animal was rented at Hackenschmidt's and driven towards Concord, where it was found dead in the road. Such episodes are deplorable, and the authorities should pay them some serious attention.

The heat won't bother you if you are dressed in a summer suit from the McEwen Clothing Emporium, located at Railroad Avenue and Main Street.

GODDESS OF LIBERTY CONTEST
MISS JOOST THE CLEAR WINNER

At last the voting in the Goddess of Liberty contest has come to its conclusion, and Newtonians can take pride in the victory of Miss Hanna Joost of our own fair city. Her subjects will most certainly pay the homage due her as she reigns over the splendid days to come. The final totals for the highest vote getters are as follows:

Hanna Joost (Port Newton)	2,649
Isabella Thayer (Crockett)	2,516
Bessie Swift (Benicia)	2,102
Genevieve Hurley (Martinez)	1,945

While some have objected to the decision of Mr. John Glass, chairman of the Goddess of Liberty Committee, to assign a few damaged ballots to the total of Miss Joost, it seems to us a wise and just policy as they were all cast for Port Newton girls in the first place. Congratulations on your victory, Hanna.

MEETINGS AND EVENTS
Town Trustees–Tonight

The Board of Trustees will meet this evening, seven p.m., at the International Hotel to discuss the cost of having the main streets of the town macadamized. The poor condition of the sidewalks on Park Street will also be discussed as will repairs to the footbridge over Railroad Avenue.

Ladies Aid–Wednesday Afternon

The Presbyterian Ladies Aid will meet at the home of Mrs. John H. Soto at "tea time" on Wednesday. They will begin to lay plans for the annual Christmas Bazaar. As usual, the bazaar will be dedicated to raising money for the poor children of the county, of which there are too many.

35
DOCTOR SAM FULLER
President, Port Newton Athletic Club

It was early Saturday evening, two days before the Fourth of July celebration began, and Foghorn had called a practice–a final tautening of the wires, he called it, before the championship tournament. In the lean years, nobody would have shown up for a practice on a Saturday evening, but with a championship in sight every man on the team but one arrived early. And that one straggler was me: Doctor Sam Fuller, pitcher, third class.

My tardiness was, for one thing, caused by the fact that I'd felt like a damned idiot ever since I'd taken that swing at Foghorn. Now, every time the son of a bitch saw me, he'd throw up his hands and start bobbing and weaving like a boxer.

"Look out, boys! Here comes John L. Sullivan!"

For another thing, Riley Towne at the newspaper had started to call down hellfire on us, and he was right. It wasn't Port Newton that was winning all those games, it was the professionals of the "Oakland Mob": Dobbs, the McDowells, and Juan Caballero, the so-called Cuban aristocrat.

More importantly, there were rumors all over town by now–sex and sin, Lily a fallen woman, even rumors of Old Man Newton's ghost for christsakes. Worse, for Long John, were the rumors that he'd accosted Lily in McMillan's, that he'd had words with Dobbs in the Beehive Cafe, even that he was spying on her from the eucalyptus groves up Buck's Ranch Road. They were rumors that nobody seemed able to substantiate but which I felt compelled to deal with.

So I'd procrastinated, dawdled, shilly-shallied, and ended up a day late and a dollar short, as usual. The sun was sinking low in the west by the time I got to that old ballpark on the bluff, and balls hit in the air would soon become indistinct blurs in an indistinct sky.

Foghorn stood at the plate with his favorite bat and a bucket of balls, spraying grounders to the infielders.

"Double-play ball!" he called and there was wood on the ball, the good old click-slap of it, and the sizzle of the seams across the July-hard earth of the infield.

Billy Lawton, playing second base, took the ball off his chest with determination if not consummate skill. He tossed it to Booger McDowell, our shortstop, who crossed the bag with the slickness and polish of the professional that he was and fired to first.

Foghorn called out, "The other way!" He choked up on the bat, tossed up another ball, and there was that click-slap again. An old, dirty, beat-up ball cutting its way toward first. Long John, lean and supple, came off the bag, scooped and fired to Booger at second. Billy raced over to cover first, and for a moment, it seemed like old times, like that championship year again, 1888. A picture postcard of yesterday, a last glimpse of all that had been good in our lives.

Then, Foghorn saw me. "Look out boys! Here comes John L. Sullivan!"

It wasn't the lovely *then* of the old, ordered century anymore. It was the awful *now* of this new, godless one.

Now, Booger McDowell played shortstop because Billy wasn't good enough anymore. Now, Plugly McDowell played catcher because Hec Fernandez had trouble handling Dobbs' pitches. Juan Caballero, the so-called Cuban, played center field, and Hec, Cal, Charlie Meyers, and Father Noone had all been relegated to the bench.

"If he don't slide," Booger told Billy, "make the son of a bitch pay. Throw the ball right at his face. Make him hit the dirt. That's baseball."

At third, Plugly showed Ernie Luciani how to trip base runners.

"It ain't cheatin' if you don't get caught."

Buck Farrell, who'd been demoted from center field to right, swung a bat to stretch his muscles while the Cuban instructed him in the art of confusing opposing fielders when a shallow fly off one of our bats looked like it might fall in for a hit.

"If you know the jerk's name," Caballero said, "sing it out. Like 'Bob, Bob, Bob.' Or just call out, 'I got it! I got it!' Confuses the hell out of 'em."

Cuban, indeed.

On the bench, Dobbs, the master of leeches and cheats, sharpened his spikes with a fine-toothed file while our batboy–my son that is–watched like a boy in love.

"It ain't so important that they're *really* razor sharp," Dobbs told Willie. "What's important is for the other team to *think* they are. Keeps 'em respectful. But if you can cut one of 'em up a little, they respect you all the better."

Greed and hooliganism were run amuck. We had plumbed the depths of dishonor. I walked up behind Long John at first, stood in foul territory, and told him that I needed to speak with him.

"About what?" he asked.

"You know what," I said.

He nodded his head once and tucked his fielder's glove away in the baggy back pocket of his uniform–the dark, championship uniform with the big white N over the heart. He called to young Elwell who came eagerly up off the bench and took Long John's place in the field. Long John and I strolled together, up the foul line, towards our new right field fence–"Eat at Vinci's," it read.

"How are the headaches?" I asked.

Long John looked at me, puzzled. "How the hell do you think they are? You don't believe all those things they're saying about me, do you?"

"Of course not," I said, glad he'd broken the ice. "I don't think anyone does."

"Half the town does."

I told him I hoped he wouldn't go making a fool of himself. "What's done is done. Be a gentleman about things. Wish her the best and let go."

"Do you know what she thinks? She thinks there's money buried out in that yard somewhere. That's why she gardens. Didn't you ever figure that out? She thinks her father buried money there. She dreams about him. She gets the dreams confused with what's real. She dreams he watches her from up in the eucalyptus. She dreams he stands by her bed and tells her there's money in the yard."

"You should have told me."

"I couldn't, Doc. She doesn't trust you. She doesn't trust anybody. She fears the people who lost their savings in

184

the collapse will come rob her. She told me about it back when... well, back when she still liked me."

He pointed towards Dobbs. "She told that son of a bitch about the money, though. Because she was afraid he'd leave her, maybe. Like her fiancé did. Why the hell else do you think that son of a bitch would stay around?"

"He wants to settle down," I said. "He wants to open a cigar store."

"Is that what he told you? He's lied about everything from the start, and he's lying about that, too. He wants Lily for the money that he thinks is buried in her yard. Then he'll be off again."

"I can't believe that."

"Well, you'd better."

He pulled his baseball glove out of his pocket and thrust his hand into it. "See you later, Doc." As he trotted back towards the infield I was left standing in foul territory with a ponder. Long John was our protector and defender, a fellow who was honest as the day was long. His rival was a savage of the east, a liar and cheat, the same man who now sat on the bench showing my son how to spike his opponents.

"Hey Pop! Look at me!" Willie had that file himself now and was sharpening the spikes on his own baseball shoes.

When I reached them, I told Willie baseball wasn't about hurting people.

"It's about not getting caught. Right Chief?"

"Damn right," Dobbs said.

Willie grinned. "Damn right."

I told him his language was atrocious.

"Like father like son, eh, Pop?"

I almost belted him one. "Go make yourself useful. Go take some grounders. Go shag some flies. Something."

"Damn it, Pop."

"Willie!"

When, at last, I scared him off, I sat down by Dobbs on the bench and asked him about his elbow.

"It's been worse," he said.

I asked him if his fingers hurt. He said they didn't. "Well, sometimes maybe."

"Can you make a fist?"

"Yeah, sure."

He made a fist with his left hand, and I asked him about the tournament. "Do you think you can pitch three games in three days?"

"If we're gonna win, I got to," he said.

I asked him about Lily. "Sophie told me about her visit with Doña Rosa. She's not imagining things, is she?"

"Hell, Doc, you see ghosts, too, don't you? When you've drunk too much of that elixir crap, I mean?"

"That's different," I said.

"Like hell it is."

I asked him about the money. "You know there isn't any."

He shrugged his shoulders.

"Sure there's money. If we win, there's money."

"No, I mean in Lily's yard. Apparently Lily thinks her father buried money from the Savings Association there, but there isn't any. It all went down with the Savings Association. You do know that, don't you?"

He threw me a dangerous glare.

"What did Sheets tell you? I saw you two having your little chit-chat."

"He says you're only after the money."

"You don't believe that lying son of a bitch, do you? Or is it that he's white and I ain't? You figure a nigger like me couldn't love a white woman so you figure I got to be after money? That's it isn't it?"

"You know me better than that."

"I know *all* you white eyes. And it's none of your damn business either. Not yours. Not Sophie's. Just let us be."

"I'm Lily's physician, Jack."

"Not any more."

That hit me hard and, for a moment, we just sat, watching Foghorn hit infield. The grass was dead and dying. The sinking sun was a red egg in the west. The pop flies Foghorn hit disappeared into the coloring sky.

"Sorry, Doc," Dobbs said. "She's going to a doctor in Oakland now. She should have told you."

"In Oakland? Who?"

186

"Some woman. Bailey's her name. Lily says she understands her better."

"Oh," I said, feeling as if I'd lost another of my children just as surely as I'd lost Jimmy Catlett and Peggy McCann and all the rest.

"She's all right, isn't she?" Dobbs said. "A lady doctor and all?"

"I've met Dr. Bailey and she seems fine. Women are very good at taking care of other women, you know. Female problems and all that. Good with children, too."

An awful thought flashed through my brain. "God, she's not... you know, is she?"

"If she is, she ain't told me."

Foghorn called to me from home plate. "Hey, Doc. Get off your behind. Come pitch some batting practice."

"Just a goddamn minute!"

Foghorn raised his hands like a boxer again and began to bob and weave. "Don't hit me, Doc. Please don't hit me."

Dobbs laughed. "Go ahead," he told me. "Go ahead and throw a few. Play some ball. Pitch a little. Try to relax."

"You sound like the doctor, yourself," I said.

He tossed me a ball that he'd turned almost black with tobacco juice and licorice. "They'll never see it in this light, Doc. Just go out there and throw. You think too much."

"So do you," I told him.

36

THE PORT NEWTON NEWS
SUNDAY, July 1, 1900

EXTRA EDITION–SCHEDULE OF EVENTS

MONDAY, JULY 2
8 a.m.–Firing of the National Salutes by Mr. P.R. Levine

BASEBALL
Four Contests Beginning at 10 a.m. at Newton Field
Pacheco vs. Concord, Martinez vs. Black Diamond
Crockett vs. Port Newton, Hercules vs. Benicia

TRAP SHOOTING–FIRST ROUND
Beginning at 11 a.m.–Founder's Park

NOON–PICNIC AT FOUNDER'S PARK

FIREMAN'S TOURNAMENT
Hose Cart Races and Other Competitions, 2 p.m., Main and
Newton

BICYCLE RACES
4 p.m., commencing and finishing at the Depot

OPEN AIR VAUDEVILLE SHOW–FOUNDER'S PARK
8 p.m., CROWNING OF THE GODDESS OF LIBERTY
Vaudeville performance featuring eight talented artists will
follow

TUESDAY, JULY 3
8 a.m.–Firing of the National Salutes by Mr. P.R. Levine

SAILING RACE
From Benicia and Return
Time depending on the wind

BASEBALL
Two Semifinal Contests
Beginning at 10 a.m., Newton Field

NOON–PICNIC AT FOUNDER'S PARK

TRAP SHOOTING–FINAL ROUND
Beginning at 1 p.m.–Founder's Park

BALLOON ASCENSION
By the redoubtable David Drake, 2 p.m., Founder's Park

AN EVENING OF THEATER
Featuring *H.M.S PINAFORE* as presented by the Port Newton
Dramatic Society
Performance at 8 p.m.

WEDNESDAY, JULY 4
8 a.m.–Firing of the National Salutes by Mr. P.R. Levine

THE GRAND PROCESSIONAL PARADE, 10 a.m.

Order of March
First Division–form up by the depot. Port Newton Silver
Cornet Band, the Officers of the Day in carriages, the Board
of Supervisors and the town trustees, the float of the
Goddess of Liberty.

Second Division–form up along the Front. The Crockett
Brass Button Band, the equestrian teams including the Noble
Brotherhood of Redskins, the floats of the Native Sons and
Daughters, the Dante Society and the Veterans.

Third Division–form up at the east end of Newton Street,
The Benicia Marine Band, the fire departments and the Fire
Queen, the Republicans and Democrats in separate columns,
the decorated rigs, the float of the Angel of Peace.

ORATIONS FOLLOW AT THE REVIEWING STAND
The Declaration of Independence, as recited by Hanna Joost

NOON–BARBECUE AT FOUNDER'S PARK
Followed by the Tug of War, the Fat Man's Race
Greased Pig Contest, Sack Race and Races for Boys and Girls
Women's Races, Men's Sprints and Dashes

THE CHAMPIONSHIP BASEBALL GAME
Beginning 3 p.m. at Newton Field

OPEN–AIR CONCERT
Commencing at 6 p.m., Six Brass Bands and all the
Vaudeville Artists!

THE GRAND MASKED BALL
Commencing at 8 p.m., Pimental Hall

THE FIREWORKS DISPLAY
Along the Waterfront, When Darkness is Complete

AT MIDNIGHT–THE UNMASKING OF THE REVELERS!

37
SOPHIE FULLER
Senior, Port Newton Union High School

Dear Diary,

The world is turned upside down. It is not amour or fairy-tale kisses anymore. I know the lower classes sometimes strike their women, but no one strikes *us*. No one strikes *Lily Newton*. I don't understand, but I will try to keep things in order for that, at least, is something I *can* do.

Mother was nauseating this morning, as always, but I expect this, so it didn't bother me.

"You can't go to the ballgame, Sophie. You'll tire yourself out for Hanna's coronation. You have a responsibility to the whole city now that you're a Handmaiden."

"Oh, Mother," I said. "All the Handmaidens have to do is look pretty."

She said, "Thank God for that."

She hurts me, Diary dear, over and over and over, when she says things like this. Why does she do it?

I insisted that I be allowed to go to the game, and she relented, at last, and said I could, but only on the condition that she went with me. "So that you'll stay out of trouble."

Just to show her, I cheered and whistled and stomped my feet at the game and all the time Mother badgered me and badgered me.

"Don't yell like that, Sophie. It isn't ladylike... Don't whistle like that, Sophie. That's even less ladylike."

We won easily, of course, and I especially enjoyed watching the Cuban. His skin is like the purest of chocolate that melts in one's mouth. In the outfield and on the bases, both, he is like a great sorrel stallion, so I paid little attention to Long John and the savage. Long John made a couple of hits, for the first time in months, and the savage pitched wonderfully, despite Daddy's worries over his elbow. But I did not notice if anything passed between Long John and the Indian. They played the game, that was all, seeming neither civil nor unfriendly.

Later, Mother insisted on helping me dress for Hanna's crowning as if I was a child. I was never so embarrassed. Why does she do these things to me? Then, when I was at last ready to go, I asked Daddy if he would hitch up the buggy and drive me to Founder's Park so I wouldn't get dirty walking.

I said, "It wouldn't look right if a Handmaiden to the Goddess showed up on shank's mare, would it Daddy?"

"Perish the thought," he said.

He is a sweetheart, and I know that he, at least, loves me, but why does he say nasty, belittling things, just like Mother?

As we passed down the hill, Daddy insisted on stopping at Lily's to make sure she was all right. I told him he was being a mother hen and that she could take care of herself, which, I realize now, are my own feelings about how he treats *me*, not Lily.

But instead of telling him what bothered me, I teased him, saying that Lily isn't the only one in Port Newton who drinks too much.

"What's that supposed to mean?"

"If the shoe fits, Daddy."

He must know I am just teasing, in the same way I would tease Calvin or any boy that I like and, well, yes, love.

But as it turned out, Daddy was right. There was Lily, as we drove up, cultivating her awful garden with a hoe. At first, I was happy to see she was wearing a big straw hat, but then I realized that it was six o'clock in the evening and the sun was not why she wore it.

"Lily!" Daddy called. "You're going to miss all the festivities. The vaudeville show is tonight, you know."

She looked up. "Oh, you know how I hate crowds."

And that was when I saw it, despite her efforts to keep her head turned away, and let the sun hat hide it; the thing that turned the world on end; the bruise and swelling on her cheek; the black and blue of her eye.

Daddy absolutely leapt out of the buggy.

"Lily, what happened?"

"Oh, you know. It happens all the time. Whacked myself with the damn handle." She held the hoe up, as if for Daddy to see, but he wanted to look at the cheek, itself.

"Let's go inside where we can get some light on it."

"Oh, don't be silly. I'm fine."

"No you're not," Daddy said.

He reached out towards the cheek with two fingers, as if he intended to turn the bruise towards him, in order to see it better, and that was when Lily's temper flared.

"Don't touch me!"

She put the hoe across herself at an angle, as one might hold a weapon, and Daddy backed away.

"Just go," Lily said. "Just go away."

And so we left. What choice did we have? As Daddy and I drove towards Founder's Park both of us were very quiet, but then I couldn't stand it anymore.

"Daddy? How could she hit herself with the handle of a hoe?"

He just shook his head. "It was her left cheek," he said, which puzzled me.

"Do something, Daddy."

"I can't," he said. "I'm not her doctor anymore."

He turned to me and smiled, put an arm around my shoulders and pulled me towards him in an ever-so-nice hug.

"But this is a special night," he said. "A night for dreams and goddesses."

I hate it when he treats me like that.

But when we got near Founder's Park, everyone who saw me pointed and waved, and I had to smile and wave back no matter how awful I felt. Firecrackers were going off all over, frightening the horses. The Benicia Marine Band, booming away, came marching up Park Street, leading a huge mass of Benicians. The whole Benicia ball team was behind them–all in brand new uniforms with matching sweaters and all in perfect step with bats on their shoulders like soldiers marching with rifles–and in the midst of them was that awful Tony Rossi, carrying that most hated banner, "Benicia, Champions 1888."

There was another roar of brass as unexpected as the last, but this time it was our own Silver Cornets with Mr. Meyers leading the way–louder and sweeter, by far, than the Benicians. And Mr. Meyers was not bearing any false championship banner, but the glorious Stars and Stripes, and even the Benicians had to cheer that. Calvin and Mr.

McMillan and everybody in town were all marching behind the band, and my heart actually stirred.

Then I saw the savage in the middle of them, a baseball held high in his left hand and, suddenly, I understood what Daddy had meant when he'd noted that the bruise was on Lily's left check.

You see, Diary dear, the savage is a southpaw but Long John swings with his right, meaning it must have been Long John who beat her, holding her with his left hand, perhaps, hitting with his right, on her left cheek.

Calvin waved at me, he is such a sweet boy, he said he wanted to see me after the vaudeville show. But it was loud because of the blaring bands, I was distracted because of my thoughts, and trying hard not to cry; so I just shrugged my shoulders, "Maybe."

It was almost dark, by then, and the air had cooled and become very pleasant. Hanna and Garnetta and I sat on some awful straight-backed chairs from Pimental Hall on the stage built for the vaudeville show. The Flying Floyds' trapezes swayed in the breeze high above us. Hanna looked very pretty, despite her hair, and that awful red, white and blue gown Mrs. Glass and Mrs. Hodapp made for her.

Mr. Bristol of the new electric company stepped up on stage to officiate and everyone cheered. It was just getting dark, and at the exact moment Mr. Bristol placed the crown on Hanna's head, he called out, "I proclaim thee the Goddess of Liberty and the Twentieth Century! In this new world, we will banish darkness forever."

Just then, all the new electric lights that had been strung through the park and along Main went on, as if by a miracle, and everyone gasped as one. There were cheers and applause and hats were thrown into the air, but all I could think of was Lily, and every time I did, it made me feel sick. She's my friend, not some low woman. My friend who I'd played ghosts with as a little girl. A fine, intelligent, and upstanding woman, beaten by a man I had once trusted and revered

Would Calvin ever do that to me? Would Daddy?

When the vaudeville show began, Hanna and Garnetta and I moved to a special box in the grandstand. The Mississippi Minstrels did their cakewalk. Hazel Fontaine, who is supposedly a famed ventriloquist, tried to amuse us, as did some banjo comedian, but it all seemed very incongruous now. At last, The Flying Floyds soared overhead like birds, almost falling time after time and eliciting squeals of fear and delight from the crowd.

Their act climaxed in leaps and drops into nets, and that was when I caught sight of Constable Sheets and Sheriff Ulshoter, patrolling the perimeter of the park. When Long John looked at me, over the heads of the crowd, his cold glance made a tremor run up my chest and into my throat.

Then, I caught a glimpse of the Indian, coming towards Long John from the opposite direction. He was surrounded by a pack of small boys, as always, and he waltzed along, eyes turned upwards intent on The Flying Floyds, and I wondered if, despite being left-handed it still could have been him that had beat her.

Then, Long John saw the Indian and stopped dead, not fifty feet away. The Indian, sensing danger in the intuitive way of the savage, perhaps, froze in his tracks and the two stood staring at each other, like duelists on the eve of mortal combat.

That big, oriental grin came over the Chief's face and, in a gesture whose meaning could not be mistaken, he took hold of his own tie, pulled the loose end of it up above his head, stuck out his tongue and rolled his eyes, in the manner of a man being hung.

I fear something horrible is going to happen.

38

THE PORT NEWTON NEWS
Tuesday, July 3

SPECIAL EXTRA EDITION

NEWTONS EDGE MARTINEZ
CHAMPIONSHIP TILT TOMORROW

Amidst the tumult of a sold-out crowd, the cries of
the beer sellers and peanut hawkers, the baseball team of the
Port Newton Athletic Club defeated the Martinez Excelsiors,
10–9, in a semifinal game of the Independence Day Baseball
Tournament at Newton Field this morning.

With the Newtons going off as five-to-one favorites,
no one in attendance was surprised when the home club
jumped to an easy 7–0 lead. The big bats were as big as
supposed, and pitcher Jack P. "Chief" Dobbs retired the first
six hitters he faced.

But by the third inning, the big Indian's curve ball
ceased to curve. His fastball grew slow and, worse still, his
fade-away lost its fade.

In the sixth Martinez tied the game as the Newton's
defense fell to pieces. With two out and runners on first and
third, Martinez slugger Talbot Green struck a shallow fly
that twisted in the high Newtonian sky and hung suspended
twixt second base and heaven.

Juan Caballero, Port Newton's dusky-skinned center
fielder, raced in calling for the ball. But shortstop Bugger
McDowell raced out calling for it, too; and so did second
baseman, Billy Lawton–who, in his other life, is a jerker of
sodas at McMillan's Pharmacy and Fountain, corner of Main
and Railroad.

All three converged on the likely landing place of
the plummeting pellet, and in the collision that resulted,
Billy, Bugger, Caballero and the baseball itself, all fell to
earth.

The Cuban sprang to his feet. "That was my ball!"
"I called you off," the hot-tempered Lawton replied.
"I'm the center fielder."

"You're a son of a bitch!"

Caballero ripped off his cap and threw it at Billy. Billy swung at Caballero. McDowell seized Billy from behind and, while Caballero pummeled the helpless infielder, the ball bounded towards the center field fence, the runners circled the sacks, and three runs were scored.

Judge Schmidt, umpiring the game, thumbed all three Newtons for fighting, tossed catcher Plugly McDowell for good measure and, when Newton's manager Foghorn Murphy stormed onto the field in protest, ejected him, too.

"He may be a judge, but he's also an idiot," an irate Murphy said later. "I could understand the ejections if our boys had been fighting with their opponents. *But they were fighting with their own teammates.* What's this world coming to?"

When asked to explain his actions to your editor, the much put-upon judge replied that Murphy's objection was irrelevant and immaterial.

"I'm sick of the bullying and intimidating tactics the Port Newton team has come to employ. It's not very Newtonian of them, in my opinion."

When play resumed, the Newtons were caught shorthanded, and acting manager Dr. Sam Fuller was forced to bring in the likes of Charles "Icebox" Meyers, Calvin Elwell, Father Frank Noone, and even himself.

"I didn't have much choice," Doctor Sam later said. "I mean, we were the only ones left."

But in baseball it is in the ninth inning that the true and epic heroes are born, and so it was at Newton Field today.

With two outs in the final frame, Port Newton trailed, 9–8, but hope reared its lovely head when Hector Fernandez, the Newtons' catcher, sent a ball down the left field line for a double. Father Noone, who'd been inserted in the outfield in place of Cabellero, was scheduled to bat next, but Noone, hitless since the Fall, was booed as he perambulated towards the plate.

Undaunted, the fearless father crossed himself, dug his cleats into the good Port Newton dirt, and promptly took the first two pitches for strikes.

Forced to swing at almost anything now, Noone selected a pitch that appeared to be nearer Japan than it was to home. But as luck, fate, or perhaps even the Almighty would have it, he managed to tip the ball just enough to cause it to meander across the greensward. Martinez second-sacker Andrew Mellus charged hard as he could and scooped up the ball.

"I should never have thrown it," he said later. "I should have just held on."

Instead, Mellus spun with the grace of a knee-less ballerina and threw so wide of first that the elusory orb sailed down the right field line towards the hill that leads to Ferry Street and the watery Strait below.

The flying father rounded the bag at first and kept on running. Hec Fernandez, on second, lumbered towards third, turned the base and headed home but, here, tragedy overtook the stocky catcher, for when he turned third, he also turned his ankle.

Meanwhile, Martinez right fielder Alf Boynton scooped up the bounding ball and threw it back towards second baseman Mellus, the relay man and goat of the hour, who propelled the pellet platewards.

"I was real excited," Mellus wept later, "and put too much mustard on it."

And hot mustard, indeed, for the ball flew high and wide of the mark, over and above the outstretched glove of Martinez catcher Nolan Warren and stuck in the chicken wire screen that hangs behind home.

Father Noone rounded third only to see before him the elephantine Fernandez, hopping homewards on one foot, his ankle all stove up.

"I saw Hec stumbling along," the clergyman confessed, "and the catcher clawing at the ball in the screen. It occurred to me in a flash that Hector would never reach home in time to tie the game, but also, that if I passed him in the baseline, I would be called out, my run would not count and Port Newton would suffer defeat."

But lo, it is written–here at any rate–that a miracle came to pass on Newton's Bluff this afternoon.

"I prayed to the Lord to give me strength," Noone said, "and when I got to Hec, the spirit entered me, and I felt myself suffused with superhuman powers."

The frail father lifted the cumbersome catcher as if his weight were air, slung him over his shoulder, fireman fashion, and carried him home. He dumped Fernandez on the plate to knot the game, tallied the winning run himself and Port Newton had earned the right to meet the winner of the Benicia, Concord game in the championship match tomorrow, on the grand and glorious Fourth.

OTHER EVENTS

The results of Monday's bicycle races, from the depot to Buck's Ranch and return, are as follows.

Men's Race: First place, Rudy Castellane, Crockett, prize of $10 and a pair of McKenzie Single Tube Tires, courtesy of McKenzie's Cyclery, First and Escobar, Martinez. Second place, T.J. Petersen, Benicia, prize of $5. Third place, Mickey Bonzagni, Martinez, prize of $2.

Novice Race: First place, Joseph Silvano, Martinez, prize $4. Second place P.P. Blum, Port Newton, prize $2. Third Place, Johnny Alton, prize $1.

The Fireman's Tournament was postponed because of the numerous fires caused by firecrackers. The unused residence at 32 Hill St. suffered considerable damage but can be repaired as good as new, according to the owner, Mr. T.P. Hale of Port Newton.

The top finishers in the final round of the Trap Shoot and the number of clay pigeons they blasted to perdition are as follows.

First Pool: 20 birds. A.C. Koch, Benicia, scored 18. Lottie Fish, Crockett, 16. Lawyer Elwell, Port Newton, 14. L.L. Dunkel, Martinez, 12.

Second Pool: 20 birds. Walter Melleer, Crockett, 19 birds. Scanlan Jones, Benicia, 14 birds. Evan Palmer, Benicia, 12. Ed Morgan, Port Newton, 8.

The prize of 1,000 cartridges donated by the Hercules Works was divided as follows: A.C. Koch, 300. Walter Melleer, Lottie Fish, Lawyer Elwell, 150 each. Scalan Jones, Evan Palmer, 100 each. Ed Morgan, 50.

At this writing, Benicia leads Concord, 3–1, in the early innings of the second semifinal game of the Grand Championship Baseball Tournament.

DOCTOR SAM FULLER
President, Port Newton Athletic Club

We were on top of the world, or at least Newton's Bluff, after Father Noone's mad dash around the bases. Half the town escorted us out of the ballpark and all were cheering. The Silver Cornets, sharp in their black uniforms of the silver buttons, led us with blaring horns. The Noble Redskins, half naked and painted for war, whooped and hollered, brandished their tomahawks, pounded their drums. A half dozen thickset railroad men hoisted Father Noone up on their shoulders, and bore him down Ferry Street.

But on the other side of our little valley, there stood an even stranger sight: Towering above the mighty oaks of Founder's Park was the red, white, and blue aerial ship of Professor David Drake. A sausage bloated on coal gas poised for an ascent towards the noonday sun.

As we marched downhill the crowd cheered, the Silver Cornets played, and the professor began his stately rise. He dropped a waterfall of ballast. The Noble Redskins waved and whooped. The professor fiddled his propellors and rudders. The big-shouldered railroaders squealed like fat schoolgirls. Professor Drake leaned over the side of the basket and tried to shout something down to us. I strained to hear, but the bands, the firecrackers, the cheering, overwhelmed his shouts.

I parted company with this victory procession downtown, where crowds of revelers debarked the ferry and the streets teemed with men in summer suits, with women sporting parasols, and pigtailed girls in sunbonnets and white dresses. At the corner of Ferry and Railroad Streets, Sheriff Ulshoter, seated on his prize blue-black gelding, kept a watch over all. He cut quite a figure up there–chocolate brown coat and vest, string tie, kid gloves, John B. Stetson hat. Even the horse, Pride of Martinez, was all gussied up with red ribbons in his mane and tail.

"Seen Long John recently?" I asked the sheriff.

"Not since last night. I figured he was at the ballgame with you fellows."

I shook my head. "He didn't make it. Most of the boys figured he was with you, what with the Fourth and all."

"Ain't seen him since last night."

The sheriff pointed upwards towards Professor Drake and his balloon, which had begun to drift towards the Strait.

"The son of a bitch is *flying*!"

"It would appear so," I said. Although my understanding, I told the sheriff, was that Professor Drake had intended to go east by south, towards Martinez and the Diablo Valley, and not northward, as he was now, towards Benicia and Solano County.

"Maybe he changed his mind," the sheriff said. "You know what a hare brain that fellow is, and for a professor and all. But, hell, Doc. *He's up there*!"

I asked him about Long John again. "I thought you two would be busy today."

"Not so far. There were duties aplenty last night with the crowds and drunks. But it's been peaceful today." He made a laugh. "The lazy son of a bitch might still be sleeping!"

I told him about how Sophie and I had stopped by Lily's the night before. I told him about Lily's eye and about how she'd claimed she'd somehow done it herself.

"That's what they all say," the sheriff told me.

I said that I figured someone, probably a right-handed someone, had thumped her a few.

"Holy Christ. You don't think it was Long John, do you? He didn't break her nose, did he? Jesus Christ that's the worst. That and teeth. Jesus."

"No. Just the eye," I said. "It's black and blue, and the cheek is bruised. She's pretty badly swollen, but there's no permanent damage, I don't think. Not physically at any rate."

He shook his head. "What about the Indian? I wouldn't put such a thing past him."

"I'm pretty sure it was Long John. I figure he left town. Made a run for it. He even told me, once, that guilty fellows always make a run for it."

"Holy Christ," the sheriff said again. "I'll go down to his office and have a look around. Then, hell, I don't know. His mother has been dead for years, but maybe he went back home to Pacheco. I'll notify the authorities there."

"Let me know what you find," I told him. "I'll be in the Exchange."

"The Exchange, eh? Go easy on the boilermakers today, will you? With the sun so hot, we're liable to have some heat stroke today. Make sure you keep your wits about you."

"What the goddamn hell? I always keep my wits about me."

"Sure, Doc."

He gave Pride a couple of clicks of his tongue, and the horse began to walk, slowly, through the crowds along the Front. "I'll let you know," the sheriff called back.

"You do that."

Inside the Exchange, the sports, the gamblers, and the painted ladies of the hotels and scows crowded around the ballplayers of the Port Newton Athletic Club, cheering, praising, buying them drinks. Everyone loves the front runner, I suppose.

Plugly McDowell, Booger, and Caballero, already changed out of their uniforms, leaned against Foghorn's polished mahogany bar–quiet, hunched over, drinking straight whiskey. Charlie Meyers–pitcher, teacher, idealist, and romantic–stood above them, on top of that same damn bar, rousing the rabble like some anarchist Frenchie.

"We can win without these whores of Babylon. We won without them today. We can win without them tomorrow. The team belongs to 'we the people'. *Liberté, egalité, fraternité!*"

I didn't much like the sound of that, but the boys all seemed to: Hec Fernandez, Billy Lawton, Father Noone. They chugged at their foaming beers and cheered, spilling suds all over the floor.

Jack Dobbs sat alone at Foghorn's poker table in back, the sleeves of his baseball uniform rolled up, his left elbow plunged in a bucket of ice. I asked him how the arm felt. He told me it was fine.

"Don't worry, Doc. I'll win your goddamn games for you."

"That's the least of my worries," I said. I asked him about Lily's eye. "Did Long John do it?

"You don't think I did, do you?"

It was an answer that wasn't an answer. "I don't know Jack, and that's the truth."

He had a bottle of whiskey beside him. He took a drink, offered me the bottle, and I poured myself a shot–Sheriff Ulshoter notwithstanding.

"The son of a bitch came by Lily's before the vaudeville show yesterday. Went crazy on her. I would have killed him if I'd been there."

"You didn't though, did you?"

"If I see him again, I probably will."

I told him not to do anything stupid. I told him that Sheriff Ulshoter was looking for Long John, that he'd be arrested, that he'd go to jail, that a man couldn't get away with something like that in Port Newton.

"Not even if he is constable," I said.

"Yeah right."

Foghorn had been over by the bar watching, askance, Charlie's shenanigans: "What profit a man to win the whole world but lose his soul?" He came over to us and asked me what I thought about Dobbs' elbow.

"He won't let me see it," I said.

"You never asked," Dobbs complained.

"Show it to him, Chief," Foghorn said.

Dobbs pulled the elbow out of the ice. It was black and blue and as fat and tender as a cooked goose. I asked him again, as I had at practice, if his finger's hurt.

"A little."

"Can you make a fist?"

"If I want to."

"Well, do it."

He tried but couldn't. "You could barely pitch today," I said. "What makes you think you can pitch tomorrow?"

"I got motivation."

I told Foghorn, "Your grandmother could probably throw harder."

"My grandmother's dead," Foghorn said.

"That's what I mean," I told him.

"Good Lord Doc, you know how much is riding on this game. Paint him with horse liniment. Drain the thing. Do *something*."

"I'm sorry," I told Foghorn. "But it's done. He can't pitch anymore. It's done. Your scheming. Your conniving. It's over."

"What the hell are you talking about?"

"The cheating. The dirty tactics. Charlie's right. Riley Towne's right. It's not our club anymore. It's *theirs*: Plugly's, Booger's, the Cuban's. It means nothing to *us* if *they* win?"

A voice came from behind us. "Glad you see it my way, Doc."

Charlie Meyers was the source, and with him were Billy Lawton, Hec Fernandez, and Father Noone, Port Newton's own little Committee of Public Safety–*Liberté, egalité, fraternité.*

"Foghorn," Charlie said. "We're calling a special emergency meeting of the main body of the Port Newton Athletic Club."

Foghorn was suspicious and rightly so. "What for?"

Charlie only said, "To win back our souls."

Billy Lawton was more specific: "I'm tired of playin' with coons."

"First we let in an Injun," Hec Fernandez said, "and now we got coons."

"Hec," I said. "You're a goddamn Mexican for christsakes."

"I'm a goddamn American and don't you forget it."

"Me too," Jack Dobbs said.

I appealed to Father Noone. "Didn't God create us all equal?"

The good Father pondered. "Well... We're all damned by original sin to the eternal flames of hell. I suppose that's created equal, in one sense, at least."

"Charlie," Foghorn said, "we got money riding on this. You're slitting your own throat. Wait till we win, *then* kick 'em out."

"You son of a bitch," Dobbs said. "I ruin my arm winning you lots of money and then you dump me?"

"Well no, not exactly."

"Exactly what the hell else, I'd like to know."

I tried to calm the situation. "Look, boys. Be reasonable. The Chief's as much a Newton as any of us. Kick the others out, but keep the Chief. There's always room for compromise, isn't there?"

Charlie said, "Haven't you compromised us enough already, Doc?"

"What the hell do you mean by that? I didn't do anything, and what I did do, I did for the good of the town."

"So, you admit it."

"Admit what?"

"You're a two-faced, mealy-mouthed, prevaricating hypocrite."

I was just about to take a swing at the son of a bitch, but Foghorn put a beguiling arm around Charlie's shoulder and played his trump.

"You know son," he said. "I sympathize with your objections, but you do seem to have overlooked something in your treasonous little plot."

"And what would that be, Foghorn?"

"*Regular* members, such as yourself, cannot call a special, emergency meeting of the main body, only *officers* can. And I'm not about to call any goddamn special meeting. What about you, Doc? Are you about to call a goddamn special meeting?"

"Not if they mean to kick the Chief out."

Foghorn took out a handkerchief and, for emphasis I suppose, blew his nose like... well, like a foghorn.

Charlie was unimpressed. "There's something you seem to have overlooked, yourself."

"What would that be?" Foghorn said, folding his hanky.

Charlie dangled the keys to the Athletic Club clubroom in front of Foghorn's eyes. "This isn't about parliamentary procedure," he said. "This is about revolution."

Charlie told us to follow, and he, Hec, and Billy led us upstairs. Me, Foghorn, and everybody else followed– everybody except Dobbs, who said he didn't feel the need to be present for his own execution.

Musty as all hell it always was in that clubroom and so, as was my habit when setting up for meetings, I went to the front of the room and threw open the windows. Spread out below was good old Port Newton–the puffing steam engines, the jolly crowds. Some goddamn marching band or other paraded across the passenger bridge up towards Main, a rainbow of brass above the tracks.

In the front of the clubroom, Charlie, sitting in my place at the officer's table, brought down that old, broken gavel of mine–once, twice, thrice. "The meeting will come to order!"

But just as he did, I heard screams and cries issuing from the populace in the streets below. I stuck my head out a window as men, women, and children all gasped as one and pointed upwards towards Professor Drake's red, white, and blue sausage balloon, still on that slow drift towards the Strait.

"My God! It falls!"

We watched as the professor fought with his ropes and rudders. We saw him become entangled in his own lines like a fish in a net. A propellor broke off and cartwheeled toward the Strait. Women screamed and pulled their children to their skirts. Sheriff Ulshoter put his spurs to Pride of Martinez and galloped off towards... well, towards nothing that I could see. The gas bag stayed aloft a moment longer then swooped low barely clearing the roof of the Newton Wharf & Warehouse, and, like a heart-struck pigeon, crashed into the chill waters of the Carquinez Strait.

"Any new business?" Charlie Meyers said.

40
Calvin Elwell
Bartender and Second Baseman

We kicked the professionals out of the P.N.A.C., just like Charlie wanted, and after the meeting was over, he appointed me to break the news to the Chief–"Him being your blood brother and all."

When I found him, he was in his hotel room, leeching his elbow. I tried to be cagey. "I don't suppose you need to do that," I said, meaning the leeches.

But he kept right on with it, even though he knew what I meant.

"Doesn't matter," he said.

I sat down with him, and we ended up sitting there half the night, the both of us drinking Electric Bitters. He leeched, and we talked and drank those Bitters and leeched some more and talked some more. Not about anything important. Not of Long John or Lily but, instead, we got to pondering the novels about Hawkeye, the Deerslayer, which were written by Mr. James Fenimore Cooper.

"Chasin' after deer in the Garden of Eden," the Chief said. "Imagine that."

We drank so much we missed the *Pinafore* show that night–which got Sophie all mad at me even though she wasn't even in it. The next morning I slept straight through the Fourth of July–missed the Grand Parade, missed the equestrian teams, missed the marching bands. We were to play the championship game that afternoon, and I had quite a head on me when I finally did arise. But I was young, then, and hangovers don't seem to hurt quite as bad when you're young.

Despite our fears, it wasn't all that hot a day–there being a breeze that blew up from the Bay and the Strait in mid-afternoon. That was lucky for me, what with that head on me and all. Everyone in town who could scatter up the price of a ticket–which Foghorn doubled because it was for the championship–went to the game. The ballpark–painted all dark green and still fresh and new–was so full with paying customers that Foghorn roped off the deepest part of left field to make standing room. Charged half price to stand–half the price he'd already doubled, that is. Supply and demand, he called it.

He put the Benicia brass band out there, in the standing room. But our Silver Cornets he put directly behind the Benicia bench, blaring away so loud those boys couldn't hear themselves think.

We were forced to put forward a scratch lineup that day, as we were missing not only the Chief and the professionals but Long John, too. Billy Lawton was at short, and I was at second, my old spot, which felt good enough. Doc started at first base. Hec was behind the plate. Father Noone was out in right.

Foghorn fungoed some balls out to the good father during warm-ups, most of which he missed. "Keep your eye on the ball, you goddamn mick."

Just like old times.

Foghorn had tried to lay off some of the bets he'd made, after the boys kicked the Chief out of the club, but no dice. Sports and gamblers aren't bumpkins from Pacheco, after all. So it was win or go broke for Foghorn and the club, too.

"Keep your hand on your wallet," I told him, but he didn't find it amusing.

Charlie pitched instead of the Chief, which was what Charlie'd wanted all along. My opinion was that he could throw well enough, if not very hard, and that his real trouble was that he lacked what the Chief had the most of–bravado. Batters were so afraid of the Chief and his fade-away pitch that it worked on their minds. But Charlie just wasn't the "Icebox" of old, anymore. Now he was more afraid of the batters than they were of him.

Worse, was that Tony Rossi had his goat. First time up, Big Tony hit one into the standing room crowd in left for a double, and as he trotted into second base, he sung out, "You won't get off so easy, next time, *Hotbox*."

It wasn't much of a taunt, as taunts go, although the "Hotbox" part was amusing, but still it was enough to cause poor Charlie's knees to begin to wobble. I had seen such a thing before, but the oddity of it is that it only seems a frailty of pitchers. Men's nerves can get to them when they bat in the pinch or when they play infield and a ground ball shoots towards them as if from a cannon. But pitchers have more time to contemplate future events–especially when they are staring in at the plate and see a big fellow with a big bat–so their knees begin knock, and it isn't a pretty sight, I can tell you that.

Charlie got hit around pretty hard for a couple of innings, and, when it looked like the third inning might go on forever, there wasn't much Foghorn could do but pull him. It all shouldn't have taken more than a minute, but since the revolution, we'd become democrats, so everybody but the beer sellers gathered in the pitcher's box to put in their two cents.

"Hec could pitch."

"Then who'd catch?"

"We could switch Billy to pitcher, Mike Luciani to short, and Charlie to third."

"Charlie can't play third."

"Hell, he can't pitch, either."

After a respectable time, Judge Schmidt strolled on out and called the question. We voted by show of hands, a plurality being all that was required, and so ended up having Doc and Charlie switch positions–Charlie to first, Doc to pitcher–which was what Foghorn wanted to do in the first place.

Doc took his time about warming up, especially as there were runners on first and second. When he was ready and just about to pitch, Billy Lawton, over at shortstop, yelled out, "Throw strikes, Doc!" Mike Luciani took up the call, "Throw strikes, Doc!"

Doc didn't pay too much attention to either of them–as he considered such advice harassment–but when Hec Fernandez called out, "Throw the old triple play ball!" I guess old Doc understood. He threw his first pitch right down the middle and Benny Canciamilla–a mechanic on the ferry–shot it on a clothesline up the right center field alley.

The baserunners took off at bat's crack, and it looked dismal as sin for the old home team. But damned if it didn't happen just like it was written: the old 8–4–6–3 triple play. Buck Farrell made a circus catch, diving and sliding on his belly, then heaved the ball back to me, the relay man.

Then it was me to Billy at second, and Billy to Charlie at first. Just like falling off a log.

"Maybe God really is on our side," Doc said, as we walked back to the bench.

"Her will be done," Foghorn said.

Next inning, however, His or Her will must have been bases-on-balls for Doc issued those aplenty. When he walked the first three batters, the Benicia Marine Band struck up "When Johnny Comes Marching Home," all bright and cheery, and when Big Tony stepped to the plate everybody knew Doc was done, even Doc. The whole team gathered in the pitcher's box again–Foghorn, Charlie, Hec Fernandez, Father Noone, the Lucianis, even Buck Farrell, the center fielder. We were up to our ears in democracy, once more.

"Charlie could pitch."

"We already tried Charlie."

"Who the hell else is there?"

Our attention was diverted, then, by the Noble Redskins–up near the top of the grandstand in their war paint and feathers. They began to whoop it up and, at first, I couldn't tell why. Then I saw the Chief sitting among them, camouflaged in turkey feathers and war paint, just like a Noble Redskin.

When he stood and made himself known, the whole crowd began buzzing. Everybody in Port Newton knew about Lily's eye and Long John being missing, and I guess the buzz was people trying to figure out what to do with him, the Chief, that is–lynch him or let him pitch.

He tossed aside his war bonnet, slipped on a Port Newton baseball jersey, and put a baseball cap on his head. He came clomping down the steps of the grandstand, already in his baseball cleats. He vaulted onto the field, and joined us democrats in the pitcher's box.

"What the hell?" Charlie said.

"The counterevolution," Foghorn told him.

Foghorn tossed the Chief the baseball, and the Chief held it high up over his head, while the crowd hushed and just watched. The Chief walked with that ball, held on high like it was, towards the Goddess of Liberty and her Handmaidens–Hanna Joost, Sophie, and Garnetta McCoy–

all sitting in this special box Foghorn had built for them right behind home plate.

The Chief stopped in front of Hanna, all painted for war like he was, and bowed low.

"My lady," he said.

I suppose all the eyes in the whole damn ballpark were on the Chief except for mine. Sophie looked just lovely, you see, sitting there beside Hanna, in a slender dress like a Greek goddess, which left her arms and shoulders mostly bare.

Because I'd missed the *Pinafore* show the night before, she glared at me with that, "I'm never going to speak to you again, Calvin Elwell," look upon her face. But our eyes caught and wouldn't let go. It's silly, I know, that such a mighty thing would happen like that–like when Lily Newton kissed the Chief as he slept on Foghorn's bar–but happen like that it did. Me and Sophie looked at each other, our eyes caught, and we haven't been able to look away since.

"I dedicate this game to the Goddess of Liberty," the Chief sung out, "to the Land of the Free, the Home of the Brave, and to our boys in the Philippines."

Hanna took the red, white, and blue scarf she had around her neck and pushed it towards him through the chicken wire of the backstop. The Chief lifted that scarf on high for all to see, just like he'd lifted the baseball, then tied it around his own neck and that was all it took. The crowd went crazy wild.

"We want Dobbs!"

"Let him pitch!"

The tom-toms began to beat a savage tune, the Silver Cornets broke into "Semper Fidelis," and that was that for democracy.

Tony Rossi waited up by home plate while all this was going on, swinging about a half dozen bats. But Big Tony liked to play to the grandstand, just as much as the Chief did, and when the Chief got back to the pitcher's box, Tony dropped all those bats but one, went over to Hanna Joost, and made a bow just like the Chief had.

"I dedicate this at bat to the white races of the world," he declared, and the moment the words were out of his mouth one of the Chief's warm-up pitches got away from him, hit Big Tony in the back of the head and coldcocked him.

Judge Schmidt, who was umpiring, pointed at the Chief. "We'll have none of that Mr. Dobbs. You can't bean a man while time is out."

The Benicia bench cleared in about two shakes. I figured on a riot, but Tony managed to rise before the count of ten. He was wobbly on his pins but so intent on showing the Chief hadn't hurt him, that he just shook himself off like a Labrador dog in the rain, and began to trot on down the base path. Only trouble was, since time was out, he wasn't awarded a base at all which caused the Benicians to get all the madder.

"It's in the book," Judge Schmidt said. "You can look it up."

Nowadays, Doc and Sophie and me sometimes sit around and drink our bathtub gin and reminisce over how the Chief used to play ball: How he scared hell out of Charlie Meyers at that first practice, how he plunked all those poor Bulls Head boys in his first game, how he coldcocked Big Tony.

"Ballplayers are pansies these days," Doc always says. He tells us how Ruth is a drunkard. How Cobb is a madman. How Shoeless Joe threw the World Series, and how Mathewson, the only one of them worth a good goddamn, got mustard gassed in the Great War. After that, and especially if he's had too much, Doc goes on about God and about how God is dead, then blames himself for what happened to the Chief.

"I should have done *something*."

Sophie usually speaks up, then, and says something like, "Don't be so hard on yourself, Daddy." She puts her arm around his shoulder and that is usually the end of it.

Once the Chief started pitching we held those Benicia boys scoreless. We even scored a couple of runs, ourselves, to make the game closer, but if you're looking for a fairy tale end, you've come to the wrong place.

There are lots of people who claim they heard the pop. I was a lot closer to the action than most, being at second base, but I didn't hear it. I don't see how anybody could have either, what with all the noise.

The Noble Redskins were whooping it up. The Marine Band and the Silver Cornets were doing their best to drown each other out. The Benicians were taunting the Chief with the Daisy song, except changing the words from "Daisy, Daisy" to "Lily, Lily, I'm half crazy," which was more cruel than called for.

So I don't see how anybody could have heard it. But you know how things like that are. When something big happens people always want to be a part of it, so everybody says they heard the Chief's elbow pop.

There was a man on second, I know that. A right-hander was batting, and the Chief threw the fade-away but just as he let go the ball, he went down from the grab of the pain.

The ball bounced six feet short of the plate, and the Chief was on his knees, holding his left elbow. We all ran to him, just like the Benicians had run to Big Tony.

All my blood brother said was, "I don't think I can pitch anymore."

And that was that for old Jack Dobbs.

He played his way up–from the Carson Indian School to the Boston Beaneaters–and found himself atop the whole world. But what goes up must come down, just like Professor Drake's balloon, and so it was with the Chief. He played his way up but then right back down again–the Washington Nationals, San Francisco Wasps, Sacramento Gilt Edges, Watsonville Hayseeds and finally, the Port Newtons, the bottom of the bottom-most barrel.

And then there came the pop.

Doc and Sophie and I talk about why he did it sometimes. Why the Chief went and ruined his arm to pitch in a jerkwater game in a jerkwater town. Sophie always brings up Lily and love. He pitched for her, she says. Doc says it was that cigar store the Chief wanted but never got. He pitched for the money, Doc says. Me, I always figure it was more like addiction. I figure maybe the Chief just wanted to be a little boy one more time. You know, cut out of Sunday school, play ball on a field of green grass, and chase after baseballs like chasing down deer in the Garden of Eden.

41

BOX SCORE
The Port Newton News

```
PORT NEWTON                      BENICIA
NAME           AB   R   BH   E   NAME           AB   R   BH   E
Lawton ss       5   2   3    0   Bennett rf      5   2   1    0
Elwell 2b       5   1   1    0   Hoffmster 3b    4   2   3    0
M Luciani lf    5   0   2    1   Casey 2b        4   0   2    0
E Luciani 3b    4   0   2    1   Rossi 1b        4   2   3    0
Fernandez c     4   0   1    1   Strentzel c     4   2   2    0
Farrell cf      4   0   0    0   Peale lf        4   1   0    0
Meyers p-1b-p   5   0   2    0   Fleagle cf      4   1   2    0
Fr Noone rf     5   1   1    1   Segui ss        4   1   1    3
Fuller 1b-p     2   0   0    0   Canciamilla p   5   1   1    0
Dobbs p         1   0   1    0
Murphy 1b       2   0   0    0

TOTALS         42   4   13   4   TOTALS         38  12   15   3

RUNS BY INNING   1   2   3   4   5   6   7   8   9   TOTAL
-------------------------------------------------------
PORT NEWTON      0   0   0   0   2   1   0   1   0     4
BENICIA          3   0   3   1   0   0   0   3   2   x  12
-------------------------------------------------------
```

HOME RUNS: Hoffmeister, Casey, Strentzel BASES ON BALLS:
Lawton, Elwell, E Luciani, Fernandez, Farrell; Bennett,
Hoffmeister 2, Casey, Strenzel, Peale, Segui HIT BY
PITCH: Casey STOLEN BASES: Lawton,; Bennett, Hoffmster,
Fleagle WINNING PITCHER: Canciamilla LOSING PITCHER:
Meyers PASSED BALLS: Fernandez 3

UMPIRE: Judge Schmidt TIME: 3:12

42
DOCTOR SAM FULLER
President, Port Newton Athletic Club

By the time evening rolled around and the Grand Masked Ball was upon us, I was worn out by it all: parades, orations, Hanna Joost's reading of the Declaration of Independence. Not to mention Long John's continued disappearance and, of course, Dobbs' elbow.

He'd ruptured a ligament, done in by years of trick pitches and abuse. I put a splint on the arm and immobilized the elbow at ninety degrees, but there wasn't much I could do beyond that.

"I doubt you'll ever be much of a pitcher again," I told him.

He said he'd figured as much and pushed himself down off my examining table. He asked what he owed me.

"A free cigar," I told him. "When you open your store, I mean. Make that a box of free cigars."

"Sure, Doc."

I stopped him. "You didn't lose everything, did you? You didn't put everything you had on the game?"

He put that big grin on his face. "Everything? Hell no, Doc. Not *everything*."

Later that evening, and despite being worn thin by it all, the Fuller family set out for the Grand Masked Ball at eight o'clock sharp. We were all in our finest as we trekked down the hill. At Edith's insistence, I'd worn my white tie and tails–"If you don't wear them now, when will you ever?"–and at Sophie's I'd worn the mask she'd gotten me–a plague doctor's mask, with a long curved beak of a nose that, in another age, would have been filled with flowers to ward off evil vapors. It covered my entire face. It was hot, I could hardly breathe, and when I tried to speak no one could understand me.

"I hate this goddamn thing," I told Edith, as we walked down the hill.

"What?" she said.

Sophie had bought Edith a mask of similar monstrous proportions. It was purple and blue, a feathered thing with a ridiculous plume that began between Edith's eyes and ran straight up over her head. We'd made the mistake of letting Willie design his own costume, and design one he had: eye mask, black cape, slouch hat. And, now, as if to make his point, he touched off a firecracker.

"Damn it, Willie!" I tried to grab them away from him, and failing in that, I tried to grab the little anarchist, but he slipped through my fingers.

Sophie, who wasn't wearing a mask, laughed at me.

"How come you're so privileged," I said slowly and carefully, "How come you don't have to wear a goddamn mask, like the rest of us?"

"But I am wearing a mask, Daddy. Don't you see?"

She lifted it up to her eyes, one of those idiotic little eye masks on a stick.

"You wouldn't want me to hide my cheekbones, would you?"

"Perish the thought."

"Oh Daddy. Don't."

She lowered her head and forged forward in a regular snit.

"What the hell's got into her?" I asked Edith.

"She's *your* daughter," Edith said.

When we reached the old Newton Mansion, Edith stopped short. It was dark and quiet, thick with brambles and bushes, peppered with holes from Lily's incessant digging. When I'd put the splint on Dobbs' arm that afternoon, he'd told me that Lily was feeling poorly.

"Sick to her stomach, eh?" Edith said to me. "Go knock on the door."

"I'm not her doctor anymore."

"Go knock on the door anyway."

I am not a hen-pecked man but merely a dutiful husband, so I climbed the porch steps and banged the knocker down, as requested. No answer. Sophie scooped up a handful of pebbles from the yard and chucked them at the dormer window high up on the roof. Most fell short. The girl had no arm.

"Yoohoo, Lily."

Still, no answer.

"Maybe the ghost got her," Willie said.

I told him there were no such things and, for the simple purpose of defying me, he touched off a whole string of firecrackers. Edith jumped. Sophie squealed. "Wilhelm!" I tore off my goddamn mask and hurled it to the ground.

"Damn it, Willie. Give me those!"

"But Pa!"

I grabbed at him again, but the boy took off running, and Edith asked me what I thought.

"We'll never catch him," I said.

"No, about Lily I mean. Maybe she's sitting in there, all alone."

"If she is there's nothing we can do. She probably started feeling better and went to the dance."

"I doubt she'd want to be seen in public with that eye of hers."

I shrugged my shoulders. "She could wear a mask."

We began our promenade downtown again, *sans* Willie, until we arrived at the fork in the road where School Street joined Main. Just beyond was good, old Port Newton, illuminated by our new electric lights and sparkling just beyond our grasp.

Edith sighed. "It takes one's breath away,"

Sophie said, "They're just lights, Mother."

Just lights, indeed, but for a moment I had a vision of miracles: houses, stores, schools, everything, all of Port Newton glowing and electric. A vision of Professor David Drake's New Age. Airships, peace, prosperity. No more dim candles, no more hissing jets of gas or stinking lamps of kerosene and coal oil.

Then, I had another, more horrible, vision. Rufus, the Negro from the Mississippi Minstrels, lay slumped against that old mother oak at the fork of the road. Blood covered his face. He held a red-soaked handkerchief against his mouth. I knelt down beside him and pulled it away.

"Let me have a look."

Two of his teeth were gone. His nose was broken. There was a gash on his forehead that poured blood into his right eye. He pushed me away.

"I'm a doctor," I told him.

"No."

He tried to rise. I told him to stay put. "You're going to need some stitches."

He got to his feet. He steadied himself against the oak, put one foot in front of the other and proceeded to weave away down the hill like a drunkard. I started to follow.

"Be careful, dear," Edith called.

He kept up a suprisingly brisk, if erratic, pace down Main towards our new electric city. Further along, Tony Rossi and a pack of Benicians, lounged on the front steps of Archer's Saloon drinking whiskey from bottles. They laughed as Rufus stumbled by.

"Got any coon songs for us?"

Billy Lawton, the little bastard, was one of them. "Is that a cakewalk you're doin'?"

Rufus just kept going.

At Main and Park Streets, Sheriff Ulshoter sat placidly atop that big gelding of his, surveying the broken front windows of Howard James' photography shop. Shards of glass littered the street.

"What the hell?" I said.

"Some fellows with too much liquor in 'em." He pointed towards poor Rufus, staggering. "What happened to him?"

"Those same fellows beat him up, probably. You ought to do something."

"Such as what?"

"Arrest them."

"I've got my hands full as it is, Sam. With the crowds and being short-handed."

"You can't let the bastards get away with beating a man for sport. They're up at Archer's. Tony Rossi. Billy Lawton. They're the ones who did it."

"Calm down, Sam."

"Calm down? *Do something!*"

I followed Rufus all the way down to the ferry and watched him board. Once on deck, he sat down, huddling like an unborn babe against the thin, white rail. The steaming locomotives heaved and clanked, shunting cars onto the deck oblivious to the fate of one, no account, black minstrel. Even on Independence Day the trains had to run, the ferry had to ferry.

When it pulled out of the slip I watched it go, then I retreated back towards the Masked Ball and ice cream and popcorn. Pimental Hall was a sanctuary that night, hung with red, white, and blue. The music of our Silver Cornets clung to the very walls. The dancers stepped lightly. Friends and neighbors, people I had know all my life. People who I would rest beside in our little cemetery through all eternity were unrecognizable to me now, hidden under their masks: A black feathered raven, a she-cat with slanted eyes, Pan and Bacchus, Medusa of the snakes.

Riley Towne leaned against a wall, drunk on New Discovery Elixir or Electric Bitters or whatever he was using to stifle his pain that night. The top of his head and the upper half of his face were covered by the mask of a court jester– green and red, topped off by three dangling appendages that contained jingling bells.

"Where's your mask?" he asked me.

"Threw it away," I told him.

"Do you suppose we ought to drag the Strait for him? For Long John, I mean."

"He'll turn up," I said, wishfully.

"Do you figure the Indian killed him?"

"I don't know. I don't think so."

I asked him if he'd seen what happened to Rufus. He said he hadn't, and I told him Billy Lawton and some others beat him up.

"Sheriff Ulshoter isn't going to do a thing about it. You ought to put that in your paper."

"If it's true, I will."

"Jesus Christ, Riley, the whole damn world is falling apart."

"Hell, Sam. It's always falling apart. Been falling apart since the beginning of time, I suspect."

I saw the ostrich plume of Edith's monstrous mask, towering a foot above the heads of the others, and following that spoor, I found her by the punch bowl. She asked about the Negro.

"I think he's all right," I said. "Well, relatively. He took the ferry to Benicia."

"My God. What a disgrace."

"Let's dance."

"You? Sam? Dance? You're not drunk already, are you?"

I made a great bow and flourish and again requested the pleasure of her hand. This granted, we waltzed. The Silver Cornets played as they had never played before–all in the same key, for one thing–and the dancers spun, ceaseless and dainty. It was old Port Newton at its best. Homey, hardworking, and embracing all who came to her–as long as they were white and had a little money, that is.

Garnetta McCoy wore her *Pinafore* costume on that last glorious Fourth. Captain Spintler, the one-armed veteran of the Philippine Insurrection, two-stepped with Eva Dunkel–she in her Red Cross nurse's uniform, he, dashing in his dress blues. Our darling Sophie spent most of the evening planted in the arms of young Cal Elwell, dancing as if they were made for each other–which they were, as things developed.

At nine o'clock sharp, the band blew a fanfare, and laughter rippled the floor. Uncle Sam himself appeared– white shirt, red pants, a blue coat, and a stars and stripes top hat. It was Foghorn Murphy under that wig and false beard– half bankrupted by gambling loses but still full of good cheer, 180 proof, I imagine.

He called to the leader of the Silver Cornets in those booming, station-master tones of his. "Captain Rice, my baton!"

From out of nowhere it flew, a silver wand such as a drum major might use, and old Foghorn caught it as sure-handed as when he was young and strong and still played ball.

"To the Front for the fireworks!"

The Silver Cornets struck up the "Stars and Stripes Forever." Foghorn did a strut brisk enough, and in two shakes Hanna Joost joined him. She offered Foghorn her arm, and we Newtonians cheered the rafters off. The band fell in behind and, like two pied pipers, Uncle Sam and the Goddess of Liberty led us out of Pimental Hall and down towards the Front.

Skyrockets flared out over the Strait, shot from the abandoned dock of Newton Wharf & Warehouse–red, white, blue. The smell of gunpowder nipped the air. The great ferry *Benicia*, a yellow-eyed monster, churned into its slip blowing whistles and ringing bells. From Railroad Avenue, the overnight train, stock-still at the depot, blew back an answer–three longs and a short, three longs and a short.

Calvin Elwell, my future son-in-law, was up on the roof of the Exchange. He hoisted an American flag up the tall pole that stood there–fifty feet across that damn flag must have been and illuminated by our brand-new electric lights.

Uncle Sam, Foghorn that is, came up beside me. "It's one hell of a sight, ain't it, Doc?"

I told him it was.

"We took a licking out there today," he said, "but we'll come back from it. Always have, always will."

"I'm not so sure," I said, but by this time Foghorn had already turned away from me, towards the rest of them– the masked faces of Port Newton: Punchinello, Puck, Merlin the Magician. I saw a red devil with slanted eyes and pointy ears and, for a moment, I thought it was Dobbs, but it was not.

Then I saw Old Man Newton. Tall and gaunt with a long white beard, he wore an old fashioned suit tight around him. He dripped with water as if he'd just stepped out of the Strait. Red-brown seaweed hung around his neck like Marley's chains. He began to dance in the street, hand in hand, with the red-faced devil. The Silver Cornets played. The masked throng backed away, formed a circle around the two and clapped in rhythm as they leaped and pranced.

For an awful moment it flashed through my mind that maybe the ghost of Old Man Newton really was running loose in the world. But then I realized that the seaweed chain that hung around his neck came from the ocean, not the Strait, and I saw it was John Glass under that false, white beard, the same fellow who'd rigged the Goddess of Liberty Contest.

Foghorn sung out, "The beer is on me!" The dancing ceased, the applause began and the one and only true inventor of the gin Martini, led us all on a charge through those swinging batwing doors of the Railroad Exchange. Inside, the railroaders and ferrymen drank their Port Newton Steam Beer, smoked their cigars, ate their hard-cooked eggs. Charlie Meyers, still in his baseball uniform, cried in his beer at the bar. Hec Fernandez tried to console him.

"I teach my students Horatio Alger every spring," Charlie moaned.

"Hell, Charlie," Hec said, "wait till next year."

Charlie shook his head. "I'm done with baseball."

Judge Schmidt, fleshy and pompous, leaned on the bar, bending John McMillan's ear: "It was, indeed, illegal of the chief to wear that scarf of Miss Joost's, but, well, I thought, 'It is the Fourth, after all.'"

Jack Dobbs was at Foghorn's poker table in back. His crippled left arm hung in a sling. He wore that same damn tuxedo he'd had on the first night I saw him. Old Rosa Paredes sat beside him shuffling a deck of cards. Both were without masks, their faces worn in the smoky light.

Edith gave me a little push of the hand. "Go find out about Lily."

I went over. I bid Doña Rosa a good evening– "*Buenas Noches*"–and asked Dobbs how his elbow felt.

"Hurts like Hell," he said.

"Rest, ice, exercise," I told him.

Doña Rosa took a card from the deck she'd been shuffling and turned it over in front of Dobbs–the eight of clubs. "*Celos*," she said. "Jealousy."

"Maybe you *can* tell fortunes, Doña Rosa," Dobbs told her.

I asked him about Lily.

"Oh, you know," he said. "She doesn't like crowds much."

Doña Rosa turned over another card, the nine of diamonds. "*Recorrido*," she said. "A change of residence, perhaps."

Dobbs laughed again. "*That* might be in the cards."

"We stopped by her place," I told him, "on the way down the hill. She didn't answer."

"She'll be all right, Doc. She's a little upset is all. Truth is, we had a little spat. And she is feeling sickly."

Doña Rosa turned over another card–the eight of spades.

Dobbs grinned. "Paired me."

"*Peligro*," Doña Rosa told him. "Misfortune. An upset."

"An upset? Well, we lost to Benicia, didn't we? That sounds like an upset to me. What was the score, Doc? Ten to three?"

"Twelve to four."

Doña Rosa turned the fourth card–the ace of clubs. "*Abundancia. Prosperidad.*"

Dobbs put on that big grin of his. "Well, that's more like it."

"But it vanishes," Doña Rosa said. "*Una quimera.*"

She began to turn over the fifth and final card but–like Foghorn's hole card on the night Dobbs floated into town–I shall never know what it was. For the next card to be played, on that Glorious Fourth, belonged to the gods of fire–the little children like Willie, like Jimmy Cattlet, like Peggy McCann poisoned by rhubarb, the little, careless children, like Foghorn and me, playing with firecrackers.

A bell tolled. Doña Rosa stopped dealing. Everyone froze as in an overexposed, flash-powder portrait–Dobbs lifting a beer to his mouth, the masked revellers dancing, Uncle Sam kissing the goddess's cheek. It was a bell like no other–sharper, thinner, more strident–the bell we all feared, the bell in the steeple of the firehouse.

Quick as thought, we Newtonians became animated again. All at once we crowded through Foghorn's swinging batwing doors and onto the sidewalk.

"Up there!" John Glass shouted. "On Newton's Bluff."

There was smoke. There was a glow of flame. The volunteer firemen among us cast off their masks and began a dash for the firehouse. Three others, coming from the firehouse but still in their dancing shoes, ran a cart of soda-acid extinguishers past us and turned up Ferry Street. Sheriff Ulshoter appeared, a black clad phantom atop his midnight-blue horse.

"We'll need every man we can get up there! If the fire gets into the eucalyptus..."

225

I told Edith, "Get the children and get home but be ready to evacuate. Don't worry. It'll be all right."

She kissed my cheek—"You be careful now"—and started up the hill. Behind me there were more shouts.

"Make way!" Jimmy Catlett's brother Bobby, carrying a torch and clearing people off the street in front of the engines, ran for all he was worth down Railroad Avenue.

"Make way! Make way!"

The rest of the Newton Fire Volunteers, all sporting their jolly, new, red leather helmets, came right behind the boy, running hard as they could pulling our inadequate, old hand-pumper. The hose company was right behind them, a wild bell clanging on the cart. A month before, the town had balked at buying a new chemical engine—seven hundred dollars it would have cost—and now we might pay a horrible price. White ash like summer snow began to fall all around us.

Foghorn came up beside me and pulled off his Uncle Sam hat, his wig and beard.

"I think it's the ballpark," I told him.

"Hell," he said. "I knew it was too good to last."

The Martinez Fire Company, in town for the Fire Tournament and the cart races, rushed past. The Benicia company was right behind. Last in the running column came the hook and ladder, pulled by eight brave Newtonians, but when they took the corner at Ferry Street, they made their turn too sharp.

The truck slid then tipped, turned over on its back and cracked into one of the electrical poles the Sierra & Bay Electric Company had put up just days before. A ladder broke free, wrapped itself around another pole and, in a shower of sparks and falling wires, the twentieth century came down—wires, poles, lights, everything. All the way up Main, the lights blinked out and old Port Newton turned black in the night.

Epilogue
DOCTOR SAM FULLER
President, Port Newton Athletic Club

We battled the fire all that night. The water pressure in the hydrants failed, but we did what we could with the old hand-pumpers and kept the fire out of the eucalyptus and away from the town. There were a few injuries–smoke inhalation, burns. John McMillan suffered a broken wrist, but other than that we got off lucky.

Still, in the morning, all that was left of our beautiful ballpark were mounds of gray-white ash and smoking, black-burnt wood. Foghorn and I stumbled through the ruins coughing on the fumes of his bankrupt dream. He pitched a charred baseball at what had once been the scoreboard.

"Don't worry, Doc," he said, "I won't go and drown myself."

Afterwards, most of the men were so exhausted they simply went home and crawled into bed. I did. Foghorn did. So did Calvin Elwell. But Calvin, from what he says, didn't get much sleep.

There came a knock on the door of his room up on the second floor of the Railroad Exchange.

"Hey, little brother. It's me."

I realize, now, that Dobbs wasn't with us when we fought the fire, but when the flames were high and the smoke was pouring, we were all too busy to notice.

Cal swung his feet out of bed and onto the floor. He sat for a moment at the bed's edge and steadied himself. The knock came again.

"It's me, little brother. I come to say goodbye."

Calvin stepped to the door and flung it open.

"Goodbye? What do you mean, *goodbye*? Where are you going?"

"Back to the big time," Dobbs said.

He told Cal some improbable story about how the Detroit Tigers of the Western League were just dying to sign him.

"They're calling the old Western League the American League now, and next year it's gonna be a *major* league. My arm'll be healed up fine by then. I'll show those bastards."

He extended his right hand to Calvin, and Calvin grasped it.

"What about the team? What about Lily?"

"I can't say it ain't been nice, little brother."

No one else saw hide nor hair of the Chief that day, and the town gossips—the menfolk milling around Foghorn's mahogany bar, the womenfolk in their sewing circles and socials–were of the opinion that his sudden flight proved he'd murdered Long John. Charlie Meyers said he knew it all along. Old Rosa Paredes said we'd find Long John dead, swollen and green down at the bottom of the Carquinez Strait.

"Un bebé del agua."

Sheriff Ulshoter and Captain Alvarado did spend the next day dragging the Strait with a hook and chain, but all they fished up was a dead Chinaman caught in the pilings under Newton Wharf & Warehouse.

No one saw hide nor hair of Lily Newton, either. The old Newton mansion was quiet that day and all the next. In the yard, a slender young apple tree, a sapling, waited to be planted in a hole Lily had dug. At night, a single lamp burned high in the dormer window where the Old Man had once had his office.

"Do you think she's all right?" Edith said to me.

"How the hell should I know?"

The next morning Edith climbed Lily's front steps carrying a wicker picnic basket with a chicken and rice casserole tucked inside. She brought down the iron knocker on the front door and waited. Lily was in her robe and slippers when she finally answered. Pale and insubstantial, she wiped the corners of her mouth with a lavender handkerchief.

"I've been sick all night," she said. Her cheek was still black and blue. Her eye seemed all the more swollen and was half shut, now.

The two of them went into the parlor. They sat in the love seat in the window bay. Port Newton was spread out below like a picture book–the broad, cold Strait, the ferry, the railroad tracks, Main Street.

"Maybe if you ate something, dear."

Lily said she was thinking of going to the hot springs in Calistoga for a while.

"My doctor recommended it. To restore my health."

"It would be good for you, after all you've been through."

"I put him out," Lily said.

"I know, dear, I know."

"He's an *Indian,* for godsakes. What was I thinking?"

About a month after the fire, in early August, Lily Newton went to the hot springs in Calistoga, just as she'd told Edith she would. But Lily did not come back until well after New Years, a period of time which gave rise to rumors of a baby being born–a black-haired, brown-eyed, baby boy. The gossips seized upon this and, apparently forgetting all about the theory that the Chief had murdered Long John, now said that the Chief's had gotten Lily pregnant and left her in the lurch, and that that explained his sudden departure from town.

But as for me, I can't believe that Dobbs would have abandoned Lily. In fact, I think it more likely that, if indeed she was pregnant, she wouldn't have wanted to keep the child and, when Dobbs opposed her, she "put him out," as one would the cat. And I don't think the big Indian killed Long John, either. The Chief talked tough, but I don't think he had murder in him. I like to think that Long John just couldn't face things in Port Newton anymore–his thankless job, his failed love–and so he'd headed for greener pastures, the goldfields of Alaska, maybe. But I don't know. No one knows and no one ever will. I know that none of the above is very satisfying, but unanswered questions do seem to be the rule these days.

As the new century rolled on, we Newtonians huddled closer and closer together, like Dobbs' little band of Washoe Indians, against the flood tide of progress. We still played baseball, trying desperately to regain the souls Charlie Meyers said we'd lost. But it was never the same. We were too old, too jaded, and more and more, the men of Port Newton, and the whole country for that matter, eschewed *playing* baseball in favor of *watching* it. More and more, we would take the train into Oakland on weekends to watch the professionals play. More and more, our democratic game, the game for which we had had such mighty hopes, became a Roman thing, a circus for the great unwashed, a tine of empire.

And so it was, on a certain spring Saturday in 1913—when the grass was green and the men and boys jammed the turnstiles of a brand new ballpark, built for the Oakland Oaks—Foghorn and I caught one final glimpse of Jack Dobbs, the great Chief.

We sat along the third base line in the stadium seats behind the dugout. Dobbs—older and heavier but unmistakable—climbed the aisle steps, dressed in a candy-stripped smock. A heavy metal bin hung like a yoke from his neck and shoulders.

"Peanuts. Get your fresh roasted peanuts."

He didn't see us—or, at least, pretended he didn't—but just kept laboring up those steps, and we pretended we didn't see him, either.

"Peanuts. Get your peanuts here."

"He'd be better off dead," Foghorn told me.

"Nobody's better off dead," I said.

A year or two later Riley Towne died. Then Foghorn. Rosa Paredes ended her days locked away in the asylum for the insane in Stockton. My dear Edith died in my arms—the influenza in 1919. Cal and Sophie married. They struggle to make a go of what's left of the International Hotel now, but most of the young folks—Willie, Garnetta McCoy, Hanna Joost—migrated to more prosperous climes.

I dwell, still, in my old house, watching over the world from my front porch. The Newton Mansion still stands on the hill, just below, overgrown and haunted. Lily still lives there, all alone and in her fifties, now, sipping her pick-me-ups and cultivating her garden. She prunes. She takes cuttings. She pulls weeds. In winter, she retreats into her parlor. In the spring, she puts out poison for the ground squirrels. At Halloween, the children throw rocks at her door.

But it wasn't the Old Man's sin that brought Port Newton down, it was something even more insidious—the natural order of things—market forces, the "invisible hand."

More and more, the farmers of Pacheco and the Diablo Valley turned from growing wheat to supplying produce to those shining cities of Professor David Drake's dreams, and truck farmers, it seems, have no need for grain ships or deep water ports. When a railroad bridge was built across the Strait in 1930, the town's last excuse for being disappeared. The depot and tracks, the waterfront and wharves, are all gone now. All that remains of our failed paradise is a dilapidated Main Street, a few forlorn families, and the cold-flowing Carquinez Strait.

And so, for whatever it is worth, there you have it all: God, baseball, ghosts, and fairy tale kisses; the coming of modernity, greed, love, and perhaps even murder. I sit on my porch, now, with a yellow cat in my arms and watch while it all fades away, no longer deluded by the myth that some shining hero will come and save us. No great god, resurrected, will rise out of the primordial waters to bring us peace, prosperity, and happiness. There are no heroes, no villains, no gods or devils—not even good and evil—only we creatures, born flawed and incomplete.

ABOUT THE AUTHOR

George Jansen is a technical writer who lives in the
San Francisco Bay Area. He spent too much of his youth
throwing curves and knucklers in pock-marked sandlots
and his right shoulder is now a complete wreck. His
first novel, *The Jesse James Scrapbook*, was published
by Hilliard & Harris in October 2003.